I'm Doin' Me 2

I'm Doin' Me 2

Anna Black

www.urbanbooks.net

Urban Books, LLC
97 N18th Street
Wyandanch, NY 11798

I'm Doin' Me 2 Copyright © 2016 Anna Black

ISBN 13: 978-1-62286-753-0
ISBN 10: 1-62286-753-X

First Trade Paperback Printing December 2016
Printed in the United States of America

10 9 8 7 6 5 4 3 2 1

This is a work of fiction. Any references or similarities to actual events, real people, living or dead, or to real locales are intended to give the novel a sense of reality. Any similarity in other names, characters, places, and incidents is entirely coincidental.

Distributed by Kensington Publishing Corp.
Submit Orders to:
Customer Service
400 Hahn Road
Westminster, MD 21157-4627
Phone: 1-800-733-3000
Fax: 1-800-659-2436

Let's Get Caught Up

Previously on *I'm Doin' Me* . . .

Tiffany Richardson, a Chicago native, moved out to L.A. to pursue her dreams of becoming an anchorwoman or radio broadcaster, but she stumbled into a writing position at KCLN for a new series called *Boy Crazy*.

Going for her interview to be the next broadcaster for KCLN's online network, she landed on the right floor but walked through the wrong door, and she snatched the position right from under Tracy Simms, a sista who lost her position because she was late for work on her first day.

Outraged and full of malice, Tracy vowed that that would not be the last they'd hear from her, even after Tiffany apologized. Not in a forgiving mood, she stormed out, but was never to be heard from or seen again.

Tiffany fell into her new, fast-paced career, and after only a couple of seasons, she was promoted to head writer and producer of the hit series. Because of her, the show rose to number one on the network; however, with the highest-ranking show at KCLN, Tiffany and her crew were baffled when their show was on the chopping block. Later, they found out it was because the brother of network owner William Keiffer, who took William's place when he was out ill, was a racist and wanted the all-black cast gone.

Quick to rise and even quicker to fall, Tiffany not only found herself in a fix at work when she learned that her show would be cancelled, but she walked in on her man Jeff in bed with the help. Close to the unemployment line and heartbroken, Tiffany became overwhelmed and on the brink of giving up.

Not sure what the future would bring and all hope lost, Tiffany ran into Kory Banks, an old crush from high school. Believing it was fate, Tiffany and her best friend Rose had high hopes that it was her chance to finally be with the one she'd loved forever—only to find out a couple of days later that he was engaged to Tressa Isabella Green, L.A.'s queen.

Fearing all was lost, Tiffany faced the reality of losing her show and losing the love of her life again, but there *was* a light at the end of the tunnel. Tressa was the daughter of Langley Green, the owner of TiMax, a huge network. To impress Kory, Tressa offered to help Tiffany bring her show over to her father's network.

This was one of Tressa's first underhanded attempts to keep Kory for herself, because she had a feeling there was more to Tiffany and Kory's relationship than just friendship.

Moving forward, Tiffany stayed focused and gave up on the idea of her and Kory ever being together, especially after she learned Tressa lied to her about the interview at her father's company. Tired of the drama, Tiffany wished Kory well on the night of his engagement party. Later that night, he showed up at her door, asking for a friendship that Tiffany knew she couldn't handle. Being friends with someone she was in love with wasn't what she wanted, so she said farewell for good.

With no show and no love, Tiffany contemplated her next move. Out of the blue, she got a call from Mr. Green and landed a new home for her series, *Boy Crazy*, at

TiMax, putting her show back on the air and pissing Tressa off.

Determined to make it to the altar with Kory without him running back to Tiffany, Tressa had to also face the fact that her father was developing a relationship with Tiffany. Feeling the pressure of losing her man and her father to the woman she despised the most, Tressa's old drug habits became hard to conceal. Tressa thought she had everything under control . . . until Kory found out she was using again. At the same time, her secret of paying actor Colby Grant to seduce Tiffany was revealed.

Kory broke the engagement after he found her stash of coke, but Tressa failed to tell her father a thing about the wedding being called off. Her trust fund money depended on her marrying Kory and staying married for a year to receive it.

After all the drama, deceit, and schemes, Tiffany won. Colby was exposed for his dirty dealings with Tressa, and his career was on the line for the decisions he made. Tressa's evil conspiracies caused her to be stood up at the altar and lose her inheritance. Kory and Tiffany—well, let's just say they lived happily ever after, until . . .

Night of the Live Interview

Tressa

"Mommy!" Tressa's voice blared when she burst through the doors. She was in a foul mood, and she could not believe that her own father had thrown her out and disowned her. She was furious and knew her mother would be the only one to talk some sense into her daddy. "Mom! Where are you?" she continued to shriek as she walked from room to room looking for her mother. She was on fire, and all she wanted was her money and sweet revenge. She wanted to make all of them suffer at that moment, including her father. Throwing her out of the studio was one thing, but not giving her, her trust, after all of those years of waiting, pleading, and begging, was the ultimate betrayal. All Tressa could see was red, and the only thing on her mind was getting back at those who crossed her and everyone that betrayed her.

Finally, she found her mother out on one of their decks, relaxing. "*Madre,*" she blasted, and her mom sat up quickly.

"*Isabella, qué está pasando? Porque estas gritando?*" her mother questioned, wanting to know what was going on and why she was yelling.

"It's Daddy, Mother. You have to talk to him. He threw me out of the studio, and he—" she cried, but then realized her mother was looking at her like a deer caught in the headlights. Her mother hardly ever spoke English. She understood some words, but she had never made an effort to even learn the English language, so Tressa paused, wiped her face, and started over. She began to explain everything to her in Spanish. By the time she was done, her mother was crying with her and assured her she'd talk to her dad.

"Gracias, Mama," Tressa said when her mother put ten crisp one hundred-dollar bills in her hand. She stroked her daughter's face and told Tressa to give him a couple of days to calm down. With that, Tressa left and headed straight to Stephen's. Her mom gave her whatever she wanted, just like her father did at one point, but those days were gone, and she knew she had to handle Tiffany and somehow win back her father or he'd have to suffer the same consequence as Tiffany. There were no other options, and she needed to be around her friends. The ones who supported her and had her back, so she drove to Stephen's. He was always there for her, not like Amber's snitching ass. Amber was supposed to be her best friend forever, but since she had gone to rehab, cleaned herself up and married a doctor, she didn't party anymore, and Tressa thought she was now a lame uppity bitch, and she severed their friendship after she found out she had sold her out to Kory. Amber had broken the code, and Tressa had nothing else to do with her. She and Stephen were now best friends forever, and she was glad he was always there for her.

"Take it easy, Tressa. You're hitting that shit too hard, and you are not going to OD in my house, bitch. Not on my fucking watch!" Stephen said. He spoke like a drama queen, not like the sexy stud he pretended to be out in public, because only he, Tressa, and his lover were there.

"Yes, gurrrllllll," his lover cosigned.

"Fuck you, Lavender," Tressa roared at Stephen's flamboyant mate. "This is a private party, and this my shit, so shut the fuck up," Tressa barked and took another line.

"Stevie, baby, you betta get yo' bitch before I euthanize her ass," Lavender snapped back.

"Calm down you two. Damn! You catty bi-otches fucking up my high. I get tired of hearing you bitches yap at each other. Damn! You bi-otches are total buzz killers!"

"That's your little girlfriend fucking up our high," Tressa countered. "Calm the fuck down and let me enjoy myself."

"Look, bitch, I've had just about enough of your funky-ass attitude. Keep on." Lavender rolled his eyes. Tressa took another line and shook, and didn't respond. She rolled her neck in a quick circular motion and took the palm of her hand and made circular motions with the tip of her nose.

"So are you going to tell big Steve what the fuck is up with you?"

"Tiffany Richardson!" Tressa snarled. Her eyes burned, and her face was hot at the thought of that bitch, and she wanted her dead. It was dramatic, but that's what Tressa wanted. She wanted her gone.

"Reesy, please tell me you are not still hell-bent on getting back at her. You didn't want Kory's ass anyways. Your wedding fiasco is old news now that Ava's in the limelight. No one's even talking about you or that shit anymore. This is L.A., bitch. There is a new dose of drama and folks to talk about every other day, so get over it!"

"I know that, you asshole, but I want my money. I need my money, and now my daddy has cut me off, Stephen. Off!" she yelled. "That means I get nothing, and I don't know what I'm going to do," she sighed. Now her eyes were watering, but then she got in touch with her emotions and toughened up. "So fuck that bitch. I'm going to destroy her, Stephen, no matter what it takes or how long it takes, I'm going to fuck that bitch and Kory's life up so bad, they're going to wish they never met me."

"Tressa, let it go. What you need to do is work on making things right with your father, so he's not going to write you off. Your daddy loves you, and I know he will get over this minor hiccup. I mean, what you did was majorly stupid, but your father will come around. He adores you, and he has never left you out in the cold. He'll calm down, and things will work out."

"You didn't see his face, Stephen. My father had this look in his eyes, a look I've never seen before, and I can't just go and say I'm sorry and cry and beg and plead this time. My father was outraged, and he isn't going to forgive me. He isn't going to give me my trust, and the only way for me to get even is to get Tiffany."

"Whatever, Reesy. I think you and this 'destroy Tiffany' is insane. When are you going to move on and get yo'self together? I mean, your daddy is wealthier than fucking life. Win him over, get back into his good graces, and he'll take care of you. If you fuck with Tiffany and get caught, you are going to lose Langley for sure. I say, work on straightening things out with your father."

"How, Stephen?"

"First, you might want to go back into rehab. Show him that you are truly trying to change. Clean up, and then your daddy will do what he always does . . . put it all behind him and welcome you back."

Tressa thought about what Stephen said, and he was right. Her daddy was always happy when she was doing the right thing, but tonight wasn't the night to start. She took another line and reclined back on the sofa. Her thoughts were jumbled, and she couldn't form a complete thought, so she decided to just enjoy her high and worry about Tiffany and her dad later. What she did know, and her last thought before she completely zoned out, was she would get even and somehow or some way, she was going to make Tiffany pay.

Several Weeks Later

The Night of the Premiere

Colby

Colby left fuming and outraged. He was so angry for what had gone down and even angrier with himself for allowing Tressa to involve him with such foolishness. He didn't stop and think about the outcome. He just went with it. He never stopped to think about his actions jeopardizing his career or what bad publicity he'd bring on himself. With Tiffany on the road to success and now one of Mr. Green's favorite persons, there was no way he would get a series on TiMax. Definitely not after all of the drama that had occurred.

"Why did I listen to your crazy ass, Tressa?" he mumbled as he got into his car. He wanted to choke the life out of her. He never thought things would spiral out of control as they did, and he definitely had lost Tiffany for good.

Never intending to fall for her when he signed up for the bogus affair, he slowly but surely fell for Tiffany. She was like an around-the-way girl, down-to-earth, smart and sexy. She was flirty and funny, and he remembered the way her eyes used to dance when she was excited about something.

Very low-key and drama-free he had the best times with Tiffany, and he was going to miss it all. "I just wanted to apologize, Tiffany, and say I'm sorry, but as soon as I blinked, you were back with your high school honey. Man, I want to beat yo' ass, Kory, and that cheap shot you got in on me was just a lucky punch. Next time I see you, you gon' learn who I am, that's for sure," he rambled on. He was heated and wanted to turn his car around and head back to the party and wait for Kory's ass.

"Son of a bitch," he grumbled. "That's okay, though. I got you, and I'm going to get Tiffany back." He continued to mentally battle with Kory and apologize to Tiffany when his phone rang. He looked at the screen in the dash. It was Tressa.

"You gotta be kidding me," he said, and then hit ignore. A few short moments later, his cell rang out again, and again he hit ignore. The next minute he got a text alert.

I need 2 tlk 2 u ASAP!

He hit delete on the screen and continued on, but Tressa started to call and text him back to back. Ignoring her, he went home . . . to find her at his gate.

He pulled up, but her car was blocking the drive.

"Tressa, move your car now!" he demanded. Tressa looked at him with a look of refusal, and then placed both hands on her hips.

"Not until we've talked, Colby. I paid you to do a damn job, and you fucked up."

"Tressa, if you don't get yo' ass in your car and get the hell out of my drive, I'm going to call the law."

"Call them, Colby. Be my damn guest. I don't have shit to lose at this point, and I know you want exactly what I want. Just like me, I know you want to get back at them."

"No!" he yelled, even though she spoke the truth. He didn't want to have a thing to do with Tressa, not anymore. She had caused him enough troubles. "I don't want to get back, get even, or do anything of that nature. I want to move on with my life and pretend that this ignominy never happened, Tressa. I'm at the height of my career, and I'm not going to allow such foolishness anymore. I will not let you or Tiffany, and that punk ass Kory make matters worse for me, so I'm asking you nicely to get in your car and get the hell out of my drive. I don't have shit to say to you, and I don't want to be a part of your schemes and scams. Go find another sucker to toy with, Tressa."

She stood there for a few seconds like she hadn't heard a word he had said. He then examined her closer and wondered why she looked a mess. Like a prom date from hell. She wore a lovely gown, but it was hanging off of her as if it wasn't the right size, and her hair looked like she was going for an updo, but she didn't have enough pins left to finish pinning it up. Her makeup was a completely different look for a princess, and it dawned on him that she was high. He really wanted her as far away as possible at that point. "Don't make me call the law, Tressa. I'm serious, I will."

"You will never work in this town again!" she yelled. Huffing and puffing, Colby looked at her with a look of confusion. She had turned into a lunatic right before his eyes, but he wasn't having it.

"Save your empty threats, Tressa. You are a nobody, a laughingstock. Everyone in this city knows you are a joke. You're yelling, but nobody's listening. You are a fucking cokehead, Tressa. You look like a homeless idiot in that dress. You are washed up, and not even your daddy wants to claim your ass right now, so get your crazy ass into your vehicle and get off of my property. If you don't go now, I'll have you locked up for trespassing," he threatened, and then reached for his phone.

Tressa stood there with her chest rising and falling as she breathed deeply with rage.

"Okay," he said and dialed 911.

"911, what's your emergency," his wireless headset blared, and he knew it was loud enough not only for Tressa to hear, but also his neighbors. In an instant, Tressa dashed to her car and cranked her engine.

"No emergency, ma'am. The problem is now leaving," Colby said and watched Tressa back out like she was trying to get away from a robbery. He waited for her taillights to speed down the road before he drove up and keyed in the code to get into his gate.

He felt foolish, thinking back on his actions of how he allowed Tressa to talk him into dating Tiffany for money and a lead role at her father's network. He knew the bad press was going to taint his image, so he decided he'd get on top of the game by apologizing in person to Mr. Green, and then working with his publicist to make public apologies for his actions, because he had come too far in his career to be suddenly washed up. He had worked too hard to be placed on the has-been list. He was too young and had a bright future, and he instantly went into the save-his-career mode. Tressa was the loser, not him, and Tiffany and Kory were not going to be a sore spot in his life.

He made a conscious decision to let them be, get over Tiffany Richardson, and squash the plans to whip Kory's ass.

After the Premiere Party

Kory

"Are you ready to go, my love?" Kory asked Tiffany.

"Yes, my feet are killing me, and I'm so ready to get out of this dress."

"And I'm ready to get you out of it too," he hissed, admiring her backside. "I mean, baby, you look so good, I can't wait to get you home so I can—" he began, but someone called out Tiffany's name. They both turned toward the voice.

"Tressa," they both said in unison.

"Yes, it's Tressa, you bitch," Tressa slurred.

"How on earth did she get in here?" Tiffany said in a panic.

Tressa looked a mess. Hair mangled, makeup on like she had done it in the dark, and although her gown was gorgeous, it didn't fit properly. Most of the press was gone because the night had winded down. Kory looked around for security, but there was no security guard in sight.

"Tressa!" Kory hurried over to her to turn her the other way. She looked horrible, and Kory did not want her to make a scene or cause any trouble. "Come on, Tressa, you're a mess. How'd you get in here?" he said trying to grab her arm, but she snatched away.

"Don't touch me, you asshole," she spat. Kory knew she was as high as a kite on something, but he had no idea what.

"Oh my Lord, Tressa, what did you take? What did you use? You need some help," he said, concerned and terrified. She didn't look well at all, and at that moment, he wanted to help her.

"Don't tell me what I need, you bastard. I came to settle the score with you and that bitch," she shot at Tiffany, giving an unstable arm gesture in Tiffany's direction.

Tiffany rushed over to assist Kory.

"Oh my God, Kory, she's wasted. Should we dial 911?" Kory heard the panic in Tiffany's voice when she asked.

Tressa tried to move forward, but stumbled and fell. Tiffany and Kory both went down to the ground to aid her. She was unconscious. Kory took her up into his arms, and they both yelled her name, shaking her limp body, trying to get her to respond.

"Kory, I'm scared. She doesn't look good at all," Tiffany said with dread.

"Someone call 911," Kory yelled.

"Yes, please, somebody call 911!" Tiffany yelled. Kory knew his phone was dead, and Tiffany didn't have a phone on her. Others gathered around and tried to assist.

"An ambulance is on the way," a man in the crowd yelled.

"Come on, Reesy, open your eyes," Kory said, shaking and tapping her face.

Tiffany slapped the back of her hand and pinched her skin and yelled out her name, but she didn't respond. They thought all the press and media were gone, but within seconds, cameras were flashing as if it was a glam set. "Please, no pictures, no pictures, please. Someone, anyone, please, somebody find Mr. Green," Kory yelled in panic. "Come on, Tressa, come on," he said shaking her and slapping her cheeks with light taps. "Wake up, Reesy, wake up!" he yelled, but she didn't respond. He checked her pulse. It was faint.

"Please, no pictures, please!" Tiffany cried as loudly as she could, but her cries were ignored. Finally, the ambulance arrived, but Tressa was still unresponsive. She was still breathing, but didn't open her eyes. Unfortunately, Mr. Green had already left the party, so Tiffany phoned him as soon as she and Kory got into the limo. They instructed the limo driver to follow the ambulance.

She put the phone on speaker, and Kory saw her hands trembling while she waited for Mr. Green to answer. "I'm so sorry, Mr. Green, but it's Tressa," she cried into the phone as soon as he said hello. "I hate to call you with this news, but Tressa showed up tonight. She was high, Mr. Green, and passed out. She is unconscious and unresponsive. We called for an ambulance, and we are now on our way to Good Samaritan Hospital. She was unresponsive, sir, and I'm afraid it's not looking too good."

"Oh no, oh my Lord," Mr. Green gasped. "Let me go home and get my wife. We'll be there right away."

"Okay, sir, and I'm so sorry."

"Thank you, Tiffany," Mr. Green said, and then disconnected from the line.

Tiffany hung up, and Kory noticed she was still shaking. "Baby, relax. She is going to be all right."

"Somehow, I don't feel too confident about that, Kory. You saw her. Her eyes were cold like she wasn't even there. How she managed to get there is more than a shocker to me. I mean, who drove her? I can't imagine her driving in that condition."

"I don't know, baby, I can't either. I've seen Tressa high, but tonight, it was something like a dream. She was in a zone. I don't know, baby, let's just hope for the best."

She nodded. "Yes, as much as I hate the sight of her, I don't want her to die, Kory. Mr. Green would lose it.

Tressa may be a lot of things, but Mr. Green loves his daughter. If she doesn't make it . . ." Tiffany cried.

"Shhh, don't cry, baby. Tressa is a trooper, a fighter. Hopefully, this will be a wake-up call for her."

"I hope so."

They pulled into the parking lot, parked, and rushed inside. They had wheeled Tressa off, and Kory and Tiffany had a million-and-one questions.

"The doctor will come out as soon as he knows something," the nurse repeated for the third time. They finally gave in and went to sit and wait. Twenty minutes later, Mr. Green and his wife rushed in.

"Where is she? Where's my baby? How is she?" Mr. Green questioned. Kory stood.

"Mr. Green, I'm sorry, they took her back about twenty minutes ago, and we don't know anything yet," Kory said, and then looked at Tressa's mother. She was a soft-spoken, humble woman that always treated him with kindness. The fear on her face was enough to make Kory tear up. Kory held it together, took her by the hands, and spoke to her in Spanish. He wrapped his arms around her and told her not to worry, and he guided her over to have a seat by Tiffany.

He walked back over to Langley, who thanked Kory for stepping up and aiding his daughter.

"I know Isa is not your favorite person, but I am so grateful that you and Tiffany didn't just leave my princess behind. Thank you for helping her."

"Mr. Green, there are no thanks needed, and I am so sorry," Kory offered.

Tiffany stood to greet Langley after she gave Mrs. Green a tight hug. "Yes, Mr. Green, we are so sorry," Tiffany added.

"No, Tiffany, don't apologize. This is not the first call my wife and I have gotten, and I pray my daughter pulls through, but at this point, I'm at the end of the road. If Isabella pulls through, she has to get help on her own. I know cutting her off was drastic, but I just wanted her to take some responsibility and do the right thing." He paused. His eyes welled, and he choked up. "But if I lose my little girl—" he tried to say. Tiffany immediately hugged him tightly.

"Mr. Green, I'm sure Tressa is going to pull through," she encouraged. "Please come and sit down." She guided him to the seat next to his wife, and she sat on the other side. She held his hand. "Mr. Green, let's not think the worst." Then she turned to Kory. "Baby, can you get some coffee for Mr. and Mrs. Green," she asked, and Kory nodded.

Before Kory could walk away, the doctor walked in.

"Green, Green," he said loudly. They all stood.

Mr. Green moved rapidly and reached out his hand quickly to shake the doctor's hand. "How is she? How's my baby?" he inquired. No matter what had transpired before that night, Kory could see the fatherly love in his eyes.

"She is stable, but not out of the woods. We were able to stabilize her, but it doesn't look good. The next twenty-four hours are critical, so we'll keep a watch on her and see what happens, but we've done all we can."

"Thank you, Doctor," Mr. Green said, and then turned to his wife and repeated everything to her in Spanish. "Can we see her?"

"Not tonight, but in the morning. I suggest you all go home, try to get some rest, and if anything changes, I'll call you."

"Thank you, Doctor," Mr. Green said and shook his hand again, but held it this time. "Listen, whatever it takes, whatever the cost, if she needs a kidney, lung, or whatever . . . I don't care. Just don't let my baby die. I will give my soul for her, and money is no object. I'll pay for whoever to fly in, whatever specialist. I need the best that you got!" Mr. Green cried. His sniffles had them all with wet eyes.

"I understand, sir," the doctor said. "We are giving her the best care we can, as we do all of our patients. If a situation arises above our control or expertise, we will get the best in here, Mr. Green. I assure you that we will take good care of your daughter."

"No, you don't understand. Treat her like the president. If you got to fly someone in, wake up the top specialist out of his sleep. I don't care. I want the best for her," Mr. Green reiterated. He held the doctor's hand and would not let go.

"Whatever we need, Mr. Green, I give you my word, we will do it for her. Don't worry."

Mr. Green released his hand and put a hand on his shoulder. "Thank you, Doctor. My wife and I will be back first thing in the morning."

"Yes, sir. Good night," the doctor said and walked away.

Kory and Tiffany stood there and waited for Mr. Green to turn to them. "Thank you so much for getting my Isabella medical help."

"Mr. Green, again, you don't owe us any gratitude or thanks. We sincerely hope she pulls through," Kory said.

"So do we," Mr. Green said. Kory knew he was not confident how things would turn out. Mr. Green was always cocky, strong, and had a tough stature, but Tressa seemed to break him down.

"Mr. Green, if there is anything you need, please don't hesitate. I'm here for whatever you need," Tiffany added.

"Thanks, Tiffany." He pulled her in for another hug.

"Yes, Mr. Green, we are here. I know Tressa and I have had our differences in the past, but the past is just what it is, and we will be praying she gets better."

"I know, son." Mr. Green hugged Kory.

Kory and Tiffany gave hugs to Mrs. Green, and then they departed. They rode home in silence, holding hands tightly. When they got in, they showered and got into bed. An hour later, Kory rolled over to find Tiffany was no longer beside him. He got up to look for her. He found her out on the terrace with a glass in one hand and an open bottle of Pinot Noir on the little round table next to the chaise she was relaxing on. He cleared his throat.

She looked up at him.

"Baby, what's on your mind? Why are you out here alone?"

"I couldn't sleep," she answered.

He walked over to join her. He took a seat at her feet and put her sock-covered feet on his lap.

"What's up, babe? Talk to me."

"I'm worried about Tressa and Mr. Green and this entire situation, Kory. You know Tressa has always had a history with drugs and alcohol, and Mr. Green and his wife have suffered time and time again for her addictions. If they lose her, it will be horrific."

"Awww, baby, don't you worry. Tressa is going to be okay. She's going to pull through."

"And what if she doesn't, Kory?" Tiffany said, raising her voice. Kory wondered why she was feeling so emotional about Tressa, a woman who despised her.

"Tiff, where is this coming from? Tressa has been a thorn in our sides for months. I don't wish her dead, but you and I both know Tressa is an addict and a major headache. She's done nothing but cause drama and pain for us in the last few months since her daddy threw her out of TiMax," I said, trying not to sound heartless. Tressa being gone would not have bothered me one bit. Yes, I was engaged to marry her, and, yes, I once thought I loved her, but I fell in love with a fraud. When I learned the truth, I had no problem leaving her standing at the altar.

She did the most to destroy what I had with Tiffany and even after she lost that battle, she still kept trying to make our lives a living hell. Tiffany and I came home from our honeymoon, well, the honeymoon Tressa and I were supposed to go on, and she busted out all of the first-floor windows of the house. We had to get a restraining order because she kept showing up at the jewelry store harassing customers, telling them that KBanks Jewelers sold blood diamonds.

"And let's not forget when we came out of Patina's after having a beautiful romantic dinner, she had spray painted the Benz. The list goes on and on. We have suffered, endured, and put up with so much crap from that woman since the live interview, and I don't want her to die, I'm not that cruel, but Tressa was a nightmare."

"I know, and I know there's a long list of things we can name that she's done to us. It's petty and childish, yes, but we weren't nice, Kory. We got just as ugly as she with the wedding, and Mr. Green giving me all of this money that was meant for her, Kory . . . I feel horrible because I got you *and* her inheritance. I mean, I feel like shit. If she doesn't make it, I am going to feel like it's my fault. Tressa had this thing in her mind that I even stole her daddy from her, Kory, and that's what drove her to rock bottom. We didn't have to play the game like she did. I could have given the money to her; I don't know, Kory, I, I, I," she cried. "If Tressa dies, I'll feel partly responsible."

"Shhh," Kory said and moved to hold her. "Tiffany, please, baby, Tressa has done all of this to herself. She brought her fate on herself. Now I agree the church scene and the inheritance was a bit much, but Tressa had the wedding thing coming for playing all of those games, and you didn't ask or force Mr. Green to give you the money, Tiff, so that is not your fault. Please don't blame yourself, sweetheart."

She sighed. "I guess." She took a big gulp, and that cued Kory to pour more into her glass.

"Tiff, baby, please. Let's not think of the worst right now. Tomorrow, we'll get up and go check on Tressa."

"Okay," she whispered and nodded.

"Now I know you're in a not-so-good mood, but I know how to make you feel better."

She smiled. "Do you really?"

"Yes." He took her glass and took a swallow of his own.

"Kory, I hope you are not trying to get ass after this evening's drama."

"I am," he smiled even brighter.

"It *has* been a minute since the planning for the premiere party, the wedding, and work," she smiled at him.

He leaned in and kissed her and her nipples immediately became erect. Kory felt the tingle of his manhood grow, and the more he kissed her, the harder it became.

"Let's go back inside," he said after breaking the kiss. He stood, reached for her hand, and she grabbed her bottle of wine and followed him inside.

The Next Morning

Tiffany

The sound of her cell phone woke her. She was in the middle of a dream, but the phone wouldn't stop ringing. "Hello," she grumbled.

"Tiffany, good morning," Myah sang.

"Good morning, Mee-Mee. Why are you calling so early?"

"I'm sorry, I thought you'd be up."

"No, I'm not, what's up?"

"I just called to check on you. I know I left the party before the big Tressa scene, so I wanted to know what happened. I can't listen to the news and TMZ. That shit be on a slant, so I wanted to know what really happened."

Tiffany rolled over and noted that Kory was not in bed with her and wondered where he was.

"I would love to fill you in," she said getting up and going into the bathroom to relieve her bladder.

"So is Tressa okay? Did she die? I know Mr. Green is a private person, and that is something so personal."

"No, Mee-Mee, she is not dead, but she is in critical condition. Once we got to the hospital and they learned who Tressa was, they went to work, giving her the best possible care. We didn't even get to see her last night, not even Mr. Green was allowed to see her. Of course, the cameras and tabloids and reporters swarmed the hospital, but luckily, no one got past security."

"Well, they were all over the studio. I mean, it was bombarded with the media."

"How do you know? We are all off today."

"I know, but I left my tablet in my desk, and, girl, I'm reading *From Main Chick to Mistress* by M. Skye, and, honey, I wasn't going to go the rest of my weekend without my book."

"You and your books, girl. You should join our team of writers."

"Nah, I'd rather read about it than write about it," she said.

"Listen, as far as we know, Tressa should pull through. I'm going to head to the hospital soon. I need to see where Kory is because we agreed to go together."

"*Excuse me?* Why? I mean, like everyone knows you and Tressa are enemies."

"We are, but I want to make sure she's okay, and you know me and Mr. Green are like," she was going to say father and daughter, but said, "good friends now. It's only right to support him."

"I guess you're right, but you will keep me posted, right?"

"I will."

"Okay, girl, I'll talk to you soon." They hung up, and Tiffany got up and went to look for Kory. She grabbed her robe and went downstairs, but he wasn't in the house. She headed for the kitchen, and then he walked in.

"Out running?" she asked. He was in his athletic attire, and his chest area was soaking wet.

"Yeah. You were sleeping so peacefully. I didn't want to wake you."

She chuckled. "Even if you had, it would not have made any difference. You know running is not my thing."

"I know, baby," he said. He went for a bottle of water, and then went over and planted a wet kiss on her cheek.

"Kory, not saying this out of insecurity, because I love being a full-sized diva, but when I think of Tressa and how slim she—" she tried to say, but he cut her off.

"Hey, don't start that shit. You are beautiful, and I love you, *all* of you."

"But you work out daily, and you are fit. Your stomach, baby, your abs could be featured in a magazine."

"And you, my love, can also grace a magazine. A cover, I might add. Don't start this, Tiff. You know that is not an issue in our relationship."

"Okay, okay." She went for the cabinet and grabbed the coffee. "What time are we going to head over to the hospital?"

"I guess after breakfast, babe. I called Mr. Green this morning, and he said there has been no change. He said she is still considered critical."

"Well, maybe we should wait until after lunch. To go there and not be able to see her would be a waste, right?"

"Yes, I guess you're right. I'm going to go shower. If you want, I can come back down and make breakfast."

"No, baby, I got it. What would you like?"

"Omelet with everything and toast will work."

"Omelet it is. Go on up." As soon as he cleared the kitchen she called Rose.

"Hey, girlfriend, what's going on in L.A.? Facebook is blasting that the Queen of L.A., whom I refer to as the Wicked Witch of the West, is dead of an overdose."

"Well, good morning to you too."

"I'm sorry, good morning. Is the Wicked Witch of the West a goner?"

"Rose, that is so not nice to say."

"Since when? You know whatever my bestie hates, I hate, and I know Tressa is public enemy number one."

"Look, she is not dead, okay? She is in the hospital, and she's holding on for dear life," Tiffany said.

"Wait a minute, it almost sounds like you care."

Tiffany blew out a breath of air and went for the fridge. "I *do* care, Rose. That is Mr. Green's only daughter, and for him, I care, okay? He gave me a chance of a lifetime. Gave me over forty million big ones. That man has a heart of gold, and as much damage as Tressa has done, he loves her, Rose, so my heart goes out to him and his wife." Tiffany proceeded to get the eggs, green peppers, tomatoes, onions, mushrooms, turkey ham, and cheese. Rarely did she add milk to her omelets, but today, she wanted to add a little.

Kory said toast, but when her eyes landed on the strawberry cream cheese, she decided she'd do bagels instead.

"So now you care about Tressa Hell-Raiser Green?"

"Rose, I don't care about Tressa, but I care about Mr. and Mrs. Green. I don't want them to lose their one and only daughter," she said while placing everything on the island. Then she went for the drawers that housed the cookware and pulled out a pan, then went for a mixing bowl.

"Well, Tiff, as your best friend and the person you have shared every intimate detail about that woman with, they lost their daughter a long time ago."

"That may be true, Rose, but this time, they may have to bury her, and no parent wants to bury a child. Do you remember how much hell my brother gave my mother with slanging drugs, his two baby mommas, and momma having to go down to the county for him every three or four months to bail him out and all the bullshit? Terrance put my mother through hell, Rose. I know you remember that. Yet and still, when he was murdered by them thugs, my mother lost her mind, Rose. Remember she became so depressed and for a while, she would not let it go. My mother was a basket case after that, Rose, and it took a very long time for her to heal from his death. I don't wish that on nobody, and even though children become problem children, no one wants to bury their daughter," Tiffany said and wiped her eyes. The flashback reminded her of her mother's pain and the pain of losing her big brother.

"I'm sorry, Tiff. I didn't think of it that way. I don't have kids, never lost a sibling, and have no idea what it's like, so I didn't mean to be insensitive."

"It's all right, Rose, I know you didn't mean any harm, and if I was as stone cold as Tressa, I'd probably not give a fuck either, but God gave me a heart. I'm not the Tin Man, or should I say, Tin Woman," she laughed.

"Neither am I, but I just know how much drama and tragedy that woman has put y'all through. Don't get me wrong, she brought everything on herself, but I don't wish anyone dead, not even your archenemy."

"Me either," Tiffany said. She grabbed the cutting board and started to dice the veggies.

"So how are you and Kory?"

"We're good, Rose. I'm so happy, and you know Momma has been blowing me up about wedding planning. She's going to drive me crazy."

"I can't wait, girl, and I'm so happy for y'all. I can't wait to find my soul mate."

"I know, Rose. Finding love isn't easy, especially finding that right one. Just look at my past relationships and that damn Jeff, girl. There's not a time that I enter my bedroom that I don't get a flashback."

"Well, Jeff was a stone-cold idiot. And you are putting that house on the market soon anyway, so that will be a distant memory."

"Yeah, you're right. You should come out here, Rose. I mean, we haven't visited for a while. Why don't you visit?"

"Girl, you know I'm between jobs. Since I lost the gallery, I'm trying to sell a piece here and there, just to have a few dollars in my pocket."

"Even more of a better time, while you're off. You know I'll get your ticket; you can stay with us. Kory's place is huge, and the guest bedroom has its own bathroom. And you know I got you in whatever thanks to the check Mr. Green gave me. You can come and stay as long as you want . . . hell, move here. You can start over. I'd love to have you."

"Tiffany, come on, I don't want your money. You know we had this conversation ten times before. When you got the money, you paid off my truck to keep me from losing it, and I deeply appreciate it, but you know how I am. I can't accept money from you."

"That's because you're foolish and stubborn. You're not working now, Rose. Your art is beautiful. Come out here. Stay at my house if you want privacy. We can shop for some spaces, and you can have your own studio. Once these L.A. peeps get a look at your work, you'll be selling pieces left and right."

"You think so?"

"Rose, I know so . . . Please, for the hundredth time, come out here. You've said it a million times that you want to leave. Before Mr. Green gave me this money, I couldn't help you, couldn't help my mom, but now I can. Momma is shopping for a condo now because I want her to have a doorman and some security and not have to worry about fixing things in that old-ass house I grew up in and having to pay for someone to shovel snow and mow all that damn grass. You know I'd do anything for you, girl, so please come. You know you love my place, and it's yours if you want a new start in L.A. Until you get your business up and running and your art starts to fly off the walls, I got you."

"Okay, okay, okay. I'll think about it. You know I want to . . . I just think you're doing too much, so consider it all a loan, and I will keep a tally and give you back every cent. That's *if* I decide to come."

"Please, Rose, I was blessed with something I know I didn't earn. It will be my pleasure to do this for you."

"Okay, I *will* think about it. Living here with my sister isn't what I planned to do, but when my pieces stopped selling, I just couldn't afford to maintain my house and bills. I just don't want to be a burden or dependent on anyone. You know how I am, Tiffany. I'm self-sufficient."

"I know, and I respect that. Just think about it. I got a few connects, and trust, L.A. is going to love your works."

"You think so, Tiff?"

"Honey, I *know* so," she confirmed. She continued to chat with Rose, and then Kory came down just as she was finishing up. She said her good-byes to Rose, they ate, and then hung around the house for a while before leaving. Later, they went out for lunch, and then headed over to the hospital.

Rehab

Tressa

It had been a couple of days after her overdose, and she was feeling good and doing better, but they refused to let her leave. She had a mind to walk up out of there, but security was everywhere, and she wondered why she was forced to stay there. She needed a hit, a line, a taste on her tongue, but they were not complying with her request. She knew that the last time was close to her last time living on this earth, but she had this under control. She only went hard when she was angry, and Tiffany made her angry. The sight of her made her mad, and she just wanted to go home, hit a line or two, and get back to living.

Hell, that night she was so enraged, and she hated Colby for not supporting her. Him not stepping up and carrying out their mission, she lost her mind. She drove to the party, sat in her car, and did every last grain of the coke she had on her. What she wanted to do that night took balls, and the powder gave her wings. She parked right in front and ignored the bastards who insisted she couldn't park there and marched right inside. She was a motherfucking Green. Her father was the reason for everything, so she could park where the fuck she wanted. As soon as she laid eyes on them, she was ready, but her head spun and her limbs were wobbly. But she was determined. After barely telling them two bitches a piece of her mind, her body abandoned her, and she blanked out . . . and then woke up there.

"Good morning, Ms. Green," the nurse said upon entering the room.

"Bitch, don't good morning me. I want to go home. Why are they keeping me here?"

"Ms. Green, when you come close to fatality from drugs, it's standard to keep you for a while. We just want you to get better and not end up right back here again. You made it this time, darling, but we can't risk there being a next time."

"But you are holding me against my will. Isn't that illegal?"

"I imagine it is, but your father has a lot of influence, and he wants you better."

"My *father*? Did you say my father?" Tressa hadn't seen her father at all. She wanted them to get her father so he could tell them she could go home.

"Yes, Mr. Green has been here every day. He and the doctors talk, and he just wants you better before we release you, that's all."

"So my father is keeping me here. That's not fair," Tressa cried. "I'm a grown-ass woman, and I will sue this hospital."

"Tressa, you really don't know where you are, do you?"

"No, I thought this was the hospital in L.A., right?"

"No, dear, this is rehab. We are in the Hamptons, sugar. L.A. is on the other side of the map, and you can't leave unless your father allows it."

"How is that possible? I'm grown. You can't keep me against my will."

"Well, according to the power of attorney signed by you, in case of any emergencies or endangerment of your well-being, your father is the sole custodian over you."

"I never signed nothing like that or I, I, I," she stuttered, and then went silent. She had signed so many things over the years that her father gave her without reading them, so she may have. "So you are saying I gave my father the power to admit me here."

"That is exactly what I'm saying. If you'd like, I can let your father know you'd like to see him."

"Yes, you do that," Tressa said as a matter-of-fact. She couldn't wait to tell her father a piece of her mind.

The nurse left, and Tressa paced. How was she back in rehab against her very own wishes? She went to the window, and it dawned on her that she was a few stories up, and even if she wanted to, the window wasn't made to be opened. The grounds were beautiful, and she wondered how long she had been in rehab. She always figured she was at the hospital in L.A. She didn't have any memory of how she even had gotten there. She remembered everything, including going to Stephen's house and him trying to convince her to not go to the premiere party. She remembered going to Colby's to ask him to join forces with her, and when he declined, she knew she had to battle them alone. But she didn't remember boarding a plane, and she wondered how in the hell had they whisked her to the other side of the map with no recollection. Was she in a coma, was she sedated? So many questions ran through her mind.

All she wanted was answers, and she wanted them now. She began to bang and yell out for someone to come, and after five minutes, she realized her efforts were useless. She went for the call button and began to press the button insanely.

The nurse returned to her door. "Ms. Green, please," she said, "you need to calm down."

"I want to see my father! Now!" Tressa demanded.

"And I told you I will relay the message. Now, you're going to have to calm down."

"I will *not* calm down. I don't want to be here, and you can't keep me here against my will. I will sue this hospital and your ass too, now get my father, this minute!" she yelled through the door.

"Ms. Green, if you don't stop, we are going to have to use other measures to tame your actions."

"Do it and this entire facility will be shut down. As soon as I get out of here, I'm going to sue this place, and you're going to be the first one out of a job," she continued to yell.

"I'll take it from here," a baritone voice interrupted.

"Mr. Green," the nurse said letting out a sigh of relief.

"Open up for me, please."

"Daddy!" Tressa yelled through the door when she saw her father through the tiny glass window.

The nurse unlocked and opened the door, and Mr. Green stepped in. The nurse was sure to tell him to buzz when he was ready to leave, and she locked the door from the outside.

"Daddy, Daddy," Tressa cried and hugged him tightly.

He hugged her back tightly, and they held on to each other for a few moments.

"Daddy, I'm so glad you came for me. I'm ready to go home. Please tell me that you're here to get me outta this place," she pleaded, but then looked at his face. His face was serious and stern, and she felt a scolding coming on and figured he wasn't there to take her home.

"I'm afraid that's not going to happen today, Isa. You're going to be here for a while. I'm not going to let you out of here until you are truly clean. You've given your mother and me the last scare of our lives, and you are not going to kill yourself with drugs and only God knows what," he added.

"No, Daddy, please. You can't make me stay in this awful place. Where am I? This is not a familiar place. Where are we?"

"Far from L.A., far from your circle of friends, and far away from the life you once knew, and, yes, I *can* leave you here, and I am. Your mother and I made a decision to help you and the last time we were called to the hospital, Isa, *will* be our last time."

Tressa slumped down onto the bed. She put her head down. "I'm so sorry for what I did, Daddy, I am, and I know that I gave you and Mommy a scare, but—"

He cut her off. "But *nothing,* Isabella. You're not fine, and you won't ever be fine until you are clean and sober, and you are going to stay here and complete the entire plan, and stay even longer if I have my way. I'm not going to bury my daughter."

"Since when did you start caring? You threw me out, Daddy! You cut me off! You gave my money to that bitch, Tiffany!" she cried.

Mr. Green swallowed hard and took a moment before he spoke. He walked over and sat beside her. He moved her wild strains of hair from her face and spoke to her tenderly. "You're right. I tossed you out of my studio and took the money that I had set up for you and gave it to Tiffany. Most of my actions were out of hurt and anger, Isabella, but I don't regret my decisions. At the time, you didn't deserve a cent or respect or another chance, but when I got that call that you overdosed, I drove to that hospital prepared to hear that you were gone.

"When we arrived and found out you were in critical condition, but we couldn't see you, it broke my heart, and all I was thinking is if my daughter doesn't make it through the night, I would not have had the chance to say good-bye or tell her how much I truly love her. The next morning when your mother and I arrived at that hospital and saw that tube down your throat and the machines and your color had left your face, baby, I didn't recognize you, Isa. My heart ached so much. It was maybe the worst pain I'd ever felt in my life. Worse than my heart attack, any breakup, or love lost.

"Your mother and I prayed and prayed and begged God for another chance, just one more chance, and a final and last chance to have our daughter back. For more time with you. Four days later, you still hadn't responded, and your mother and I prepared ourselves to say good-bye, but we got that call that you opened your eyes, and there was physical evidence that you were going to recover. Your mother and I immediately transported you here. The next day, I had the doctor sedate you, and we flew you here. He was kind enough to make the trip with us to make sure you were okay.

"We wanted you to have another chance, so we both decided that you would only have a fighting chance here, and I know that there are some things neither of us can undo, Isa, but I'm ready to offer new terms."

Tressa lifted her head and looked at her daddy. She could see that he was honestly making an attempt to help her and from the tears in his eyes, she knew this was his final attempt.

"New terms, Daddy? What do you mean?" she inquired. She'd hoped it was something that would motivate her to want to stay and clean up for good.

"We can move forward and start over. Not for me or your mother, but for you. Stay here willingly and get clean, Isa. Clean up and give yourself a new beginning, a new start, a new lease on your life. I know I have always denied you a spot at TiMax, but it's time you learned the ropes. Now, I'm not saying you can have my seat, of course, because I'll be around for a while, and there is a lot to learn, Isa, but I want to give you a position and give you some control. Underneath all of this L.A. girl image, you are smart, Isabella, and as far as your trust, the new terms concern a payment plan."

Thrilled with everything he was saying she still needed to know what he meant. "Payment plans and a position at TiMax, what does all of that really mean, Daddy? What are you saying?"

"It means you will get your inheritance divided into monthly payments. As long as you are doing well and living drug-free and dedicating yourself to truly learning the business, you will get your money and a spot at TiMax."

Tressa hugged her father's neck tighter than she ever remembered hugging him before. "Do you mean it, Daddy?" she asked, and then sniffled. How could she not change? How could she not accept his offer? She was back in her father's good graces, and she would be awarded the money she always knew she was entitled to.

"I mean it, Isa. You are the apple of my eye, Isabella, and I love you so much. I just want a daughter that I can be proud of. I know you were jealous of the relationship I built with Tiffany. It's understandable, but you must know that I never wanted you to feel that I was replacing you, and I know you are hurt and ticked off with Kory and Tiffany, but I need you to let that go, Isa. My company is my baby, and I won't have strife in those walls, so you're going to have to get along with Tiffany, because in spite of your differences, she is good at what she does, and once you come aboard, you will be seeing a lot of her."

"Daddy, do I have to play nice with her? I mean, she and Kory—" he cut her off again.

"And the first step to healing is self-reflection, Isa. Take responsibility for what you've done. You know you never loved Kory, and you only cared about the money, so let this thing with Tiffany and Kory go."

Tressa looked at her father. She was determined to prove that she was better than Tiffany and that she was just as talented and just as driven. "Okay, Daddy, I hear you, and I want to clean up my act. It's going to be so hard, Daddy. You have absolutely no idea how this feels, or what it feels like to want another hit or a drink. It's all you think about. It's all you crave," she said and swiped a tear from her eye.

He put his arm around her. "I know, pumpkin. I know this will be the ultimate battle for you. But you can do it, Isa," he said.

Tressa smiled. Her father hadn't called her pumpkin since she was a child.

"Your mother and I have your back, and we will be here every step of the way. We are going to help you. Whatever you need."

"Thank you, Daddy," she said. She hugged her father tightly, and they talked for a while longer. Mr. Green told her that her mom was back at the hotel and would come by the next day. He explained to her that she knew Tressa would explode when they saw her for the first time being trapped in that place, and she didn't have the energy to deal with her.

Tressa smiled because she knew her mother was right about her behavior, so she vowed to herself she'd change and make her parents proud. She hugged her father and made him promise they'd come the next day, and he promised her that they'd come every day until it was time for her to go home.

With that, Tressa felt confident that she was going to be fine, but two days later when that withdrawal kicked in, she knew she wasn't strong enough, and she had doubts she'd make it.

One Year Later

Time to Pay

Episode 1

Tracy Simms

Tracy double-checked the mirror five times before she got out of her car. She looked gorgeous, she noted, with her natural curls straighten and her individual lashes. This was her first date with Mike, and she was still gloating and admiring how well she had conquered her quest to get close to one of the network owners of TiMax. Langley was her first target, the one she wanted to pursue, but he was a dead target, because after doing her research, she learned that he had never had one affair, not one that anyone could confirm, and he was not enticed by sexual promises or sexual advances from young and beautiful women. She had tried on several occasions to get within five inches of him, but her advances were ignored, and she knew it was a lost cause to pursue him.

She was smart, glamorous, and desirable, but Langley had looked past her as if she was invisible. Mike, his partner, on the other hand, was a different story. He liked the ladies, didn't hide his affairs, and he was known for bedding a woman, or twenty, outside of his marriage. She didn't like the idea of seducing Mike because Mike wasn't a handsome man. Powerful, wealthy, and intelligent, but he had a face that was not striking, in her opinion, but her obsession to ruin, Tiffany Richardson's life made him look as fine as Colby Grant.

"All I have to do is imagine I'm with Colby Grant," she said and closed the visor that housed her lighted mirror. "Colby, Colby, Colby, just think of Colby Grant," she coached herself and got out. She walked into the restaurant feeling anxious and excited. She had a foolproof plan to get what she wanted, and she wasn't going to stop until Tiffany knew how she ruined things for her.

She was supposed to be the new writer for *Boy Crazy,* and she had left her previous job for that position. Just because she got caught in traffic, she lost her spot to Tiffany, someone who at the time didn't even qualify for the job. She had to admit the show was good, but she knew her show would have been ten times better, but being late left her jobless and close to being homeless. After three months of living off her savings because she couldn't land another gig, Tracy grew more infuriated with Tiffany. She wanted Tiffany sad, lonely, hurt, distraught—the way *she* felt when she lost everything. She wanted her depressed and at the end of her miserable rope. She wanted her to pay and wanted her job.

Shortly after she lost her spot, she began to follow Tiffany, scope out her life, and when Tiffany became involved with Colby Grant, Tracy grew even more enraged and wanted to make Tiffany pay for her losses. She should have been evicted, but she exchanged sexual favors to her old-ass, funky landlord to keep a roof over her head. Just when she thought she'd swallow a bottle of pills, UVN called her back and asked if she wanted to be part of a new show idea. She was grateful to join the workforce again and accepted it without any negotiations.

Going back to work was the best thing, because Tracy had gotten so depressed, she began to inflict pain on herself. She'd punch her thighs until they were black and blue. She'd slap her face over and over again until it no longer stung. She'd throw herself against the wall, and she'd graduated to cutting herself—right before she got the call. Going back to work helped her from causing any serious harm to herself. Although she'd occasionally self-inflict, she no longer broke the skin. She no longer used sharp objects to pierce her skin. That's where she wanted to send Tiffany Richardson. She wanted her to be in a dark place, just like she was when Tiffany swooped in and stole her life from her.

Tracy still had a deep-seated desire for revenge, and if she could seduce Mike, get in good and gain some control at TiMax, Tiffany would surely be the first to go.

"Good evening, my lady. Do you have a reservation?"

"I do. I'm meeting Mike Harrington," she purred. She was in a sexy mood, and she had to get the mood right for her to stomach an evening with Mike's ugly ass.

"Sure. I have your reservation here. Right this way, madam," he said. She followed, closely making eye contact with the handsome men that were already seated. She knew she was eye candy, and she welcomed the looks and stares from the women as well as the men. Once she was seated at a great table, she noted the host offered her a drink, and she immediately ordered a white wine spritzer. She had to alcohol-induce herself so she could look at Mike and see Colby Grant's face and not Mike's horrid face.

The waiter, not the hostess, approached with her drink. "Would this be all, madam?"

"No, bring me another in about five minutes."

"Yes, ma'am." He hurried off, and five minutes later when he returned, she had finished her first one. "Here you are, madam. Would you like a menu?"

"No, I'm waiting for my party, but in three minutes, you can bring me another drink. And the tab. I want to pay for these now before my dinner date arrives."

"Of course, madam, I'll be back in three."

"Yes, thank you," she said with a slow nod. She had arrived twenty minutes earlier than her companion just so she could be more relaxed. Mike was wealthy and powerful, but he just wasn't pleasant to the eyes. He had dark skin that didn't bother Tracy, but he had large pores and bugged eyes. She'd not want to see him in a dark alley, because he'd make a person piss their pants, he was so far from attractive.

Three minutes later, as promised, the waiter was back with a glass and a bill. She took it, gave him her card, and then told him to come back in ten with another one, and that one will be billed to the evening. She gave him a generous tip, and by the time Mike made it, she was on her fourth, but Mike assumed it was her first.

Buzzing a little, feeling good and more relaxed, she was in kitten mode, purring and holding on to Mike's every word. She flirted, touched him under the table, and made Mike's cheeks flush a couple of times. Tracy was so focused on accomplishing her mission that Mike was starting to look fuckable.

"So, Tracy, what can I do to steal you from UVN?" he asked with a tone of fascination, she thought. After a few drinks and heavy flirting, Tracy had him eating out of the palm of her hands. She made a point to talk about work, her ideas, and how UVN wasn't allowing her to push her talents to the limits. She wanted to appear brilliant and full of impressive ideas, and Mike was falling full speed ahead into her trap. She could tell from the eye contact, the compliments, and his constant mentioning of how talented he thought she was that led her to believe that he was eating up all of her words.

"Steal me? You want to steal me? I'd rather you take me as your lover than your employee," she stated boldly. Inside, she hoped it wasn't too much. She didn't want him to recognize her game.

"How about both?" he smiled.

She beamed back and knew she had him. "How about you take me somewhere to make me scream first, and then we talk business later?"

"Young lady, you don't know me," he said leaning in closer to her and lowering his voice. She didn't know why his tone changed. There were no others seated near them, and there were no servers in plain sight.

Inclined to hear where he was going she replied, "What's to know?"

"There are some things I like to do behind closed doors that some women are afraid to try."

"Well, as long as it doesn't put me in the hospital or in a body bag, I'm game."

He chuckled. "Really?"

"Really. I don't scare easily, Mr. Harrington, and I'll try anything once."

"I'll tell you what, Ms. Simms. I will have my driver pick you up in two hours. Come to me tonight, naked."

"Naked? You mean walk to the car totally nude?"

"No, you can walk to the car in whatever you like, but when I open the door, I want you completely naked. You look average enough, and I have what I want you to wear if you're game."

Tracy paused but tried to keep a straight face. This old ugly-ass bastard was into some weird shit, she just knew it, but she was so hell-bent on bringing Tiffany Richardson to her knees, she quickly said, "I'll be wearing stilettos, and I will put on whatever you want to see me in."

"That sounds good to me, baby." He waved for the server. He made sure I was satisfied and didn't want anything else, and then handed the server his black card.

"Sir, would you like your ticket first?" the server asked.

"No, whatever it is, it's fine, and take out 30 percent of that amount for your tip and hurry back with my card."

The server bowed. "Yes, sir, right away." He hurried off.

Mike just sat there and licked his lips as he examined her chocolate skin. Yes, her breasts stood up, and she had plenty of cleavage exposed. After all the drinks she had, she welcomed it, and her pussy was speaking on her own behalf. She was wet and said to hell with his face, we want to meet his dick.

The server returned and said his good night. Mike stood and reached for her to help her from her seat.

"It was a pleasure. Dinner and company were both extraordinary," Tracy said.

"It was my pleasure, and I look forward to continuing our night. See you in two hours," he said, and they made their exit.

Tipsy but good to drive, Tracy raced home, showered again, moisturized her skin, and made her face all over again. She waited for her ride and rode to a place on the ocean outside of town. She removed her sweats and T-shirt and put on her sexy black five-inch heels, and then made her way to the door. She rang the bell, and when he opened the door—in an adult diaper and baby bonnet and adult-sized bib, it took every muscle in her body to keep from laughing her ass off in his face. He had an oversized pacifier hanging around his neck, and she thought she was on a set for real. She wondered where the cameras were hidden.

What in the fuck have I signed up for? were her last thoughts before entering into his adult day care.

"Can you handle *this?*" he asked with his arm stretched out, moving it in the direction of the room.

Trying to keep a straight face, she whispered, "Yes, baby, I can handle anything you'd like."

"Are you sure, because if it's too much, you can leave right now."

Determined to follow through she smiled. "Ask me that again and I'll have to spank you."

With that, Mike went into character. "I'll be good, Mommy, please don't spank me," he whined like a two-year-old. Tracy wanted to fall to the floor in laughter, but she decided it was too late to turn back. As weird as it was, she enjoyed nursing her grown-ass baby, because he latched on well, giving her nipples more pleasure than she ever felt before.

When he whined about being hungry, she asked, "What do you want to eat, baby?"

He mimicked a child when he spoke. "Kitty kat, I want to eat kitty kat."

She followed him to a giant high chair, made for adults, and the tray was a full-sized table. He slid the table over to the side and climbed into his seat and rolled the table back in place. Tracy looked at the table wondering how the fuck was she going to lie on a hard-ass table, but when she climbed on to it, it was soft and comfy, so she lay back and let him feast on her hot spot, and she climaxed over and over again.

Like Taking Candy from a Baby

Episode 2

Tracy

After a week of wiping Mike's ass like he was a toddler and letting him feast on her like she was Gerber in a jar she was finally getting a tour of TiMax. She walked around with a smile plastered on her face, and she couldn't wait to get started. She was finally in her office. She looked around. It was just as prestigious and upscale as she'd imagined it would be. After her tour guide had left her alone, she crept back to Tiffany's office. Now they were on the same floor, four offices apart, and since there was a lot going on, she decided she'd check on it another day.

Since her official start date would be Monday, that weekend she went in on a Sunday, a day she knew no one would be there, and set up her office. After adding a few personal touches to her office, she eased down to Tiffany's office and was pleasantly surprised it wasn't locked. Their offices were close by each other's, but Tiffany's office was a corner office, and Tracy could see it was a lot larger than hers. She took her time and explored by looking in cabinets and drawers and realized Tiffany may have had a few more perks than she, so she'd have to have a talk with Mike. She was just as talented and good as Tiffany Richardson, so she wanted an office equal or even better than Tiffany's.

Realizing she had spent too long in a place she should not have been, she slowly cracked the door open to make sure no one was in the hall, and then headed back to her office. She looked around. Now she was definitely not happy with her mediocre space, although it was very nice, something she'd love in a heartbeat . . . if she had not seen Tiffany's corner space. She pulled out her phone and dialed Mike. He answered on the fourth ring, just as she was about to hang up.

"Hey, this is, Mike." He sounded businesslike, not like they had been sucking and fucking for the past week and change.

"Why is Tiffany's office larger than mine?"

"Excuse me?"

"You heard me, Mikey," she called him on purpose. That was the childlike name he liked when they were in his adult day care.

"Ms. Simms, I'm in the middle of something. Can we meet in maybe two hours?"

"Yes, we can," she shot at him. She knew that meant he was with the wife.

"Good and be sure you come prepared to bounce around some ideas. I am anxious to play around with your ideas."

"I will, baby, believe that." She hung up and laughed. That meant she needed to be ready to bounce him on his oversized bouncer, the one she rode his face on. He was so sick with it; she'd bounce on his face until he fell asleep if that's what he wanted. Having her pussy in his face all night would have suited her just fine. It had only been a week and a few days, but she had nursed him almost every night since the first night. What he told his wife she had no clue, but all she knew is she'd take his temperature in his ass, bounce on his face, or let him suck her nipples until he fell asleep like a baby, if that meant an office that was analogous to Tiffany's.

Tiffany had won once, but Tracy was determined to come and take her spot at TiMax and produce killer shows that would put Tiffany's ratings down to zero. "Yes, let me go and clean up for my grown baby." As weird as what Mike wanted, he teased her body right, so she was starting to get into it too. "Damn, am I weird?" she asked herself when she got onto the elevator.

When she hit the bottom floor and the doors opened, there *she* was standing, waiting to get on, and Tracy's heart pounded. She wasn't ready. She didn't want to see Tiffany, not yet, not now. She wanted her to notice her on set or in a meeting, or after she became her boss—not getting off of the elevator.

She told her feet to move, and she stepped off. "Hello," Tiffany said.

"Hi," Tracy said and kept moving. She took rapid strides, hoping Tiffany wouldn't call out her name, but then she heard the elevator doors shut, and she was relieved she hadn't recognized her. She then let out a breath of relief that she had vacated Tiffany's office moments before, and she hadn't caught her in there.

"You have to be more careful, Tracy," she told herself and hurried out to the parking lot instead of calling for a cart. There were three options at TiMax: park and walk, park and go to the booth on that level, or call for a cart or valet. Since she parked and walked, by the time Tracy made it to her car, she was sweating and out of breath. She got into her Volvo, cranked the air-conditioning, and headed home. She showered and changed, and then headed to Mike's place. She was starting to think she was just as weird as he, because she was beginning to like what they were doing. It was crazy at first, but the pleasure was so good she found herself anxious and excited to get back to "Mikey," and his adult nursery to play around again.

She rang the bell and heard him say come in. When she walked in, he crawled toward her fast, like a little baby boy really happy to see his mother. "Mommy, you're home, Mommy, Mommy, you're home," he cheered in his baby voice.

She knelt down when he reached her and caressed his cheek. "Yes, baby, I'm home. Your mommy's home. Did you miss Mommy? Did you miss me, baby?" she returned, getting into character. This not only turned Mike on, but she was also starting to like it just as much as him, and she wondered how she would ever find another man who was into being in diapers and spankings. If she'd find another one to devour her hot spot and suck her tits as good as Mikey, that was easier on the eyes, she'd be all in.

"Yes. Milk, Mommy, milk. Eat, eat, eat, Mommy," he fussed like a hungry baby and tugged on her top.

"Okay, okay, baby, calm down. Mommy knows you're ready to eat, baby. Mommy knows what you want, so come over and let's get on the rocker so I can feed you, baby. Mommy's breasts are full, and my nipples are hard enough for you to feast, baby." She undid her buttons and walked toward the love seat-sized rocker and still wondered who he had to make all of those oversized furnishings and who had he hired to turn his living room, kitchen, and spare bedroom into an adult-sized day care.

He crawled behind her, and she removed her top and unlatched the nursing bra. Yes, Mike had given her nursing bras, nipple pads, and you name it to stay in character. She sat, and they got comfy, and she held her left breast to put it in his mouth, and he latched on. He rested a hand on her breast as to hold it in place and looked up at her while he sucked her nipple like he was waiting for some milk to quench his hunger and thirst.

She stroked his head and talked to him in a tender tone. "There you go, baby. You were hungry, huh?" He stared up at her like a baby enjoying his mother's breast milk. After a few moments, her center tingled, and she loved the sensations his suckling gave her erect nipples. "Come on, baby, let Mommy switch," she said, and they repositioned themselves for him to latch onto her right nipple. It felt so good she tried to focus on cuddling him and talking to him like a mother would her child, but she really wanted to tell him to suck harder, baby!

After fifteen more minutes of him feasting on her nipple, her center ached, and she wanted to give him his dinner. "Come on, baby, that's enough for now." She pulled away.

"No, Mommy, eat, eat, eat," he cried.

"I'm going to feed you, baby, but Mommy wants to feed you some jar food, okay? You can nurse later."

He nodded and climbed down. He crawled to the kitchen and climbed into his high chair.

She went into the pantry, undressed completely, and put on a costume that looked like a jar of Gerber baby food. Yes, it was a strapless, tight-fitting, body-hugging mini that had the Gerber baby on it, and it said rice and chicken. After grabbing the jar that she planned to smear on her clit, she went to the fridge and grabbed the "Mommy juice," which was the red wine, and poured a glass. She took two swallows, then Mikey whined and banged on his cushioned table, the table she rested on as he ate her to orgasm after orgasm.

"Hold on, baby, Mommy has to heat up your food. After I've had my Mommy juice, your food should be good and warm for you, baby."

He kicked and started throwing a tantrum.

"Listen, young man, behave yourself and wait. Mommy is heating up your food. If you don't behave, I'm going to spank you," she admonished, and her adult baby calmed down and put his massive binky in his mouth and sucked.

It took everything in her to keep from laughing, and she again wondered why she was even more turned on. Her clit ached. After she polished off her glass of wine she climbed onto the soft table. She opened wide, popped the top on the jar food, and shook it over her opening, and then smeared it with her fingers. "Your dinner is warm now, baby, come and eat," she said. He dove right in, doing things to her clit and opening no man had ever done. She was loving the crazy and erotic things that Mikey was doing to her.

"Yes, Mikey, baby, eat all of your food, baby, eat it all. Mommy loves it when you eat every last drop of your dinner, baby." He slurped and sucked and after her third orgasm, she was done. She wanted the dick, so she knew she had to close the role-playing down, and that was by simply changing his diaper. Mikey had always come on his own, and the semen in his adult diaper was the end of "Mommy and Mikey" fun. They then went into his master bedroom, showered, and then fucked. She'd once asked why he couldn't fuck her as Mikey, and that sick motherfucker had the nerve to say it would be weird to put his dick into his mother. But eating her was just like her doing what was natural to feed her baby, like when a mother gives her child her breast.

She didn't ask any more questions after that.

"So now can we talk about work?" she asked while she rested in his arms.

"Yes, go ahead."

She was falling for this Mike, not Mikey, although Mikey is the one who pleased her tits and clit right. But she loved when he wasn't crawling around in a damn diaper. He was smart and talented and about his business. Not the baby-babbling fool in diapers.

"I need to talk to you about my office."

"What about your office?"

"I got a peep at Tiffany's office, and if I'm correct, we have the same job and title, right?"

"Yes and no. Tiffany is my partner's number one producer, and you just started."

"Okay, how can I become your number one producer?"

"Well, produce your first show. I hired you because I know you have potential, but Tiffany has proven herself, and her shows are doing well, but . . ." he paused. She assumed he could see the frustrated look on her face when she lifted her head to look at him. "An office is just an office. The office right below Tiffany's office is a corner office, and that office is free if you want to move."

It was a corner office, but the thought of being beneath Tiffany didn't sound good. "What about above?" She knew it was juvenile, but it seemed Tiffany was already five steps ahead of her.

"I'm sorry, darling, but that one is not available. There are other offices, but they are not corner offices, but larger."

"No, it's okay. I'll keep my office," she said disappointedly.

"Tracy, baby, it's just an office. No one's in competition at TiMax; we are one big family," Mike said. He was so wrong. Tiffany wasn't her damn family, and she planned to leave her job-stealing ass in the dust. Getting Tiffany fired was her ultimate goal in the end.

She smiled. "Yes, you're right," she agreed. She didn't mean that shit, but Mike didn't need to know that.

Work as Usual

Episode 3

Tiffany

"Hey, boss lady, are you free for a minute?" Mee-Mee asked, sticking her head into Tiffany's office.

"Yes, but only that. I'm heading to meet with my new cast members for the *Love On Top* series."

"Okay," she said. She backed up to exit the office, but Tiffany called out her name.

"Myah, what's going on? Did you need something? I have a few moments to talk."

"No, not really. I was just looking for an update on Tressa. I mean, you and Mr. Green are tight, and I heard Tressa will be coming to work here soon."

Tiffany shook her head. "Come on in, girl, and shut the door." Tiffany decided to make time for this conversation. She got up and poured them both a drink and handed Myah a glass, and then went back to take a seat in her chair. "Now, you know besides Rose and Asia, you are one of my best girlfriends, and I've trusted you before with info, Mee-Mee, so if I give you the truth, you have to promise you won't say a word."

"Tiffany, you know me. You know I'd never say a word to anyone."

"Okay, yes, Tressa, will be coming aboard soon, but I don't know any dates or official details yet."

"So she's fine now? After rehab and what . . . like a year of laying low she's rehabilitated?"

"As far as I know she is."

"Okay, I guess that's good." She took a swallow.

"What do you mean you *guess?* That *is* good, Myah."

"You say that like she's not public enemy number one."

"That she is, or should I say, was. That is old news. She hasn't caused any trouble in my world. My husband and I never even discuss her, and so, for Mr. Green, I'm happy. I mean, the overdose . . . damn near losing his daughter and the extensive measures of rehab, I'm glad that after all of this time she is better."

"I guess you're right, because no matter how bad my munchkins are, I love them to death, and if ever something should happen to either of them, I'd go insane."

"And I'm sure that is how Mr. and Mrs. Green feel about Tressa, so this stays between us. Until Mr. Green makes the official announcement, we did not have this conversation. Now, I must get to my meeting. I hope you remembered to upload all of my show ideas to my tab."

"Yes, ma'am, I did."

"Fantastic." Tiffany got up, polished off her drink, and headed out. She hurried down the hall, then stood and waited for the elevator.

"Good afternoon," Tracy said.

Tiffany turned to acknowledge her new coworker. "Hey, Tracy, how are you?"

"I'm good. Finally going to meet with my new cast today, and I'm so excited."

"I bet. I remember my first show," Tiffany smiled. The elevator doors opened, and they both stepped on.

"Well, this isn't my first show exactly. You know I was the executive producer for *Back to Life* on UVN?"

"Okay, I'm familiar, just never got a chance to catch it."

"I'm sure. I mean, it wasn't as popular as *Boy Crazy,*" she said.

Tiffany detected a little sarcasm in her voice, but she didn't comment. "Well, no worries. You're here now, and I heard some good things about your show *Grapevine*. I'm sure it will be great. TiMax rarely produces a dull show," Tiffany said looking at the floor numbers light up as they descended. She didn't know Tracy well, and they hadn't talked much, but in the couple of months since Tracy had been there, Tiffany always had gotten bad energy from her.

Like the day when they had their staff meeting to welcome her to the network, Mike made a comment that she should link up with her, and that Tiffany could show her the ropes. Tracy quickly declined and said she'd be fine. Afterward, Tiffany greeted her and told her if she needed anything just ask, and Tracy's response was, "I got this. This isn't my first rodeo." Tiffany shrugged it off, but she didn't get good vibes from Tracy—ever.

The elevator finally hit the bottom floor, and they both headed toward their sets. Tiffany stopped in her tracks when she saw Colby enter the building. "Colby," Tiffany said in a huff, "what are you doing here?"

He smiled and looked past her. "Tracy, hey, darling. I was on my way up to your office."

"Hi, Colby," Tracy said, and they exchanged a quick hug. "I was just on my way to set. Are you excited?"

"You bet your ass I am," he replied.

Tiffany couldn't help but interrupt. "I'm sorry. Why are you here, Colby?" she inquired. She wanted to knock that huge grin off his smug face.

"Oh, you didn't know? Colby is the lead for my series *Grapevine*. It was last minute, but after some negotiations, Mike and I worked it out, and now he's here."

"Son of a bitch," Tiffany let slip in a whisper. She cleared her throat and spoke up louder. "Congratulations. Good day," she said and hurried off. As soon as she got on the other side of the door she called Mr. Green. He was still on leave dealing with Tressa, and she hated to bother him, but he knew the history with Colby.

"I'm so sorry to disturb you, sir, but did you know Colby Grant is the lead for Tracy's new show?"

"Yes, I know now. Didn't find out until after contracts were signed and deals were done. I suggest you just be professional, Tiffany. Mike and I are equal partners, and he has the same power I have, and he wanted Colby, so we have to put our personal differences aside and conduct business."

Tiffany didn't like it, but what could she do? It was Mike's and Langley's network. "I know, Mr. Green, and again, I'm so sorry for bothering you. I know you are out for medical reasons. How are you? And I hope Tressa is still doing well."

"She is doing well. We will be headed back to L.A. in a couple of days. My doctor allowed me to travel so we want to spend some family time together. I can finally say I'm a proud father."

"I'm sure you guys needed it, sir, and I'm so happy to hear that everything is better now. I mean, the last time I saw, Tressa she was in bad shape."

"She was, but I have a strong feeling that she is finally going to be just fine. With that, I have to ask you something. I'm asking something huge."

"Sure, Mr. Green, anything. You have been more than a boss to me and a friend to Kory."

"Indeed, Tiffany. You and Kory are like my children from another mother," he joked and laughed out loud at himself.

Tiffany laughed a little too, not to be rude. "I guess you're right, sir."

"Well, we should be home in a few days, and when we come in, I plan to groom you and Tressa to be my successors. I'm not going to live forever, and with the health issues I have going on now, it's time to groom you two. Tressa is my blood. She is going to need help wearing the crown after I'm gone."

"Mr. Green, don't talk like that. You're not going anywhere." She tried to sound light and not so serious. The idea of Mr. Green dying was something she didn't want to think about.

"Well, I wish your words were true, but we both know better. What I need from you in the meantime is to let Tressa shadow you. Show her the producing side, the casting calls, story line creations, etc. I want her to start from ground zero. Running the company is pretty much a breeze, because we have some strong, good, loyal, and knowledgeable staff members that make Mike's and my life a lot easier, trust and believe, but I want her to have hands-on experience with the things like Mike and I did before we turned our company into what it is today. Mike and I created, produced, funded, even built sets with our own hands to start this company, and I want Tressa to be groomed properly. Can you do that for me?"

Tiffany bit down on her bottom lip. No way could she tell Mr. Green no. He had done way more than she could imagine for her and Kory, so she said, "Yes, of course," in a rush. She wanted to eat those words, but she couldn't refuse him.

"Wonderful. As soon as we're in L.A., I'll have you and Kory over for dinner and go over some things. I truly believe my daughter is ready now. I'm confident that this will be good for her."

"Sounds good, Mr. Green, but does Tressa know what your plan is? I mean, I'm not her favorite person."

"Well, if she wants to be a part of this team, she's going to have to put her personal differences aside and do what's best for TiMax. There is no competition at TiMax.

We are family, and Tressa is ready, so she won't be a problem, trust me."

Tiffany let out a silent sigh. "Okay, Mr. Green. I'm heading to set. I'll see you soon." She ended the call, climbed into a cart, and called Kory. This was news she had to definitely share with him.

I'm Finally Ready

Episode 4

Tressa

"Good morning, Myah," Tressa sang. Myah looked up as if she'd seen a ghost.

"Tressa . . . I mean, Ms. Green," she stammered.

"Relax, Myah, I come in peace. I'm supposed to meet Tiffany here at nine."

Really? Tiffany didn't tell me, she was about to say, but Tiffany came out of her office.

"Tressa. Hey, good morning. You look well," she smiled.

"I feel good," she smiled back at her. She had been clean for a little less than a year, and she really felt like a new person. She and her dad had bonded and rekindled their relationship, and she was dead set on making him proud of her. After returning to L.A. from rehab, her dad offered her a final do over. He convinced her to rid her head of the extensions, and she went over the edge and got a new pixie cut that she had to admit gave her a sexy appeal that she didn't know she owned. Her dad gave her a new beginning with a monthly spending limit.

The terms of her trust were a monthly check, and it was more than enough for her to do what she needed because now that she was clean, her perspective on life, money, and spending were different. Mr. Green would give her a payment each month, only after she tested clean for drugs. Even if she wanted to complain or dispute it, she couldn't because her parents had given her countless chances, and she planned to take full advantage of this last one. She was not only grateful to be back in her parents' good graces, she thanked God that she was alive.

"Shall we?" Tiffany said, and they went into Tiffany's office. "Have a seat," she offered, and Tressa sat on the other side of Tiffany's desk. "Coffee, juice?" she offered.

"No, I'm good," she smiled. She looked at Tiffany as she fidgeted with papers and other items on her desk. Tressa could detect her uneasiness and uncertainties, so she said, "Listen, Tiffany, given our history, I can imagine this is awkward for you. The other night at dinner with you and Kory, I will admit it was odd, but I now get what my father has been telling me for years, and you can relax. I'm done with the past, and I'm only thinking of my future in life and at this company. I'm ready for a new beginning, and I can only do that if the people I hurt can forgive me. If you can't forgive me and move forward, I'll let my dad know this bright idea for you to teach me the ropes was a mistake, and he can assign me to someone else."

Tiffany opened her mouth, but she didn't say anything.

"But before you say no, I know why my father hired you, and I know why he wants to groom you for his seat because you are smart and creative and ambitious. All the things I was not for a very long time, Tiffany. You didn't grow up with things handed to you like I did, yet you are here, and my dad tells me you're the best, so I want to learn from the best." When still she didn't speak, Tressa was sure Tiffany didn't believe a word she said.

"Okay, thanks for your time. I understand." Tressa stood to leave.

"No, Tressa, wait, please. Sit, don't leave."

She eyed Tiffany for a second or two, and then she slowly slid back into the chair.

"You're right, and I'm sorry. Forgive me, but I sit here across from you looking at this external makeover, from head to toe . . . You look gorgeous, but I'm not going to lie. I'm still a little nervous about the internal you. I want to trust you, Tressa, but I'm not Mr. Green. Your father may always see the diamond in you, but I've seen the coal, so, yes, I have my doubts, but I promised Mr. Green that I'd show you everything I know, so that's what I'm going to do."

"Thank you. All I suggest is we take it one day at a time, Tiffany. You don't owe me shit, neither do I owe you, but I owe my father my life, and no matter what issues I have with anyone on this planet, I'm going to make my parents proud of me. That is my ultimate goal right now, and I really don't give a fuck what people think of me. I've let go of a lot of people that I once called friends, Tiffany, and that was as hard as kicking my habits. I know this is not what you ever expected, but we are here now, and I don't care if you still see me as the old Tressa, Tressa the addict, or Tressa the ex of Kory's. I'm not here for you. I'm here for me and for my dad and my family, and the rest of my life is all that I care about."

Tiffany smiled. "With that, let me show you to your office." She stood and showed Tressa to the office directly across from hers. It was the office that Wallace had before Tressa cost him his job.

"Talk about karma," Tressa said.

"Well, this is the only office on this floor that's empty."

"I see. Maybe I'll talk to my dad about bringing Wallace back on. It's my fault that he got booted out of here."

"Well, last I heard, Wallace moved to New York, and he produces the news."

"I had no idea. Good for him."

"Yes, it is. For now, we will share Myah, but you have a few candidates to interview next week for your own receptionist."

"I get a receptionist?"

"Yes, ma'am. Who's going to take your calls when you are on set or remember the 101 things that you'll definitely forget?"

"I know, right?" They laughed. Tressa was familiar with the studio. She had been hanging out there since she was a kid, but Tiffany took her around to some of the new sets and introduced her to some of the new people, and then she introduced her to Tracy.

"Hi, Tracy, it's a pleasure."

"No, the pleasure's all mine, Ms. Green." Tracy had a little more enthusiasm than Tressa cared for so she pulled back her hand before she shook it off her arm. After the day was done, she made it back to her office. She realized she was going to have to purchase some sensible shoes. Her Red Bottoms were hot and stylish, but they hurt like hell. She kicked off her shoes and powered on the iPod Myah had given her that morning. Myah showed her some basic show materials, so she clicked on a few links, and then she stood and went over to the fridge. She knew all the offices were normally stocked with liquor, but her father made sure she had a variety of flavored waters, sports drinks, iced coffees, and juices.

She grabbed a Minute Maid Cran-Grape and went back to her desk. She twisted it open and hit the music link. Myah had shown her how to turn on the wireless speakers, and as soon as she rocked her head to an old Blackstreet cut, "Tonight's the Night," a tap on her door frame made her jump.

She had thought everyone was gone. She looked up, and it was Tracy. Surprised to see her, she invited her in and lowered the volume on her sounds. "Hey, Tracy, come on in. I didn't know anyone was still here."

"I was on my way out, and I noticed your light."

"Yes, I'm going to leave in a few moments. I was just trying to take in today's adventure. I had no idea so much went into producing, and I definitely didn't know one scene could take that many hours to tape."

"Yep, it's a long and stressful job, but I love it."

"Well, I'm going to learn to love it. I mean, for a long time, I just wanted recognition and a title, but now I see that doesn't come easy."

"It doesn't," she giggled a little.

"Forgive me, would you like something. If you want liquor I recommend you go to your office, but I have tea, juice, water," she offered.

"No, I'm fine. I honestly came down to ask you about something nonwork-related."

Tressa raised a brow. She didn't know this woman, and she was sure it was going to be a personal question about her addiction. She was about to get up in her business, Tressa thought. Now that she was clean and sober, she was learning to manage her anger in therapy, but Tracy was going to get a tongue-lashing if she stepped into her personal lane. "What about?"

"No, I shouldn't," she said waving her hand.

Tressa hated when people did that shit. It was obvious she was in her office after hours for information on something.

"Okay, Tracy, you might as well spit it out. I mean, I just met you today, and I'm sure there isn't much you don't know about me. I'm the boss's daughter, a rehabilitated addict, and my face is still plastered on tabloids, so out with it."

"Well, I wanted to know how you are able to work with Tiffany, after what she and her husband did to you. I mean, if that were me, I'd still be pissed, and no way I'd want to be anywhere near her. After all, Tiffany . . . she is this . . . this . . ." she stuttered, and then she let out a breath expressing her total distaste for Tiffany. "Let's just say, I wouldn't be too forgiving," she said.

Tressa noticed her fists were balled up when she spoke of Tiffany, and the frown lines in her forehead showed that Tracy was not frustrated with Tiffany over her drama, but she may have had some personal issues as well.

Curious about what she was about, Tressa went with, "You've heard the saying, 'keep your friends close and your enemies even closer.'" After she had said those words, the tension eased from Tracy's face, and she smiled.

"I *knew* it. I knew you couldn't possibly like that evil bitch," she blurted, and Tressa went along with her.

"Well, for my job's sake, I'm going to play nice." Tressa was still trying to feel her out, and she definitely wanted to know what Tiffany had done to Tracy to make her so angry.

"Wow, I'm so glad I came to your office. It's late, but we should get together and have dinner one night. I mean, if you'd like. One thing we both have in common is hating that bitch, right?" she said.

"Well, let's just put it this way . . . She won't be around here long, not if I can help it."

Tracy smiled brightly. "Yes, you and I *definitely* need to get together." She dug in her bag and gave Tressa a card. "I know I'm on the employee roster, but here is my card with my cell phone number. Call me." She stood. Tressa took the card and gave it a once-over. She assured her she'd buzz her.

Tressa powered off the music, downed her juice, called for her car, and prepared to leave. She headed to the bottom floor, and when her car pulled up, she noticed Tracy was with a very familiar face. It was Colby. He shut the door and hurried around to the driver's side to get in, and they drove off. "What the hell?" She had been away too long. She was out of the loop, but she declared that she was going to get to the bottom of this bull.

"Where to, Ms. Green?" her driver asked.

"My parents' estate, Johnny. It's been a long day. I need a soak, some herbal tea, and the remote."

"Yes, ma'am."

They exited the TiMax parking lot, and Tressa scrolled through her phone, and every name was trouble. Every name did drugs and drank like a fish. She started from the top again, and there was Amber. She was her only true friend and the only one she knew that was clean and sober and always wanted the best for her. She had written her off and cussed her out like a dog for telling Kory everything behind her back, but that was the past, and she had to call and make peace with her. She hit Send and on the third ring, she answered. "Hello," she said softly.

"I'm sorry, Amber," were the first words out of Tressa's mouth.

Amber said nothing.

"If you don't want to talk, I understand, but please just hear me out." Still Amber said nothing. Tressa swallowed hard, and then continued. "I was a dumb-ass addict bitch, and you were my only true friend, and I wasn't in my right frame of mind back then. No matter how hard I wish I could go back in time and take back all of those horrible things I said to you, I can't. I love you, Amber, and I miss you. I don't blame you for blowing the whistle on me. I brought that upon myself, but I know you, and I know you have already forgiven me because you are a soft-ass Sagittarius," Tressa said, and Amber laughed. Tressa's burden felt lighter. "I know it could never be the way it used to be, and I don't want it that way, because how it was, was dysfunctional, but I want my friend back, and I'm sorry for everything, Amber."

"Me too," she replied and from there, they talked Tressa's entire ride home and agreed to meet for lunch the next day.

Thanks, but No Thanks

Episode 5

Colby

He just looked at Tracy from across the table as she continued to try to convince him to join forces with her in her quest to destroy Tiffany. He didn't understand for the life of him how so many hated Tiffany, and over petty shit.

"Again, Tracy, I'm done with revenge, getting back, and all that jazz. I got so much backlash from the rumors and the scheming I did with Tressa, and I'm not for no more drama. I lost quite a few opportunities behind that mess, and how you got Mike Harrington to even give me the lead was a miracle. My agent was ready to drop me, Tracy, so, no, I won't be a part of your *Destroy Tiffany Richardson Mission*. I'm focused on my career, and all that extra shit—nah, I'm not interested."

"So you're not the least bit salty about her going back to Kory?"

"I was at first, but you know what? That was the main reason Tressa hired me. To keep her and Kory apart, but that is who she was meant to be with."

The disappointed look on her face let him know she knew him getting on board with her was out of the question.

"But, Colby—" she said.

"But nothing. Tracy, you are the producer of an amazing show. *Grapevine* is a kick-ass show. Let that old shit go and move on. So what Tiffany has a handful of shows right now? You will get there, and you can be just as great as she is."

"I *am* just as great as she is!" she barked. "As a matter of fact, I'm *better*. I would be where she is now if she would have never showed up and took my spot. She is where she is today because she took my position at KCLN," she shot back with venom.

Colby wondered why something that had happened so damn long ago still had her so angry. "Tracy, listen to yourself. News flash . . . Tiffany's life and fortune is her own. Have you ever stopped and asked yourself this one question?" he said with his index finger held up in the air.

She downed her drink and said. "What question is that, Mr. Grant?"

"What if you had not lost your spot to Tiffany, and you showed up on time, and you joined the *Boy Crazy* team back then? Would you have had the same success? Maybe, maybe not. We'll never know the answer to that question, Tracy. You have to let this rage go. You and Tressa are the most vengeful women I've ever met in my entire life. The only difference between you and her is you're not a drug addict."

She snorted in irritation and waved for the server. "I'm nothing like that cokehead. Tressa had it easy compared to me. I lost everything. I was close to being homeless. By the grace of God, that one show brought me back from damn near living on the streets."

"So count your blessings, Tracy. Fuck where you almost landed. *Almost* doesn't fucking count. Look where you are now, and I promise you if you keep up this madness, it will backfire on you. Trust me, I know."

"Well, I don't have a dick, so I don't get caught up or sidetracked. I just want to knock her off of her high horse. She looks at my face every single day, and do you know that bitch has no clue who I am. She doesn't even *remember* me, Colby, and I stood in her face at KCLN the day she stole my spot."

"Is she supposed to know you, Tracy?"

She opened her mouth to answer, but then the server approached. She ordered them another round, and he promptly shifted the subject to the show. He wanted to work, not get back at anyone. Showing up at that premiere party was the worst mistake other than joining forces with Tressa. Cameras caught Kory's sucker punch, and the tabloids flipped the script on him like he was some lunatic ex-boyfriend stalking Tiffany and got handled by her new fiancé, and once the media got the leak of the real story of him being paid by Tressa to seduce Tiffany, they ate it up, and every morning he dreaded what would be said next about him.

They tried to say he was on drugs, made comments about him, Tressa, and Stephen, being lovers, all kinds of negative publicity, and his agent was on the verge of dropping him. He managed to hold on to his agent due to contract and legal matters, and then his agent got the call for *Grapevine*. If he hadn't landed the lead in *Grapevine*, he would have been right back where he started from in the very beginning. He was grateful that celeb gossip didn't last long, and things died down after they confirmed that Tressa hadn't overdosed and was alive and in rehab.

It wasn't long before the focus moved from him, Tressa, Tiffany, and Kory to another set of actors, athletes, and stars. He was grateful and had no intentions of speaking to Tiffany again. That day he saw her in the studio, he should have been a little more cordial and maybe apologized again, but the look of panic on her face was his hint not to say a word to her. Little did he know his new producer invited him to her office purposely at that precise time so he could run into them. He didn't put two and two together until after she confided in him that she hated Tiffany.

"So that's why you told me to come to your office and not the set. You knew I'd run into Tiffany at that time."

She shrugged her shoulders. "I honestly forgot. I mean, I figured I'd see you on my way down or on set."

"Yeah, okay," he said. He instantly regretted signing with Tracy's show. At dinner that night he made it a point to tell her that he'd never say anything to Tiffany about Tracy hating her, and she promised she'd keep their relationship professional and keep him out of her plans to get back at the other woman. With that, he dropped her home and headed to his place.

Reunited

Episode 6

Tiffany

Tiffany eyed all the faces that were coming her way at LAX. Finally, after all the begging and pleading, Rose agreed to join her friend out in L.A. Tiffany had tried convincing her over and over again to come out there, but Rose was stubborn and set in her ways. She had turned down Tiffany's attempts to help her and stayed in Chicago with her sister, but after the fiasco of her sister thinking that her husband and Rose had something going on, it was the straw that broke the camel's back. "Rose, over here," Tiffany yelled out when she saw her friend. They both moved in each other's direction.

"Tiff, girl, look at you. You look like you're Hollywood, damn L.A.," she said, and Tiffany went back in for another hug. She hadn't seen her best friend since her wedding, and the first thing she noticed is that Rose had put on more than a few pounds. They both had always been a little on the larger side, but Tiffany had managed to maintain a twelve/fourteen, while Rose looked like a twenty or twenty-two, but Tiffany didn't say anything.

"Girl, stop it, you always trying to blow up my head."

"No, I'm telling the truth. I've gained a million pounds since your wedding, and you still look the same."

"I see, girl, what have you been doing?" Tiffany said. Since Rose brought it up, she thought it was then okay to address it.

"Hell, depressed, eating, and depressed. No man, no steady work, living in hell with my sister and her husband. And did I say no man?"

"You did, but you are still gorgeous as ever, and like we said before you got here, new beginnings. A new start. What your sister accused you and James of was foul."

"Yes, but it was time for me to go. I just hope Roslyn and I will be sisters again. She didn't even want to hear me out, Tiff."

"I know, Rose." Tiffany rubbed her arm. "Listen, we're not going to talk about that right now. We are going to focus on your future. Come on, let's get your bags. Asia is driving around; she's going to meet us outside."

"Wow, I'm dying to meet her."

"And I'm dying for you to meet her too. Her mom took ill when Kory and I got married, so she couldn't attend or even be in the wedding."

"Yes, she had to go to Jamaica, right?"

"Yes, and I'm happy her mom recovered, but still hate she missed the wedding."

Rose continued to follow Tiffany to the baggage claim. "And I advise you to take off some of those layers. You are in Cali now, baby. It's not cold at all."

"I see you showing skin, Ms. Flawless."

"I try," Tiffany teased and primped. They walked over to the belt and got Rose's oversized bags. Since she was moving, she had extra luggage. She sold her car because Tiffany said she could use her Benz until she got another one. Her other items would be coming by movers in a week. "Girl, I can't wait for you to see Kory, and, girl, we have so much to catch up on," Tiffany said, dragging two pieces of Rose's luggage on wheels with ease. Rose fell a few steps behind her with the other luggage, her carry-on, coat, sweater, and purse. Tiffany slowed her pace so Rose could catch up. Rose's face was drenched with sweat, and she was out of breath. She had packed on some pounds, and Tiffany didn't like what she saw, but declined on commenting. They made it outside as Asia pulled up in Tiffany's Escalade.

"Damn, Asia, pushing some nice wheels."

"You like? It's mine. Asia just drove because I wanted to come in to meet you."

"Okay, girl . . . I like this. This is nice."

"Well, you can use this one if you'd like, or the Benz. This was a splurge, trust me."

"I'll take the Benz. I'm not picky. I just appreciate everything you're doing for me, Tiffany."

"Girl, please. I know if the roles were reversed, you'd do the exact same for me."

Rose brightly smiled. "Yes, you're right."

The hatch went up slowly, and Asia got out. She went around and greeted Rose.

"Hi, Rose, nice to finally meet ya," she said with her Jamaican dialect.

"You too, Asia."

"Now move your pregnant behind aside, so Rose and I can load these bags."

"You're pregnant?"

"Yes, and big mouth over'ere was supposed to keep ya mouth shut!" Asia said and slapped Tiffany's arm.

"My bad, Asia, I forgot. Please don't be mad. Rose don't know nobody here to tell."

"No, Asia, you don't have to worry about me," she said and put the last bag in the back.

Tiffany hit the button, and the hatch slowly started to close. Asia walked to the back passenger side. "Asia, you can ride up front."

"No, ma'am. You can sit up front with ya gal and get caught up. Mi, don't mind to sit in the back," she said and got in. Tiffany got into the driver's seat, and Rose climbed into the passenger seat. Rose immediately hit the A/C control to make her side cooler.

"This is definitely not the Windy City."

"It's not, and all them layers you wearing are going to have to come off."

"Well, I packed wrong. I didn't bring many summer clothes."

"So that means a trip to the mall after we go and drop these bags off."

"Not me," Asia said. "I have an appointment with my wedding planner. You know since this pregnancy, we moved everything up before I start to show. I'm six months already, and thank God I barely have a pouch. God, I wish I would have found out early."

"Six months, Asia? You look amazing," Rose complimented.

"That's why the wedding is rush-rush. Edward and I planned a long engagement, but this little 'hiccup' changed all of that, so I have to exchange vows before I look like a whale."

"I doubt that," Rose said looking over her shoulder at Asia.

"Thanks for the kind words, Rose, you're sweet. But, Tiff, no mall for me. I have an appointment."

"I know, Asia, I didn't forget. I'll drop you home first, and then we will go by my house so Rose can see Kory, and then hit the stores."

"Sounds good."

"By the way, you are welcome to spend your first night with us, or do you want to stay at your new place? I had my personal items packed and moved already months ago after the honeymoon, because, as I recall, you promised at the wedding that you'd be here a lot sooner."

"Awww, come on, Tiff, let's not rehash the past. The point is I'm here now, and I'd like to go to my new place and enjoy a long quiet bath and a glass of wine tonight, if you don't mind. The last few days at my sister's has been hell, and I couldn't wait to get on that plane this morning, so we can go by your place, but I want to spend a night by myself."

"That's fine. The furnishings are still there. It's basically a clean palette for you to decorate any way you like."

"Well, until my paintings get here, and we get the business up and running, and I make some cash, I'll just have to live with the blank palette."

"Nonsense, Rose. I told you I've got you."

"I know, but you've done enough already."

"Rose, stop it, okay? You have to get sheets, towels, rugs, and just a few personal items. I left all of the dishes and cookware; didn't need any of that. It's like a furnished home waiting for your fabulous finishing touches, plus, you can always look at some of the things I put in storage and if you want them, we'll just take it back to the house. I only took all of the personal stuff so you can make it yours. I don't want you to feel like you're living in my house. It's now your house."

Rose smiled, and her eyes welled. "Thanks, Tiffany. It's been a rough patch for me, and I finally feel like life is going to be better."

"It is, Rose, don't worry. I have a better idea. After we drop Asia off, let's go by your place, take your bags in, and you can kinda get an idea of what you wanna do. If you see something you like while we're out, get it, and I'll sleep over with you tonight."

"Are you sure Kory won't mind?"

"Nah. I'll go home, pack a quick bag, you see Kory, and then we spend some girl time."

"Well, if that's the case, I'll come over tonight too, if you ladies don't mind. Rose, I know you haven't seen your friend in a while, so if you'd prefer I not come, I'll totally understand."

"Nonsense; please, the more, the merrier."

They dropped Asia off, went by Tiffany's old place and dropped off Rose's things, and Tiffany put the key in her hand. She told Rose if she needed anything, even groceries, she had her back, and then they headed to the mall. Rose got a few items, but Tiffany could tell she was saying no to a lot of things to keep Tiffany from purchasing so many items.

When Rose said no, and Tiffany thought she'd looked nice in it, Tiffany said yes. After the mall and a couple of home stores, the back of the SUV was packed with goods. Then they headed to Tiffany's, and Kory greeted them both at the door. He cooked and after they caught up, reminisced on high school memories, Tiffany packed a small bag, and Rose followed in Tiffany's BMW. They got to Rose's new place and unloaded. They both paused to shower, and by nine, Asia had arrived.

Tiffany and Rose enjoyed wine while Asia drank lemon tea. Rose unpacked all of her clothes and stored her luggage in the spare room's walk-in closet. They put the task of hanging things on the wall for the next day, and they made the beds. Tiffany felt weird at first going to the guest room to sleep, but she was a guest in Rose's house.

"Tiff," Rose whispered.

"Yeah," Tiffany said. She blinked her sleepy eyes. The digital clock on the nightstand showed it was after two.

"Are you asleep?" Rose asked softly.

"Yes," Tiffany said. But then she sat up. "What's wrong, Rose?"

"Can you come in the other room with me?"

Tiffany turned, and her legs dangled over the side of the bed. "Why, Rose, what's wrong?"

"I'm not sleepy, or I just can't fall asleep."

Tiffany stood. "Sure," she said. She and Rose went into the master suite, and Tiffany climbed into bed. Rose got in on the other side. After a few moments, Tiffany asked, "Rose, what's really going on?"

She let out a sigh. "Do you think I'm ugly?"

"What, Rose?" Tiffany sat straight up and turned on the lamp. "Rose, why would you ask me something like that? Of course not!"

Rose's eyes welled. "I know I've gained a lot of weight since the last time we saw each other, and today," she paused and put her face in her hands. She began to sob loudly, and Tiffany was confused.

"Rose, sweetheart, talk to me. What's wrong?"

"When you saw me today, you gave me this look, a look that you've never given me before, a look I've gotten from strangers, but never in a million years did I think I'd get it from you. It's like you bodychecked me. And when we were at the mall, I felt so uncomfortable trying on clothes with you, and I, I, I . . . I mean, you've never made me feel insecure before about the way I looked—ever!" She cried, and Tiffany felt horrible.

"I'm so sorry, Rose. I am so, so sorry. Yes, when I first saw you I was blown away, and I was shocked because you've changed. I don't think you are ugly, and I'm sorry for making you feel that way, Rose. I love you like a sister, Rose, and you know I'd never do or say anything to hurt you, and I'm sorry if I did. The weight just caught me off guard, and I'm really sorry if I hurt you in any way. That was so not my intention. You and I grew up being on the chubby side, and you know I'd never intend to make you feel bad about the way you look or your weight."

Rose dried her face and sniffled, and then said, "Thank you for everything. Thanks for opening your home to me and offering me this opportunity, but I think it's better if

I go back to Chicago. I don't think I'll fit well out here in L.A. I don't feel like it's for me."

"Rose, no, please don't say that. I'm so glad you're here. Please don't leave. I'm sorry, Rose." Tiffany wiped her eyes. She knew she had given Rose a few looks that day, but she didn't mean to hurt her. "Please say that you'll stay."

"I don't know, Tiffany. L.A. isn't for me. I looked around at these L.A. natives today, and I don't know how I'm going to fit in."

"Rose, just give it a try. You said you'd love a new start, and you got one here. Just please, just give it a chance. Give it six months, just six. We will start your business, and you will adjust. Just don't leave, Rose. Once you get back to painting and taking beautiful photos, you will have your rhythm back, and you are going to love it here. A new start for anyone is scary, but you have me and Kory, and we will do whatever it takes for you to get things going, Rose. Please don't go. I finally have my best friend in the same city, and just a short car ride away versus a plane ride away, and I am begging you to stay."

Rose was quiet for a few moments. Tiffany stared at her with pleading eyes.

"Okay, I'll try it."

"Thank you, Rose." Tiffany hugged her tightly. "I love you so much, and I've missed you so much, Rose, and I am sorry if I hurt you."

Rose smiled a half smile. "I forgive you, but I just couldn't sleep without telling you how I felt."

"I know, Rose, and I'm glad you told me. You are beautiful inside and out, and I guess a little L.A. has rubbed off on me, and I was wrong. I have no problems with how you look. You are my best friend, and again, I'm sorry." Tiffany didn't think she could apologize enough.

To think she'd do that to her best friend made her feel like a horrible person.

"I forgive you, and I love you back. I am going to give L.A. an honest chance, and we have to find a studio as soon as possible because I only want to move my equipment once, understood?"

"Yes, ma'am. We can start as soon as you'd like. I have some places in mind, and you are going to do well. You are supertalented, and I have no doubts in my mind that you will shine."

Rose gave Tiffany a confirming smile that she agreed, and then slid under the covers. Tiffany turned out the lamp. The next morning, the two friends slept in, and after they had dressed, they went to the studio. Tiffany took Rose around and introduced her to everyone, including Tressa. Rose smiled and got a good vibe from Tressa she later told Tiffany.

"I thought I'd instantly hate her," Rose said tossing the salad. They were at Tiffany's preparing dinner.

"Well, Tressa has changed. A remarkable change, I might add. But I keep watching and waiting for her to relapse."

"Well, she seems harmless."

"That's because you were not here for Hurricane Tressa," she laughed, and then Kory walked in.

"Dinner smells good, ladies."

"Thanks, baby, it will be ready soon."

"Cool. I'll be in my man cave. Just give me a holla."

"Okay, babe." Kory gave Tiffany a quick kiss, and then vacated the kitchen.

"I still can't believe you and Kory are married after all these years."

"I can't either sometimes, Rose. I sleep with that man every night thinking tomorrow I'm going to wake up and find out it was a dream."

Rose laughed. "I hope you don't, because that would put me back in cold-ass Chicago, living with my sister and her horrible tribe. Last night was emotional for us, but I welcomed the quiet."

"I know that's real." They finished making dinner, ate, and talked for a good while. It wasn't that late, but Rose wanted to get home, shower, and relax. She promised Tiffany that she could make it home with the navigation system on her own.

Tiffany gave her another quick lesson on the alarm system and told Rose how to turn on the hot tub. Rose said she was going to go home and pour a glass of wine and embrace her new home, new environment, and be ready bright and early to go check out some spaces to possibly open her very own gallery.

After a thirty-minute drive, she had made it and called her friend to say she was home safe.

New Beginnings

Episode 7

Rose

Rose walked out in her robe, carrying a tray of wine and snacks. Never had she owned a hot tub nor had a private pool, so she smiled when she stepped into the water. "Oh my God, this is heavenly," she said and relaxed in the hot tub. She had enjoyed Tiffany's company last night, but she welcomed her solitude that evening. She had been living with her sister and her four kids for two years, so she felt like she was in a resort. She hated how she left, with her sister thinking she'd stoop so low and mess with her husband. It often made her tear up. It was a big misunderstanding, but her sister was too crazy and insecure to hear her out.

It's like God set the whole scene up for her to leave, or get put out, she thought as she replayed the events. She had come home only to find her brother-in-law drunk and passed out on the sofa that was her bed. In her attempts to wake him and get him off the couch, she fell on top of him, and at that very moment her sister walked in. Shocked to see her sister, Rose panicked. "Roslyn, it is not what you think," she said, quickly getting up. Since she was caught off guard, it seemed it was harder to get up.

"Like hell, you trifling bitch. What the fuck were you doing on top of my husband?" her older sister demanded. Her voice roared, and Rose trembled in fear. Roslyn always intimidated her.

"It's not what you think. I came home, James was out, and I tried to pull him up, and I fell on him."

"Is that the best you can do, you ho . . . huh? Yo' fat ass can't get a man, so you try to seduce mine?"

"No," Rose cried. "I'd never do something so foolish."

"Whatever, bitch. Get your shit and get the fuck outta my house!" Roslyn blasted.

"No, sis, it's not like that—" Rose tried to defend herself.

"Get the fuck out!" Roslyn yelled and started going for Rose's personal items. The den had Rose's artwork, easel, and paints and supplies, and when Roslyn started to destroy some of her pieces, Rose reacted and tackled Roslyn to the floor. The fight got bad, and out of breath, they both gave in.

"I want you out by morning." Those were Roslyn's last words before she left the room. Her drunk-ass husband was still passed out on the sofa and hadn't even awakened from all of the commotion. Rose sobbed and went for her phone. She called Tiffany. "The shit has hit the fan, and I need to leave. I have nowhere to go, Tiffany, and she wants me out by morning," was all she said, and that night, Tiffany didn't ask any questions. She just said okay. Later, Rose packed all of her things and loaded her cousin's car with all she could carry, and just said to hell with all the rest. She had a small storage unit that Tiffany paid for every month, and she was grateful that the damage Roslyn had done to a couple of her pieces were minor.

Her cousin took her to Western Union, and she got the money that Tiffany sent. She paid her cousin $250 for gas and helping her move her things, and then checked into a nice hotel room. Tiffany had sent her the max for

Western Union, which was $2,999. Two days later, she met with a moving company at her storage and paid them a cashier's check, and then they loaded a truck. Tiffany called and said her first-class ticket will be waiting at the counter and the following morning before she departed at six a.m., she went to her sister's place. She had a money order for one thousand written out to her sister, and she dropped it into her mail slot. It wasn't much, or enough to truly tell Roslyn thank you for letting her stay, but it was all she could give so that she still could have a few dollars in her pocket when she arrived in L.A.

She looked out of the plane window and bid Chicago farewell and put her headphones in her ears. When the attendant tapped her arm and offered her a mimosa, she smiled brightly and accepted. Her flight was nice, and being in first class with unlimited drinks, snacks, and upscale customer service, she noted she'd thank her best friend again.

Returning back to the moment and the present time, she let her head fall back, and she closed her eyes and tried to forget the horrible episode that went down with her and Roslyn. She loved her sister so much and missed talking to her and missed the friendship they shared. Why Roselyn turned on her and didn't believe her continued to stomp her brain, but since Roslyn wasn't talking to her, she knew she'd never get an answer.

With her eyes closed and her head back she was disturbed by a male voice. Her head jerked up—and there was a police officer standing over her with a flashlight in her face. "Ma'am?" he said again.

"Yes, Officer, what is it? You scared the living crap out of me."

"I need you to step out of the hot tub, ma'am."

"Why? Why are you here? I didn't call you."

"A neighbor called us, ma'am. What is your name?"

Rose was shaking like a leaf. "Rose, Rosemary Jennings," she recited with her hands up.

"I'm going to need you to come out of the water. This house belongs to a Tiffany Richardson. Not a Rosemary Jennings."

"Yes, she's the owner. I'm her best friend. She knows I'm here."

"Anyway, can we clear this matter up?"

"Yes, sir. I'll be happy to give you her number. And I'm naked, so please don't make me come out of this water."

He turned around. "Please come out. I need your ID, ma'am."

Rose stood and got out as quickly as she could and rushed over to her robe. She put it on and proceeded to go inside of the house through the patio doors off the living room. She went into her bedroom and retrieved her license from her purse. She didn't know the officer followed her inside, so she was shocked to see him standing near the French doors. She handed over her license and stood there feeling uneasy and wondered who decided to call the police. She wasn't disturbing the peace, playing loud music, so what nosy neighbor called?

After examining her ID, the officer talked into the radio attached to his shoulder, and Rose was trembling. "Yes, I need you to check a Rosemary Lynette Jennings, Illinois state-issued licensed," he said and read off the license number.

"Really, Officer, you can just call Tiffany; she'll verify that I'm here," Rose said going for her phone that was on the kitchen island a couple of feet from where they stood, and the officer yelled at her not to move. Rose jumped and instinctively put her hands up. The officer didn't even reply. She slowly turned with her hands up and saw he had drawn his gun. "I was just going for my cell phone and my keys are over there on the kitchen island. I have the keys to this house and the car in the garage." She was now shaking like a leaf.

"Just stay where you are, ma'am," he ordered.

The bass in his voice made Rose tremble even more. She was hoping he wasn't trigger happy, because she definitely didn't want to be a cop's next innocent victim, so she stood as still as her shaking body could stand. A few seconds later, the radio cleared Rose of any warrants or violations, and then the officer cooled his stance.

"I'm sorry, ma'am, you can relax. This is just protocol. I didn't mean to frighten you." His voice was now gentle, and he put his gun back into his holster. He handed her back her ID. "You said you have the keys, ma'am?"

"Yes, right over there, on the island."

"And how long have you been here?"

"Since yesterday. I flew in yesterday morning, sir."

He nodded. "All clear. She is a houseguest, not an intruder," he said into the radio.

Rose exhaled. "Thank you, Officer. I'm just so shocked. I'm thinking maybe I should get a lock for that fence. I mean, you scared the hell out of me."

"I'm so sorry, Mrs. Jennings. A neighbor called saying she knew the owner of this place had moved out awhile ago and that no one should be here. She was concerned that someone had broken in."

"Well, I appreciate her concern, but the owner Tiffany, Tiffany Banks, knows I'm here. She and I are best friends, and I'm permitted to be here."

"I understand, Mrs. Jennings. I'll let you get back to your soak."

"It's Ms., and thank you, Officer Brady," she said reading the name on his name tag.

"Not a problem. Can I leave a card with you? I mean, you *are* new to the area, so if you'd like a tour guide . . ." he smiled.

Rose's brows raised. She was shocked. She just knew he wasn't flirting with her. No makeup, wild natural curls, and she was as big as a house her insides screamed. "Excuse me?" she said as if she didn't hear him.

"I didn't mean to be too forward. I mean, if you don't want to . . . I can—" he tried to say, but she interrupted.

"No, I'd like your card, sir."

"It's Levi," he said handing over his card.

"Thank you, Levi, and everyone calls me Rose."

"Well, Rose, it was nice to meet you. My cell number is there so call me or text me if you'd like. My shift ends at eleven."

"Okay, I will." She stretched out her hand, and he gently shook it. They walked out the French doors, and she walked him to the gate.

"Yes, I suggest you get a lock for this gate. I mean, this is an upscale neighborhood, normally safe and quiet, but a beautiful woman like yourself can never be too safe."

"Thank you," she blushed. "I'll pick up one tomorrow."

"Great. Good night, Rose," he said and walked out the gate.

"Good night to you too." Rose examined the card and ran in place to express her excitement. The officer was a walking calendar boy. Tall, tanned medium brown skin, and dark black eyes. He was clean shaved, and when he removed his hat inside the house she saw he had a tight fade. Before getting back into the water, she went for her phone.

She texted him a quick message.

Hi, this is Rose . . . It was nice meeting. This my num. Enjoy the rest of your night. ☺

Within moments, she got a return text.

You too. If you don't mind, I can text or call after my shift.

I don't mind; either is fine. Be safe.

After that, she went out and got her goodie tray and turned off the hot tub. She locked up, set the alarm, and then dialed Tiffany. She had to tell her what happened, for one, and tell her about the miracle of her getting a man's number. She was superexcited and talked to Tiffany until her other line rang.

"Oh my God, Tiff, it's him."

Tiffany yawned. "Okay, Rose, good night and don't let him come over, understand? You are not easy," Tiffany repeated.

"Okay, bye," Rose said and answered her other line. After the first ten minutes of nonstop chatter and laughs, she went for a glass of Pinot and stayed up half the night talking to her new L.A. friend, Officer Brady.

I Need a Plan

Episode 8

Tracy

Tracy paced her office back and forth, mind racing and her heart was pounding fast. She had just left a morning meeting with Mike, Mr. Green, and a couple other producers, and everyone had mind-blowing ideas that had both Langley and Mike smiling and nodding approvals. When it was her turn, she hadn't had anything new; no updates or any new show ideas. Her answer simply was "*Grapevine* is on schedule and is going to be a sure-fire hit." Mike's face glowed, but Langley only gave a swift nod and turned to his superstar, Tiffany.

"And you, Tiffany?"

"Well, I have two new show ideas, but the one I want to propose is a sexy after-hours series that I'd like to call *Chocolate Legs*. My idea for it is to have an escort service that provides more than dates, like some sexy sexual adventures. The main character who I want to call Passion is introduced to this lifestyle by her new roommate when she relocates to New York to be closer to her ailing mother. In need of extra cash, she goes and not only does she make more money than she could ever imagine, but she becomes the one that all men desire. Eventually, this life will become routine until her mother dies and she finds the man of her dreams and wants to leave it all behind."

The corners of Mike's and Langley's mouths both curled up. "Again, Tiffany, I love the concept and idea, but the title, I'm not feeling," Mike said. "Chocolate is bringing us back to an all-black cast, and we want diversity."

"I agree," Langley said. "The main character can be a young, beautiful, black woman, but I want this agency to offer a variety of women from different ethnic groups and since *Sin City* is coming up on its last season for after dark, this idea can be placed in that slot, or if we keep the title, we can put it on TiMax Black. That way, it can have an all-black cast if you like." He turned to, Mike. "What do you think about that? 'Chocolate Legs' is catchy."

"That sounds good, but we should ping-pong it a little more before we finalize the direction, so have Myah coordinate a meeting with my assistant so we can revisit this in, say, a week."

"Yes, sir," Tiffany smiled brightly.

I'll be damn, Tracy said to herself. *This bitch always wowed the crowd, always has a great idea and always has Mr. Green eating out of her hands.* When everyone stood, Tracy stopped Tiffany. She was fuming on the inside and still could not believe that Tiffany didn't know who the hell she was. She was totally pissed that that bitch could take her gig and not even remember her face.

"Ummm, Tiffany, do you have a second?"

Tiffany paused, and then turned her attention to her. "Sure, what's up, Tracy?"

Tracy knew that addressing this issue right now was probably crazy, but she was tired of ogling at Tiffany, hoping it would hit her. "That show idea was great," she said.

"Thank you, Tracy, and again, congrats on *Grapevine.* I've heard good things."

"Yeah, thanks," she said. She stood there looking at Tiffany, wanting to reach out and choke the life out of her, but she blinked and shook off that urge, and then continued. "I was just wondering and been wanting to ask you a question."

"Okay," Tiffany said. She shifted her weight to her left side and tilted her head awaiting Tracy's question. Tracy could sense she wanted to get the conversation over with, and she may have been a little irritated with her taking up her time.

"You don't remember me, do you?"

"Remember you? What do you mean, Tracy? You've been here for what, a couple of months? I see you every day, so I'm confused. What do you mean remember you? Remember you from where?"

"KCLN," Tracy said.

Tiffany still looked puzzled and confused. "Yes, I was at KCLN for a few years. That's where *Boy Crazy* originated. Did you work there?" Tiffany looked at her, studying her face. Tracy could see that she had no clue or even remembered their brief encounter.

"No, but I was *supposed* to work there," Tracy said matter-of-factly. Now her arms were folded across her chest.

"Okay, I don't follow," Tiffany said, folding her arms across her chest, not moving her gaze from Tracy. Their eyes were locked on each other.

"Tracy Simms, Tiffany, I'm Tracy Simms."

It took a couple of seconds, and then clarity must have dawned, because Tiffany's mouth dropped open. "Oh, Tracy, you were supposed to be the new writer for *Boy Crazy*. Now I remember you. You are *that* Tracy?"

"Yes, I'm *that* Tracy. I was late, but you showed up and like pulled the rug right from under me."

"Oh, Tracy, I'm sorry. I had no idea back then, and I didn't want to just take your job, but Todd insisted. I needed a job at the time, and that's how it went down. I'm sorry, it wasn't calculated or personal. I had no idea that the spot was for you, nor did I know that Todd had mistaken me for you until you walked in. It was unfortunate, but you know how it goes in this business."

"You're right, I do know, so no hard feelings, right? I just wondered how you didn't remember my face or recognize me. I mean, you *did* take my job."

Tiffany relaxed her stance and unfolded her arms. "Tracy, come on, you can't still hold any ill feelings over that. That was ages ago and look where we are now. At TiMax. KCLN is like skid row compared to this place. Tell me you're not still sore about that."

Tracy put on the fakest smile she could muster up and said, "No, not at all. I'd be crazy to still harbor ill feelings, right? Like you said, this is how it goes in this world. One day you're hot, and the next you're not." She laughed.

Tiffany agreed and laughed too. "That is so true." Tiffany continued to giggle, and then placed a hand on Tracy's shoulder. "Well, it was nice, Tracy, but I have to get over to set. Enjoy the rest of your day," she said. She hurried off, and Tracy's smile slowly faded as she watched Tiffany happily saunter away in her designer suit and Red Bottoms. The curls that cascaded down Tiffany's back swayed to the rhythm of her strides. Everything about Tiffany, from her head to toe, spoke volumes, and Tracy's anger had gone from simmering to boiling.

She snarled, "Yes, bitch, I *am* crazy, and as soon as I figure out a way to knock you down from that throne you sit on, trust me, I will."

Incensed, she headed for her office. It was ten in the morning, but she needed a drink. Hell, she had the ingredients for a mimosa, so she hurried to make one. She downed it and made another one, and then she snatched open her office door and headed to Tressa's office. Tressa was her only other option at that point. She was the only person she knew that hated Tiffany as much as she did.

Tressa's new secretary was there, and she stopped Tracy from walking into Tressa's office unannounced.

"Excuse, Ms. Simms, but Ms. Green is not available."

"What time will she be back in?"

"I'm not sure. She's in a meeting with Mr. Green. I was told to contact Mrs. Banks if an issue needed immediate assistance," the young beauty said politely.

The sound of Mrs. Banks's name made Tracy's skin crawl. She had never met Kory and didn't want to, but that was another thing Tiffany trumped her on. A husband. That bitch had a husband. Tracy refocused and quickly said, "No message, I'll come back." She hurried to her office and said between tight lips to her assistant, "Get Mr. Harrington on the line, now!" Then she stomped into her office, and her chest heaved up and down. She realized she had to get a grip. Her horns were showing, and she didn't want anyone to know that she was on a mission to take out Mr. Green's star child, and she didn't mean Tressa.

"Ms. Simms, Mr. Harrington is on line one," she heard her assistant announce from the intercom on the desk phone.

She snatched the receiver from the cradle. "I need to see you now!" she blasted into the phone.

"Ms. Simms, need I remind you that I'm the owner of this company, *and* I'm your boss?"

She paused before she spoke. Mike was right, and she couldn't afford to be thrown out on her ass. "Mr. Harrington, I must apologize." She changed her tune quickly. "I didn't mean to be rude or out of line."

"I'm sure. Now I have a meeting in five. I'll get back with you later, Ms. Simms." With no more words, he ended the call. That pissed Tracy off so bad she wanted to throw the phone. She was lost in her own mission, lost in her own unorganized conquest to destroy Tiffany Richardson-Banks or whatever that bitch's name was. She had no master plan, nor did she know her next move.

She got up from her desk and went over to the sofa and flopped down. Then she grabbed the unfinished mimosa and savored the flavor as it trickled down her throat. Too exhausted to plot or devise a plan at that moment she said, "Tomorrow. Yes, I'll come up with something tomorrow."

No Way

Episode 9

Tiffany

Tiffany hurried off, trying to get to the studio as soon as she could. She could not believe she had just had a face to face with the one she screwed out of a job. For a while, she had carried guilt about what had happened that day when she landed her job, but her intent was never to take anyone's spot. She harped about it to Asia a few times, but Asia would always assure her that it was her destiny to get that spot at KCLN, and she had nothing to feel guilty or sad about.

It had been Tracy's misfortune, but it wasn't something that Tiffany had set out to do. It just happened that way. She had addressed how bad she felt to Todd, Darryl, and anyone that knew how her job came about, and they'd all said the same thing. "This job was meant for you to have, so stop feeling bad." Even the sound of Darryl's voice rang out in her head when she thought of him saying those words to her.

Tiffany was out of the golf cart before it could make a complete stop. She hurried inside and searched for Darryl. Now that he had the opportunity to produce his first miniseries, she didn't see him as often as she used to when they had worked side by side.

"Dee, where's Dee?" she asked a passerby. She didn't want to take forever finding him.

"He's in the sound room," the worker replied.

Tiffany was off and yelled thanks over her shoulder. When she got to the door, she paused to catch her breath. She didn't realize how fast she had been moving until her breathing increased. "Calm down, girl. This is no big deal," she told herself. She wanted to consult with Dee before jumping to any conclusions about Tracy. Tiffany had to see if Dee had heard any rumors before she made it about her. She opened the door, and Darryl had on a headset so the engineer that saw Tiffany come in gestured to let Darryl know she was there.

He removed the headset and looked around to see her. "Hey, Buttercup, how are you?" he said and hurried over to hug her.

"I'm fine, darling. How are things going? How does it feel to be doin' you?"

"Fantabulous, love. What brings you to my tiny set, sugarplum? Marital troubles already, hummmm?"

"No, Darryl, damn. Why do you always suspect something is going wrong in my castle?"

"No reasons . . . I'm just being ole messy me."

"Well, Kory and I are fine. Still no bun in the oven, but that is an entirely different topic. You will *never* guess who I just ran into."

"Baby, this is L.A., and nothing shocks me. Hell, if Tressa Green can be clean and sober and have an office with this company, nothing will shock me. Because when I got that news, I thought for sure the devil was wearing a snowsuit, because hell had to be freezing over," Darryl said, making faces and doing his hand gestures. Tiffany laughed because Dee was so dramatic and couldn't nobody tell him that he wasn't born a girl.

"Dee, shut up and stop. You are *always* acting up."

"Baby, I'm always doin' me . . . you betta ask'em!"

"Anyway . . . Guess who works here—better yet, let me put it this way. *Grapevine*," Tiffany said. That was her first hint, but Darryl didn't get it.

"*Grapevine*. Oh yeah, I heard your boy Colby is the lead character."

"Yes, you're right, but not him. I ran into him a couple of months ago. That bastard, but guess again."

"Listen, Watermelon, I have a show to run. I can't play this game all morning, love, now dish."

"The executive producer?" That was Tiffany's second hint.

"Tracy, ummm, Tracy Stewart, Smith, yeah, yeah, Tracy . . . What gives?" Darryl had a look on his face that said *talk bitch or this conversation is over,* so Tiffany told him.

"It's Tracy Simms, Dee, *Tracy Simms.*" She gave the goods, hoping he'd get it.

"Listen, Strawberry, Tracy whomever—dish, give me the dirt."

Since Dee didn't guess, Tiffany figured he hadn't heard anything, so at least there were no rumors. "Tracy Simms is the one who was supposed to get the writing spot at KCLN. Remember the sister who was late, the one I jacked out of a job?"

"No way. Get outta here," Darryl said with his voice five octaves higher.

"Yes. I didn't recognize her, but she made it a point to tell me after this morning's meeting."

"Oh really? What'd she say?"

"Well, she was like, you don't remember me do you, and I was like, should I, and then she proceeded to make me aware that she was the one I snubbed for her job."

"No freaking way," Darryl said laughing.

"It's not funny, Dee. What if she's out to get back at me?"

"Chile, please . . . That was seasons ago. She'd have to be a whack job for sure if she's still harboring over that mess. Life couldn't have been that bad. She's at TiMax, so don't worry about her. I mean, what can she do—ruin your reputation? Not! If that fiasco with Tressa and that pole-dancing scene didn't destroy you, she can't, Love Bug, so no worries."

Darryl did have a point, but Tiffany felt a little uneasy still. "Darryl, are you sure? You know now I need you to keep your eyes and ears opened. If this chick has it in for me, I need to know. You can't be too careful nowadays."

"I know, Starfish, but I'm sure she's harmless and over that old mess. Now get the hell out of here so I can get back to work."

She opened her arms for a hug. "Okay, Sweetie. I'll see you later, and I'll come back and sit in on a few tapings when your recordings get underway."

"Okay, Cupcake," he said and kissed her cheek. Tiffany turned to leave, happy she had talked to Darryl about it. He was normally her voice of reason.

When she got to her set, construction was still underway, and it looked like it would only be a few more days before she and her cast could occupy the space. She headed back to her office, and then she called Kory.

"Hey, baby, what's up?" he said.

"Nothing much. A pretty easy day. Are you busy?"

"No, I'm home. I got the plans for the new location today, so I'm working from home."

"Good, baby, because I've had a morning you would not believe."

"Oh yeah? What happened?" he asked. He sounded concerned, so Tiffany first assured him it wasn't anything life-threatening, and then she filled him in. "Are you for real? No way." He was just as surprised as she and Darryl, Tiffany gathered from his shocked tone.

"Yes, baby, so if I come home, can you take a break?"

"Of course, my love, for you, I'd do anything."

"Awww, Kory, you're so sweet."

"Yeah, I am," he boasted. She could hear the smile in his voice.

"Can you fix me a sandwich, with everything, even onions, please? I got a late start this morning, and I didn't eat breakfast. And I'm starving."

"Sure, baby, no problem. Can you take the rest of the day off?"

"Ummm, I'm sure I can. I need to check in with Mee-Mee, but I'm sure I can. Why?" She twirled a curl in her hair.

"Because we can work on our baby today, all day," he said. His voice was so soothing and so sexy in her ear, her center contracted.

"I'd like that, Mr. Banks. Give me an hour, I should be there."

"Okay, honey, drive safe, and I'll see you soon."

Tiffany ended the call and hurried inside of the building to her floor. She stopped at Myah's desk first. She had an appointment with Rose that afternoon to look at a space for her gallery, so she made a mental note to call her in the car. She didn't need Myah to reschedule an appointment with her best friend.

She rushed inside her office and grabbed her purse, keys, and tablet, and told Myah to do her best not to call her unless it was dire.

When the elevator doors opened, before she could step on, there was Tressa and her dad getting off. "Hey, you two." Tiffany's smile was bright. She was always happy to see Mr. Green. He was like a father to her, and she always enjoyed being with him and around him.

"Mrs. Banks, you're the person we were about to visit," Mr. Green said.

"Awww, Mr. Green, I was headed out. Is it important?"

"It's nothing that can't wait," he replied.

"Daddy, are you sure? I think this matter is pressing," Tressa said.

"Isa, it's nothing that can't wait until morning."

"Are you sure, Mr. Green, because I can call Kory? I was just taking the day because my set is still under construction, but I'll be happy to talk if you need me now."

"No, Tiffany, you go ahead. Isabella and I will see you in the morning."

Tiffany looked at Tressa for confirmation. She knew Mr. Green was a softy with both of them.

"Yeah, Tiffany, we can talk tomorrow. Can you meet us in my dad's office, say, at nine?"

"Of course, Tressa, nine is fine."

"Okay then, that's settled. Now come and tell me more about your project, Isa," Mr. Green said, placing his arm around his daughter. Tiffany pressed the call button and watched Mr. Green and Tressa walk slowly toward her office. She could see Mr. Green's pace was slower than usual and wondered if she should call Kory with a change of plans. Suddenly, the bell chimed, bringing her back, and the doors opened. She was concerned about what Mr. Green wanted to discuss, but she also wanted to get home to her husband. Since their wedding night, they had been trying for a baby, so that trumped everything and everybody at that moment.

She walked in the elevator, and then she heard a voice yell, "Hold the elevator," but by the time it registered to press the button, the doors had closed, giving her one last peep at Tracy. She let out a sigh of relief because she did not want to ride down with Tracy and decided she would do her best to keep a safe distance between them. Tiffany wasn't sure why, but she got a bad vibe from Tracy, and thought back to how she'd catch her eyeing her in meetings. Tiffany thought it was strange, but didn't pay it no mind. Now she was wondering what was brewing in the woman's head.

Tiffany had been in L.A. for quite some time, but she was from the South Side of Chicago, and her momma didn't raise no fool. Her momma used to always say, "Trust is earned, not a gift," and she had absolutely no reason to trust Tracy Simms.

Just Me and You

Episode 10

Kory

It was almost one in the afternoon, and Kory impatiently waited for his wife. He had fixed her a club sandwich and put a few baked chips on her plate. He remembered they had potato salad from the night before, so he grabbed it from the fridge and added a couple of tablespoons on her plate. He made sure the wine cooler was stocked with her favorite whites, and he then closed all the black-out drapes in the house with the remote. It was early in the afternoon, but he wanted to create a romantic scene for Tiffany.

He lit every single candle that they usually burned when they wanted to get romantic, and then he went to his system and hit the touchscreen. He went to Spotify, browsed through his playlist, and wondered what he wanted to serenade his woman with. He went to his '90s R&B list and pressed Play. He thought the new stuff was cool, but R. Kelly's "Honey Love," Silk's "Freak Me, Baby," Next's "Butta Love," and Guy's "Piece of my Love," were more appropriate for the vibe he wanted that afternoon.

Kory wasn't always a romantic, but with Tiffany, it came so easily. He always wanted to see her smile. It pleasured him to see her happy and to hear her laugh. Flowers, jewelry, and little gifts made her smile. His attentiveness and affectionate ways made her happy, and his ability to make her laugh was too easy. Tiffany was so mellow and easygoing, he didn't have to spend a fortune or jump through hoops and hurdles to please her. And he felt like he was the luckiest man on earth. She had come into his life at the most inconvenient time, back then, so he thought, but he knew now that her timing was perfect.

To think he had been with Tressa, a stone-cold bitch. Selfish, evil, controlling, spoiled, loud, and just plain old simple. "Thank you, God. You save me from the worst mistake of my life," he said out loud.

"And what mistake was that?" he heard Tiffany's voice ask him from behind. He was so preoccupied with making sure things were perfect he hadn't noticed her enter the room.

"Hey, baby, welcome home." He walked over to embrace her, and he gave her a quick kiss.

"Hey, honey, and again, what mistake was that?"

"Tressa," he said. "I mean, every time I think that I was going to marry that woman, knowing damn well she was an addict and a narcissist, makes me want to kick myself in the ass."

"Well, before you knew those things about her, I'd say you were blinded by the beautiful face and tiny waist."

"Ha, baby, come on, you know that's not true. Tressa was just a different person when we first met. Her true colors didn't show until after the ring. I mean, Tressa was a gorgeous woman the day I met her, but looks went out the window when she began to show her ass."

"Well, all of that is in the past, my love, and I'm home to let you do what you do," she smiled. He held her tighter.

"And what is that, Mrs. Banks?"

"Don't play with me, Mr. Banks. I'm here to let you spoil me. Like you always do. I got a feeling today is our day to make this baby thing happen, so I'm going to let you feed me, pour me a glass of Chardonnay, and let you do that sponge thang you do, you know, with that bath oil, and then I'm going to take you to our bed and rock you until we both pass out."

"Really? That's what's about to go down?" He painted her neck with another tender kiss.

"Oh yes, and after our nap, you know, after we're rested and rejuvenated, we are going to have dinner, another bath, more wine, and more lovemaking. We are going to make a baby within the next twenty-four hours," she said rubbing his head. He leaned in and kissed her passionately, and his insides stirred. He wanted Tiffany, all of her, not just her body, but her mind, her soul, and her being.

He pulled back. "Baby, I love you so much, and I'm so glad that you're mine. I want you to be happy for the rest of your days, baby, and I'll spend my life doing whatever it takes to make you happy, Tiffany."

She smiled at him brightly. "Baby, you are the sweetest man I've ever known, and marrying you was the best decision I ever made in my life. I want to make you happy too, Kory, and if at any point or any moment you're not happy, tell me, baby, so I can fix it. I've loved you from the moment I laid eyes on you. I mean, you were rocking the high-top fade, Cross Colors overalls, and I know that gold chain had to be fake," she teased, and he moved his arms from around her waist.

He laughed. "Oh, babe, I remember that. You had that Salt-N-Pepa haircut with one side short and the other side long, with them big Queen Latifah earrings. Now, those I *know* was fake, but my gold chain was real, baby."

She headed toward the kitchen, and Kory was right behind her. "Kory, that thick-ass chain *had* to be fake." She examined the plate on the island, and then went to the sink to wash her hands.

"Baby, I'm telling you it was real. My family owns like eight jewelry stores; well, back then, it was only three, but every piece of jewelry I rocked back then was real. I had to cut grass an entire summer for half the cost of that chain. My pops was like, 'Come up with half the money, son, and it's yours,' so, no, baby, my chain was real," Kory boasted and poured himself a drink.

She sat at the island and pulled her plate in front of her to enjoy the lunch he had prepared. She took a bite of potato salad, and then said, "I wish you would have liked me back then. Hell, those earrings I wore . . . got them on Halsted for $12.99, and you know they were fake as hell."

He chuckled. "Yeah, I was too immature back then to handle a girl like you."

"That's what you thought?" She looked at her plate when she said that and not at him.

He noticed her tone change. "Yes, Tiff, you were like this smart, classy, honor roll, studious girl who was pretty as all get-out, but I was chasing tail back then, babe. I didn't want to mess with your head." He went for a glass for her.

"So you knew I liked you, Kory?" she asked with her eyes now glued on him. Up until that moment, he had always denied that he knew that she had feelings or even cared.

He went for the wine and didn't answer. "Kory Lamar Banks, you *knew* I liked you back then?" she asked again. Still he didn't respond. "Kory!"

"Okay, yes, baby, yes. We are too close now for me to tell you any lies. I love you, babe, and I'm sorry for lying before. I knew, okay, but I knew I'd hurt you, Tiff. I was a straight idiot back then, and I was doing some old crazy teenage pimp shit. If I had got with you back then, I know I would have dogged you, and I didn't want to do that to you." He poured her glass and handed it to her.

She took a sip, and then sighed. "So what made me so special, Kory?"

"You have to ask? You're my wife, right now, today, so *that's* what made you so special. You were and have always been special. I knew it back then, and I would have never played with your heart, Tiff. You were different." He took a sip of his wine, and then put his glass down. He went to the other side of the island where she sat and turned her to face him. "You were the only girl that I got nervous around. You were the only girl I never wanted to run game on. You were the only girl that I'd lose my cool around, that let me know that you were special, and now I am fortunate to have you as my wife, Tiffany, so how things worked out for us is perfect, in my book. We have yet to see our happy ending."

"Really? I thought our marriage was our happy ending."

"Nope, when we grow old together and watch our great-grands play in that yard is where we will have our happy ending."

He kissed her softly, and Tiffany never got back to her lunch. They didn't make it upstairs either. They made love right there in the kitchen. After their final climax, they made it as far as the family room with glasses in hand, where they grabbed the blanket that ornamented the back of the sofa in the family room and cuddled close and listened to '90s R&B.

"Baby, are you okay?" he asked holding her close as she rested in his strong arms and on his chest.

"Kory, I am perfect, baby, and I love you." A few short moments after, they both drifted off to a sweet sleep.

L.A. Looks Good On Me

Episode 11

Rose

Rose stood and looked out the bright picture window in the front of her new gallery. She had never imagined being in the heart of L.A. where the who was who shopped, and she had already turned over a dozen people away, but not before giving them a business card. The space was up for lease, but her best friend insisted they negotiate a sales price, and it worked out because they got a better deal. The cost for her to lease for ten years, if she stayed that long, would have been more than to just simply purchase the place. She was glad she listened to Tiffany. Since Tiffany was footing the bill, how could she argue, even if Tiffany wasn't right?

Paid in full, her name was on the deed, she knew she'd soon be in business. She spent most of her mornings with Levi, because he worked second shift, and every afternoon getting her gallery ready for her grand opening. The space was so huge and perfect. Her studio was in the back, so she could do her art in the same building. Overjoyed and excited, she just knew she'd fit right in.

She continued her day nonstop, organizing, opening crates, and gasping at art pieces she had forgotten about. Her stuff had been in storage for so long; some paintings brought back bitter and sweet memories.

Before calling it a night, she decided she'd stay and work on a piece. She was inspired again, and still basking in her new life. Afraid and apprehensive about moving to L.A. at first, the thought had given her the blues, but now she was glad she made the decision to just do it.

She put on her smock, grabbed a fresh, clean canvas, and went for her colors. The studio was so well put together that she had a place for everything. She was always organized and never wanted to be stuck hunting for a certain brush or tool when she was working. That would frustrate the hell out of her, but after rearranging her last place, organization was one of her top priorities.

"Thank you, God," she said before putting her brush on the canvas. "The last two and a half years of my life have been a disaster, so I thank you for this moment, Lord. This is beyond my wildest dreams," she prayed, and then blinked away her tears. She had a painting to do, and she didn't want to have tears blurring her vision.

After three hours, she was finally done, and it was after eleven. She stood back admiring her newest piece, when she heard knocking . . . okay, a loud banging. She put down her color palette and dropped the brush in water and went out to see who was banging at that hour. Her look of frustration quickly faded when she realized it was Levi. She hurried over to the door, unlocked it, and let him in.

"What are you doing here?" she asked with a smile. "What a pleasant surprise."

"I've been calling you and texting you, but couldn't get you. I mean, it worried me a little, and I went by your place, and since you weren't there, I figured you'd be here."

"I'm sorry, my phone is over here." She went for it. It was on the front counter. "I was in the back working on a piece."

"I didn't mean to disturb you. I just wanted to make sure you were all right," he said.

"No, no, it's okay. I'm happy to see you." She went over and locked the door. He looked around.

"Wow, your place is coming together; it looks nice, Rose. You have got a lot done in a small amount of time."

"Well, the sooner I get it together, the sooner I can open the doors. I'm excited," she beamed.

"As you should be. This place is amazing, and this . . . You painted this?" He admired one of her favorite pieces.

"Yes, about a year ago. I was in a funk when I did that piece, can you believe?"

"Well, they say you do your best work when you are going through the hardest times."

"I've heard that too."

He walked around and continued to compliment her collection. "Wow, Rose, you are the real deal, baby. I mean, I probably can't afford any of this, but you are in a prime location, and these rich folks are going to be in here buying paintings and photos left and right."

"I hope so, and I'd be more than happy to paint some things for you. I have to get more lighting before I start taking pictures again, but when I do, I'd love to take some pictures of you."

He shook his head. "Naw, worry about your business right now and don't worry about me."

"I insist; after all, it looks like you're working with something really nice underneath that uniform."

He blushed. "Nah, I wouldn't say all that, but I feel you, though."

"Do you want to see the one I just finished?"

"I'd love to," he said.

"Come on, follow me." She led him to the back and like her other pieces, he gave her praises.

"Rose, girl, baby, you are one talented sister. This is absolutely stunning. I don't know what else to say other than, baby, this is it!"

"Thank you." She took off her smock, dropped it in a hamper, and went to the sink to wash her hands. "Are you done for the night?" she asked. They had hung out, went to breakfast and lunch, and he showed her around L.A. Sightseeing, hand holding, and a couple of good night kisses, but that's where it ended. Rose didn't want to move too fast, but she was feeling him, and she did want some dick. It had been long overdue since she had a dick in her life.

"Yes, I'm done. I would have been home, but when I couldn't reach you, I just wanted to make sure you were okay."

"Yes, I know, and I'm fine. I'm sorry. I didn't leave my phone up front on purpose."

"It's cool, babe."

"So how about we go to my place for a nightcap? I mean, if you'd like."

He didn't respond right away. Instantly, Rose got a knot in her stomach and felt uneasy. She immediately wished she hadn't asked. "You know what? Never mind. Forget I asked."

"No, babe, no. I was just caught off guard, but I'd like to come. I'd like that."

She looked into his eyes. "Are you sure? I mean, there is no pressure, Levi. I'm not trying to rush things. I just wanted to spend a little more time with you tonight. I mean, we can go somewhere else . . . a restaurant, bar, lounge," she nervously rambled.

"Shhh, no, I want to come over. Like I said initially, I was caught by surprise, but I'd like to come over." He kissed her softly on the lips.

She smirked. "Okay, well, my car is out back."

"I'm a little ways down the block. There was nothing close."

"All right. Do you mind giving me a few minutes to allow me to clean up? It won't take long," she said moving toward the leftover paint and brushes she used to create her last masterpiece.

"No, baby, of course not. I'll wait."

She smiled brightly. "Thanks, it will only take a couple of minutes." Once she was done, they went back to the front to prepare to leave.

"So I'll meet you then?"

"Yes, let me walk you out, and then I'll be there shortly after."

Rose nodded in agreement, and he waited while she turned off everything and set the alarm. He walked her to her car. "Rose," he said before he shut her door.

"What is it, Levi?" She looked at him in his eyes wondering what he was going to drop in her lap.

"We don't have to move too fast."

"I know," she said with a grin. She put her key in the ignition. "You don't have to come if you don't want to."

"I do. And I'll be there soon. Drive safe," he said. He leaned in and kissed her again.

"You too, and I'll see you in a few." Rose cranked her car and pulled out, then she hit the button on her steering wheel and called Tiffany.

"Hello," Tiffany answered. Her voice was groggy, and Rose knew it was late.

"I'm sorry, bestie, but I need you."

"Hold on, let me get up." Rose heard what she thought was cover wrestling, and then heard Tiffany whisper, "Baby, it's Rose, I'll be back in a few."

Rose knew she shouldn't have called that late, but Tiffany was her one and only best friend. "I'm so sorry, Tiffany."

"Girl, it's okay. Kory and I have been fucking all damn day, and I am tired as hell, Rose. I bet if I tried to open my legs, I'd cramp the hell up."

"Must be nice."

"Damn, Rose . . . my bad. I didn't mean it that way, girl, what's up?"

"Well, I invited Levi to the house tonight, and, girl, he seemed a little hesitant. Now I'm thinking he's married, got a woman at home, or something. Girl, I don't know. We've been kicking it for a few weeks now, but no sleepovers, and I still have not been to his place."

"Rose, don't try to figure that shit out. Just be up front with his ass and ask. Give direct questions and demand direct answers. You know I'm not for that guessing game madness. Hell, we are too damn old not to be direct."

"I hear you, Tiff, but I like him so much, it's like I don't want to know if something else holding him back. I enjoy him too much."

"Okay, then, don't find out; wait until you're head over heels in love, and then you can't leave his two-timing ass alone. Rose, this is Basic Relationship 101. You know the drill on this, so man up and get to the bottom of this before you fall for him and things get really shitty."

Rose didn't want to admit it, but Tiffany was right. "Okay, friend, thanks for the reality check. I'll call you tomorrow and tell you how it goes tonight . . . after I confront him for answers."

"Okay, love, but be careful. I don't want you hurt. This is the first guy you've met in L.A. There are plenty more out there. You don't have to get with the first one who shows interest, Rose."

"I know, but I like this one, so wish me luck."

"Good luck, girl, now, bye. I'm going back to sleep. I have a nine o'clock meeting with Tressa and Mr. Green in the morning, so I need some sleep."

"Good night, and make sure you stop by the gallery tomorrow evening when you're done with work, because I want you to see the progress I've made. I'm almost ready to schedule a grand opening date."

"That's awesome, babe. I will, I promise. Now good night, darling." They hung up, and ten minutes later, Rose was at home. She went inside and took a shower. She moistened her skin with oils and smell-goods, put on a cute little nightie, and went for a glass of something to relieve her nerves. With a glass of Pinot Noir, she settled on the sofa and turned on the tube. The clock was ticking, and she didn't want to call him. After forty-five more minutes and her second glass, she decided to call it a night. She had her answer. He was married or had a live-in and couldn't do sleepovers. She knew his ass would be a no-show.

She turned off the tube, went into the kitchen, rinsed her glass, and then put it in the dishwasher. "Oh well . . ." she said and headed to her room. Just then, her doorbell chimed, and it made her jump. She couldn't believe he had actually shown up.

She went to the door, looked out the peephole, and then opened the door. "I thought you weren't coming," she said.

"I know, and I'm sorry I'm late, I had to run home first. I wanted to shower and change."

"Okay, come on in, Levi." She stepped aside and decided she still had to confront him. She didn't want to know the truth, but she definitely *needed* the truth. "You're married? Have a lady? Come on just tell me before we go any further," she said immediately after closing her front door.

"Can I at least have a seat first before the interrogation?" he asked.

"Come on in and have a seat."

He moved over to the sofa, but she didn't sit.

He went and sat down on the sofa in the living room.

"Can I get you something?"

"A drink would be nice."

"And then you tell me the truth?" she snarled.

"And then I tell you the truth," he agreed.

She went into the kitchen. Her heart was thumping so loud against her chest, it was like the beat was banging on her eardrums. She fixed him a vodka and cranberry, and although she didn't need it, she poured herself another glass of wine. She was afraid to hear his truth, but she had to. She went back and handed him his glass and took a seat on the sofa near him.

"You look pretty," he complimented.

"Thanks, now out with it, Levi." She didn't want to be distracted from the truth and flattery would get his ass nowhere at that moment.

He took a swallow and let out a breath. "I am married," he said.

Her heart dropped. "Get out!" she yelled and rose up from the sofa quickly.

"No, wait, wait, please . . . let me finish."

"There is nothing to finish. You are a—" she tried to say, but he put his glass down and stood. He grabbed her by the arms firmly.

"My wife is on life support!" he yelled over her.

Rose stopped and just stared. "Holy shit!" she said in shock. Those were the last words she expected to hear.

The Big News

Episode 12

Tiffany

Tiffany rushed into her office at eight forty-five. She was tired and not herself that day, and she knew it. The day before, she and her husband spent the majority of their day making love. They got in a few glasses of wine, a couple of snacks and dinner, but the bulk of the time had been spent with Kory deep inside of her.

"Mee-Mee, I gotta meet Mr. Green in less than fifteen. Please get me coffee ASAP," Tiffany commanded in a rush, and then headed into her office. She had finally gotten a weave after some pushy convincing from her stylist, and due to the previous day's activities with Kory, it was a mess. It had gotten wet in the shower and in the steam from the bath she and Kory took the night before, and the beautiful drop curls that cascaded down her back and draped her shoulders were gone. She managed to slam her makeup that morning, so it took away the attention from her messy ponytail that she tried to pull off, but it was not a good look. She was exhausted and how you feel is how you looked in her world, and she knew she needed to go to her office and give her hair one last herculean effort.

Tiffany fussed with her hair, and then Myah walked into her office with her coffee made just the way she liked it. She was down to six minutes, and she knew her hair was a hot mess. "Tiff, what in the hell are you doing?"

"Mee-Mee, I have no clue. Kory and I did the damn thing most of yesterday, and I'm not used to this weave, and I don't know how to get it back to how it was."

"Here, take this coffee and give me that brush," Myah demanded. "I'll be right back." She left, and Tiffany quickly blew a breath to cool her first sip. She needed a pick-me-up, and she needed it quick.

A few seconds later, Myah walked back in. "Now, first of all, I just called Mr. Green's assistant and told them you'd be there by nine fifteen, now sit back and let me work my magic." Myah laid a little bag on Tiffany's desk and pulled out rubber bands, hair pins, and a little miniature can of spray and a travel-sized jar of gel. Less than ten minutes later, Tiffany looked presentable.

"Oh my God, Myah, thank you. This sew-in mess ain't for me. I need to get this mess out of my head. Who needs all this long mess anyway? Not me."

"I think it suits you. You just have to take the time to learn how to style it instead of letting these hairdressers in your head every other day."

"Mee-Mee, please, I don't have time for that. I have shows to produce and a baby to make."

"Whatever. Just get to that meeting right now before you are late."

"Yes, the meeting. I'll see you later." Tiffany headed toward Mr. Green's office, and as much as she wanted to pass Tracy without saying a word, that would have been rude. Was this chick ever on set or in the idea room with her writers? Tiffany would have sworn she waited for her to leave her office because she ran into her too damn many times in a day. "Good morning, Tracy."

"Good morning, Tiffany. Looking good, girl."

"You too," Tiffany said, not knowing what else to say. She had just thrown her look together, so the last thing she expected was a compliment, especially from Tracy. She took rapid strides to the elevator, dismissing Tracy. When the doors opened, why did Colby have to be the one to emerge from it?

He stepped out. "Tiffany," he said.

She wanted to say fuck you, but instead said, "Colby." She figured he was on his way to Tracy's office. He was the lead in her series. "Whatever," Tiffany said once the doors closed. She made it to Mr. Green's office at exactly nine fifteen.

"Tiffany, come on in," Mr. Green said. He attempted to stand, but Tiffany could see that he wasn't his old self.

"No, Mr. Green, sit; no need to stand." She went around and leaned in to give him a hug and a soft kiss on the cheek.

Tressa spoke. "I remember a day when that would have made me ready to fight you, Tiffany Banks," she giggled.

"What, Isa?" Mr. Green inquired.

"Tiffany hugging you like that, but now I know we are on the same team and why you admire her so much."

"We are, Isa, and I also admire you. You have made your daddy proud." Mr. Green smiled at Tressa.

"Tiffany, have a seat please," he said. She went and took the seat next to Tressa.

"Now, ladies, let's get down to business. I wanted to meet with you two because I'll be stepping down soon."

"Mr. Green, why?" Tiffany asked. She knew he had some health issues, but not bad enough to leave. Not 100 percent, but she thought he looked well and still had it in him to work a couple more years.

"Awww, come on, Tiff, you're a bright woman. You know my health is fading, and I want to go home and enjoy my wife before I leave this place. Mike and I have been partners for a long time, and this meeting has to stay in this room, young ladies," he admonished.

"Yes, sir," Tiffany said first.

"Of course, Daddy," Tressa said.

"Well, Mike is going to sell me his shares, meaning there will be only one owner of this company really soon. His children have no interest in taking his place, so he and I have come to a handsome agreement for him to sell."

"Mr. Green, that is a lot to take on in your condition, sir," Tiffany interjected. "I mean, Mike is a brilliant man, and why would he leave now? Why would he even consider sharing?"

"He is planning to sell, and that's why you two are here. I'm so grateful that my daughter has turned her life around, and now I want to teach her the business. I want you and Tressa to both run this company when Mike and I are gone. Mike agreeing to sell is something we've thrown back and forth for a very long time. Like me, he wants to spend time with his wife and family, just like I do. With his son being an architect and his daughter a surgeon, this is not what either of them want to take on, so I want you two to keep this company running as long as you are young, and hopefully, my grands and your offspring, Tiffany, will eventually, take over after you."

"Daddy," Tressa said shocked, and then Tiffany chimed in.

"Mr. Green, us . . ." she pointed back and forth at the two of them with her thumb, "I know producing and directing and creating shows. This is a huge company. I don't know if we are capable of doing this. I mean, this company is your and Mike's baby . . . to trust us," Tiffany said doubtfully. She knew she was brilliant and destined for success and maybe becoming a CEO of her own network someday, but she was sure she wasn't ready.

"Yes, Daddy, Tiffany is right. You can't be serious about putting this network in our hands. I've only been here a few short weeks, and I'm trying to grasp as much as I can as it is."

"Yes, I know, but I'll be bringing in help. I, myself, will be active in the process, but you two will learn this business, and in a year, you two will be the heads of this company. I know you two are able to do this, Isa. You are the shining star I've always known you could be, and Tiffany is one of the hardest working, most dedicated women I know, other than your mother," he joked. "The bottom line is . . . I chose you two, and that's what I want." His tone was serious.

Tiffany swallowed hard, and then looked at Tressa with a terrified look. A look Tiffany knew she had never before displayed in a public place. Tressa hunched her shoulders. Tiffany knew she was just as unsure as she was.

"Daddy . . ." She paused and looked at Tiffany again, and then back at Langley. She swallowed hard, and the words she spoke made Tiffany even more terrified. "If you can teach us everything we need to know . . . We can do it."

Tiffany thought her ears were playing tricks on her. Had Tressa lost her mind with all the drugs she had done. But then again, she thought, if Tressa, a recovering addict and alcoholic, showed up and said she could do the job, Tiffany knew damn well she herself could. "Mr. Green, like Tressa said, we can do it," she said, and then immediately wished she could take those words back. Being CEO of a company that large was a *huge* responsibility, a level of talent that she may not have had.

"Now, listen, it will be business as usual around here because many people in this company are not going to like my decision, but it's my company, and I'll do what

I damn well please. So, in the meantime, ladies, we will have a lot of meetings with a team I've handpicked to show you two the ropes. There are only a handful of employees that know what's going on, so do not speak to a soul about my health, Mike selling his shares and leaving, or about you two taking our seats. Understood?" Mr. Green was a pillow when it came to them, but he spoke so sternly, Tiffany knew he was dead serious.

They both said *yes, sir* in unison. Their meeting went on for another hour with basic details of what's to come, and Tiffany could not believe what was happening to her. She knew why Tressa would automatically become the next in line, but for Mr. Green to pick her was overwhelming and a little too much information for her already-exhausting day. She finally made it back to her office, and Myah came in.

"Hey, boss, how did the meeting go with Mr. Green and Tressa? Is Tressa back to her old schemes and tricks? Did the precious Queen of L.A. fall off of the wagon?" Myah joked and laughed out loud at her own jokes about Tressa.

"It went well. And Tressa is still on the up-and-up, so far. Mr. Green was just making sure Tressa is on the right track and learning the business. Just a routine follow-up with schedules, budgets . . . just the basics," Tiffany lied. She was told not to say a word, so only Kory and Rose were going to hear that information for now.

"Wow . . . I still can't believe Tressa is Tressa. That woman was a mess, but she is doing good and looking damn good."

"Yes, she is," Tiffany said, and then there was an odd silence.

"Well, I'll get back to my desk."

"Hold on, Myah. I have a question for you."

Myah came closer and sat. "Yes, Tiff, what's up?"

"Have you ever thought about producing?"

Myah smiled. "*Have* I? I have so many ideas swimming around in my head."

"Really? Like . . .?"

"I can't tell you. You'd steal my ideas, go make it happen, and then what . . . It will be my word against yours."

"We can sign a clause, Myah. I'd never steal your ideas."

"I know, Tiff. I was just joking. I just think if I share my ideas, I want to be the one making my ideas into productions."

"Well, Myah, today is your day. You are no longer my assistant."

"Come again?" She looked puzzled.

"Yes, you are fired. Clean out your desk and move your things to the office way down on the other end of this building. It's small, but as of today, you are a junior producer, so go pick one of those three little-ass offices down the hall and clean out your desk. I'll get with HR. Your services as my assistant are no longer needed."

"Tiffany, stop freaking playing. You *cannot* be serious."

"I *am* serious, now move it before I change my mind."

Myah leaped out of her chair. "Oh my God, oh my God, you *are* serious!" she squealed and was jumping in place.

"Yes. You've earned it, Myah, and it's time you moved up. There is no limit when it comes to learning new things, so you will shadow Dee, and soon, you'll be putting your ideas into production." Tiffany smiled. Myah was bright, dependable, and it was time for her to grow as well.

Myah raced out of Tiffany's office. Tiffany picked up the phone and called HR and let them know her decision. Not even sure if she had that power or not, she did it anyway and was confident Mr. Green would back her up. When the day came to an end, she headed for the elevator, and when she hit the call button, Tracy appeared again out of thin air. *Not a-fuckin'-gain,* Tiffany thought to herself and was tempted to act as if she left something in her office just to keep from getting on the elevator with her.

"Long day?" the bitter one asked.

"Yes, and I'm glad to be heading home," Tiffany said. When the elevator doors opened, Tiffany stepped in first. She hoped someone else she knew would get on so she could talk to them and not Tracy's ass.

"You know, I'm just as good as you are, and I would have done just as good as you did with *Boy Crazy*," Tracy said.

Tiffany rolled her eyes. "Listen, Tracy, I was signed years ago for *Boy Crazy*, and I've produced four other shows since then. Let it go. You are at TiMax now. Work on keeping your spot here," Tiffany snapped. She hated knowing within a year she'd be CEO, because with that, Tracy's future at TiMax wasn't secure.

"I know you're not threatening me, Tiffany Richardson."

"No, baby, that's not a threat; that's advice; and it's Tiffany Banks. Get the fuck out of the past," Tiffany blasted when the doors opened. She stepped off wanting to tell Ms. Simms another thing, but she kept her cool and kept it moving. "I'm too busy doin' me to let Tracy shake my branches and leaves," she said to herself and flagged a cart to take her to her car. She was tired, but she promised Rose she'd come by the gallery, and that's what she was going to do.

Unbelievable

Episode 13

Rose

Rose was busy moving things around, jamming to Anthony Hamilton's "Since I Seen't You." *Comin' from Where I'm From* was still and always will be her favorite Anthony Hamilton CD. The music blared so loudly she didn't hear Tiffany knocking on the door. She was so busy singing off-key and rocking her head she didn't notice that Tiffany had used her key to come in.

When the music abruptly stopped, Rose jumped. "Oh my God, Tiffany, you scared the shit outta me."

"Well, I was knocking on that glass so hard, I thought my knuckles would bleed."

"I'm sorry, girl, but this CD does something good to me. It like moves me to my soul."

Tiffany scaled back the volume, and then hit Play again. Now it was low enough to hear each other speak. "I know, this is one of my favorites too, so I hear you." Tiffany put her purse down and began to walk around. "Wow, Rose, it is *so* nice. This wall color is perfect, and those lights really give this room an elegant feel. I'm excited for you."

"Thanks, Tiff. I'm just about done with opening all the crates. And I've come across pieces I totally forgot about. I'm so excited . . . and terrified at the same time," Rose expressed. "They are picking up all the empty crates and rubbish tomorrow. After I get bar codes entered and my inventory entered in the system, we can set a date for the opening, and then sell some fabulous art." She and Tiffany high-fived.

"Yes, your pieces are fabulous, honey, and you are going to make tons of money. I just know it," Tiffany encouraged. "Oh, and don't forget to call the paper to run an ad for an assistant. You have to get someone trained and familiar with the prices and the names of your pieces pronto. You want to get someone who is efficient, with a great personality and sales background, so you have to take the time to interview, check references, and—" Rose cut her off.

"Tiff, I know, baby. I know my last gallery went out of business, but things are going to be different here . . . better. The location for one is kick ass, the atmosphere is just entirely different. The timing, I mean, everything is finally falling into place, and I am more than confident about this move, this place, and my new business. I got this. You've made a good investment, and I won't let you down."

Tiffany's lips formed an enormous smile, and then she hugged her friend tightly. "I know, Rose, and I know you got this, girl, but you know me. I'm a control freak, but I trust you, and I know you will do well."

"Thank you. I remember you were the first person to buy a piece from me."

"Yes, and when I told people about your gallery, they'd frown and be like . . . a gallery? Don't nobody like art." They laughed.

"Well, that was because I started in the hood, hoping I could bring a little culture to the area, but I should have listened to you when you said the location was bad."

"No, I'm glad you didn't. You did it on your own. It failed, but you tried it. You did what you set out to do, so that is why I know you are going to rock L.A. It's yo' time, girl."

"That's right," she said, and they both continued to admire the space. "So I have to tell you about last night."

"And I have to tell you about this morning."

"Okay, you first."

"No. You. I'm exhausted, and I know you got some wine somewhere up in this upscale establishment," Tiffany teased.

"You know I do."

Tiffany followed Rose toward the back. Right before you entered the studio, where Rose created all of her masterpieces, there was a little kitchenette. Rose had had a sliding screen wall installed, so when she had exhibits, the casters could work without disturbing potential buyers.

She poured them both a glass, and after she handed Tiffany hers, they went back to the front and sat on the red, round, plush sofa.

"So, last night I called you about Levi, right? Told you I thought he was up to something because we'd hang out, and he was nice, but it seemed as if he was holding back. So as you know I asked him to come over last night, and he was a little hesitant. When I got home, I showered and waited and after a while, I just said, 'Fuck, he ain't coming.'

"So as soon as I headed for the bed, he rang the bell. I let him in, and he told me the truth. He's married."

"*What?* I *knew* it, Rose . . . damn! Did you kick his ass out?"

"No. Wait."

"No, wait, my ass! Please tell me you threw his ass out."

"I was about to, Tiffany, but then he told me she's on life support."

"*What?* He said *what?*" Tiffany yelled. "You didn't believe that craziness, Rose? Please tell me you didn't fall for that. That is the craziest shit I've ever heard. That is original, for sure. I'll have to use this bullshit in a show."

"Calm down, Tiffany. He wasn't lying."

"Rose," she said. She had one hand on her hip and her head cocked to the right with her brows vaulted toward the ceiling.

"Tiffany, he wasn't lying, okay? At first, I didn't believe him either, but this morning, I went with him to the hospital."

Tiffany relaxed her stance. She then sat back down. She leaned in as if she needed to make sure she heard Rose correctly. "He took you *where?*"

"I went to the hospital with him this morning. I let him stay with me last night, only after he promised he'd take me and let me see for myself."

"So you fucked him on his word, Rose? How could you do that? That was stupid."

"See . . . There you go, being so Tiffany. I did *not* fuck him. As much as I would have loved to, I didn't. We talked half the night, and we slept. He didn't even take his clothes off."

Tiffany drew back. She let down her defense and said. "I'm sorry, Rose. Tell me what else happened."

"Well, last night he told me that his wife was shot during a robbery at a convenience store about four months ago. The bullet was removed, and for the first few days, the doctors assured him she'd be okay. He said a day after they took her from critical to stable, she flat-lined, but they revived her, and she has been on the machine ever since.

"He says every night he goes and stays with her all night, and last night when I asked him to stay over, he panicked. He said maybe hanging out with me was a bad idea, but we are human, and he's been feeling lonely. He said when he met me, I was someone new and different and not from around here and knew nothing about him, so he felt safe to spend time with me. He said after a few days, he realized he was starting to like me, but he felt bad because Paris was on her deathbed and he was out dating.

"He said he told himself that he wouldn't see me, call me, or text me anymore, but he wanted to, so now he is confused."

"Oh, wow," Tiffany said and grabbed Rose's hand and squeezed it. "So is his wife going to pull through?"

"Most likely no, but he can't let go. I don't think he's ready, and I didn't want to put my two cents in. I mean, that's his wife."

"So are you going to see him again?"

"Well, we've decided to just be friends. Hang out and just be champions for each other right now. He's lonely, and I'm single, so we are just going to enjoy each other's company."

"But what if you start to fall for him, Rose, and she wakes up? What if—" Rose cut her off.

"Tiff, please, there is always going to be a what-if. I've decided to just be what I said I'd be to Levi. We're just going to take it one day at a time."

"That's some crazy stuff, Rose. I've never heard of anything like this in my life, and I can come up with some elaborate stuff, but *this* . . . I'll be waiting every day just to see what happens and how this unfolds."

"Tiff, my life isn't one of your shows."

"I know, Rose," she said and scooted close to her. She wrapped her arm around Rose's shoulder and kissed her cheek. "Don't worry, my friend. Things are going to work out just fine."

"I hope you're right."

"Me too."

Time to Tag Team

Episode 14

Tracy

Tracy camped outside of Tressa's office hoping to catch her. She had been trying to talk to her for a few days, to no avail. She called her several times, and Tressa had not returned her calls, and she wondered why. When she saw Tressa approaching, she smiled. "Hey, Ms. Green. How nice to see you. I've been trying to get ahold of you."

"I know, Tracy, but I've been superbusy. I have an agenda longer than my right leg," Tressa said, going into her office, with Tracy on her heels.

"I know, and I'm sorry to intrude, but I have a problem, and I wanted to talk to you about it." She watched Tressa put all of her belongings down, and then Tressa took a seat.

"Thanks, I wanted to talk to you about Tiffany Richardson."

"What about Mrs. Banks?" Tressa asked. Tracy's eyebrows slightly raised at the way Tressa said 'Mrs. Banks' as if she was giving her some respect, and Tracy hoped she wasn't making a mistake by asking her to join forces with her to run Tiffany up out of there.

"Hold on," Tracy said. She went over to the door and shut it. Then she came back and sat without Tressa offering her a seat. Tressa looked as if she was very interested in what she had to say.

"Let me give you a little background on Tiffany. You see, she wasn't supposed to get hired at KCLN as a writer. That was *my* job, *my* position, and Bill Keiffer had hired *me*. I ran a little late, and when I walked in, Tiffany had already worked her magic on the room, and *bam!* she took my job. Now, between you and me, I had a couple of rumps in the sack with Bill for that position, but after that day, he blocked my calls, wouldn't talk to me, and my life was turned upside down.

"I lost everything. I went into debt, was jobless, lost my car, and so many people that I thought were my friends just cut me off after a while. I finally got a call from UVN, and if it hadn't been for that, I would have been homeless, so, yes, I can't stand the sight of her, and I have been going out of my mind trying to figure out a way to bring her down a notch," Tracy said and waited for Tressa to reply.

"Listen, Tracy, I'm sorry to hear about the hell you went through, and trust, I have forty-five million reasons to hate Tiffany too, I can assure you, but my father is fond of her, and there is no way you are going to be able to sabotage her position here. Sad to say, but that will be close to impossible. She is the top producer here and on her way up, so trying to hit her here at TiMax will be a waste of your time."

"And that doesn't piss you off? From what I heard, your father basically adopted her. She had you thrown out, Tressa, and your father gave her your trust. She married your ex-fiancé. Don't you want to see her burn? I mean, you can't tell me that you forgive that bitch for what she's done. I'd want her head on a platter after all she's done to you."

A smile went on Tressa's face. "Yes, of course, but you have to cool your heels, Tracy. You can't go out with guns blazing. A person like Tiffany . . . You have to kill them softly. Tiffany will get hers, trust me, but you have to stop wearing your hatred for her on your sleeve. It's tacky, and it's not a good look."

"How is it so easy for you, Tressa? How could you be in the same room with her without wanting to snatch her head from her body? Or tackle that bitch to the ground? It takes every inch of my muscles to maintain when we are in the same room because I want to choke the life out of her."

"Because I'm not like you anymore. I once was, but I've learned how to channel my anger. You can take a person out when they don't know that you're coming. So, if you want to destroy Tiffany, you have to try a subtle approach. All of this extra control to keep you at bay when you are in the same room is like giving Tiffany the power. Bring it down, Tracy. And what she did to you is nothing on what she did to me, but I'm not ready to rip her to shreds."

"So what do I do? How do *you* keep your cool?"

"You calculate your steps, devise your plan, and then execute," Tressa said. Tracy followed what she was saying, but she was hoping she'd give her something more to go on.

"So what do you plan to do?"

"You do not want to concern yourself with that, Ms. Simms. My issues with Tiffany are my issues, and how I handle her and my issues is my business."

"But you do have a plan, right?"

"Just watch and you'll see."

With that, Tressa pushed back from the desk. "I have things to do, so if we're done . . ." she said with authority. She wasn't Tracy's boss, but she was the owner's daughter, so Tracy gave her respect.

"Yes, we're done, and I've heard you loud and clear." Tracy stood and hurried back to her office. She had two messages, one from Colby and the other from Mike. She hadn't gone to see Mike in a couple of days, and he was blowing up her phone. She dismissed him and dialed Colby first.

"Hello," Colby answered.

"Hey, Colby, it's Tracy," she said. She had known why he left her a message because she had called him earlier. She had been trying to bed him since day one, but she hadn't broken down his defenses.

"Yeah, you called earlier. What's up?"

"I called to go over a couple of rewrites. Can we meet at my place tonight, say around eight?"

"Just e-mail them to me, Tracy. I can take a look at the changes."

"I'd rather you meet with me, so we can go over them together and make revisions once, instead you playing ping-pong with the script."

She heard him let out a breath of air. "Okay, eight is fine. Text me your address." He then disconnected the call. She smiled, and then got back to work.

We Just Want a Baby

Episode 15

Tiffany

Tiffany paced the warm tiles of her heated bathroom floor. She had set her alarm for three minutes, and it took everything inside of her not to peep at the test. "Please, Jesus, let it be this time, Lord. I have everything but—" she was cut off.

The alarm sounded off before she could finish her sentence. With her fingers crossed tightly, she looked at the little window that only had one line, indicating that the test was negative. She picked up the stick and blinked at the test, hoping the second line would magically appear, and before long, her lashes were wet from the tears that fell. "Negative, again," she sniffled. She put the stick down and put her palms down on the granite vanity.

It had been six months and no pregnancy. "God, why me? I mean, I have everything a woman could ask for but a baby, Lord. Please, God, just bless my womb to give my husband children," she cried. She took the stick and tossed it into the wastebasket, and then she started the water to wash her face. Kory would be home soon, and she didn't want to look like she had been crying because she'd have to tell him why.

He'd told her that morning to wait until she missed her period, but she was too anxious, and knew in her gut she was, but now she had the results that she wasn't.

She headed down the steps and went into the kitchen. She wasn't pregnant—again. Again, another negative, so she reached for her favorite thing—wine. After pouring a glass and savoring the flavor, she grabbed her phone and called Asia.

"Hey," Tiffany said after hearing Asia's voice.

She also heard the sounds of a screaming baby, and then Asia said. "Tiff, mi must give yah ah call back," in a Jamaican dialect rush.

"China?" She asked, knowing it was Asia's baby girl screaming at the top of her little lungs.

"Yes, she's in a mood. I'ma hit yah back." Asia hung up before Tiffany could say okay. Asia went into labor two nights after her wedding. Tiffany didn't understand how she tried to hide it anyways, because by the time she walked down the aisle, she was thirty-five weeks and looked pregnant, so her secret was out.

Tiffany scrolled through her contacts, and then called Rose. She needed someone to vent to, to cry to, and to get answers from, because God wasn't telling her anything. The doctors said she was fine, and that Kory could impregnate a small village, so she was stumped why there was no baby inside of her after six long months of trying.

"Hey, lady," Rose sang.

"Hey, girl, why so cheery?"

"Do you have to ask?"

"It must be Levi again."

"It is, it is. Girl, he is a great guy, Tiff, and you were right. I'm falling for that man."

"I bet. I told you." Tiffany thought twice about bringing up her issue now. She didn't want to bring Rose's mood down.

"Girl, yes, so what's up? To what do I owe this call? I mean, all you do is stay in bed with your man if you're not at the studio."

"Well, Rose, you know we've been trying to get pregnant and against my husband's advice, I took a test a few minutes ago, and, of course, it was negative again."

"Awww, Tiff, I'm sorry. Maybe you took it too soon. Did you miss your period?"

Tiffany sighed because Rose sounded like Kory. "No," she confessed. "But this time, Rose, I just felt 100 percent sure I was."

"Well, Tiff, at least y'all having fun trying, right?"

"I guess you're right," she lied. Baby making was a chore, and sometimes, it caused strain and making love was now making a baby, not the old passionate take-me-away kind of sex, and as much as Tiffany missed that, she wanted a baby more. It had turned into ovulation kits, temperature taking, elevating the hips with a pillow, just anything to make her eggs and Kory's sperm come together.

"So relax, girl, it will happen. Maybe you need a break from work. A nice getaway with Kory and a change of scenery. I mean, you're practically running the company now since Mr. Green is showing you the ropes. You are his protégé."

"Yes, Rose, I know I have a lot on my plate at the station, but trust, Kory and I get it in, baby. My office, his office—hell, we've even done it on the set, so why are we not pregnant?"

"Patience, my sister, patience, even God took six days to create the world."

"Yes, but it only takes one time to get pregnant."

"Yes, for some, but not all, Tiff. Relax, girl. It'll happen."

Tiffany sipped and heard the door open. "Look, I gotta run. Kory is home. I'll talk to you later, honey."

"Okay, tell him I said hey!"

"Will do." Tiffany ended the call as soon as Kory walked into the kitchen. "Hey," she said and took another sip of her Pinot.

"Hey, baby, I didn't expect you home until later."

"I took a half day." She went for the bottle to refill.

"You didn't," he said looking at her.

"Didn't what?"

"Take another test."

"What?" she asked like he had it all wrong. She didn't want to look guilty, but there was no disguising it, and Kory knew her like the back of his hand.

"Come on, baby, it's 1:15 in the afternoon, and you're about to do a refill. I told you to wait, baby. It could be too soon, and you're disappointing yourself when we could be."

"Kory, you know I can't wait. We go through this every single month."

"And every month I tell you to wait, and every month you don't."

"And still every month it's negative."

He walked over to embrace her. She couldn't hold on to the tears, so she let them flow. She was disappointed again, and as soon as he held her she sobbed.

"Come on, baby, don't do this. It's going to happen. We are healthy, and we are going to have children. It's just taking a little bit of time."

"I know," she sobbed even harder. "Crackheads can get pregnant, teens with no idea what life is all about can get pregnant, one-night stands can get pregnant, so why not us? We are a loving couple."

"Shhh! Don't, baby, stop, okay? Don't do this to yourself, Tiff. It's just not our time, and trust, I'll keep making love to you and planting my seeds until we are blessed with a child."

"Okay," she nodded.

"Now," he said and turned her back to him and pulled her in close to him. He planted a couple of soft kisses on her neck. "I want you to take your glass, go up, and take a long hot bath, and I'll whip us up something to eat."

"Awww, Kory, baby, no. I'm not hungry. I'm not in the mood to eat, baby."

"You're not now, but after you have your bath, and I put this on you," he said and grinded his midsection against her ass, "you are going to be starved."

"Okay, I guess you're right, baby," she agreed. "Make something with cheese, baby, I want something cheesy," she requested.

"Your wish is my command. Now, go up, and I'll be up soon to work on our baby," he said and gave her a gentle push.

Tiffany smiled so brightly. It's like her skin glowed. She topped off her glass and headed up the stairs. She ran her afternoon bath and soaked. Whatever he was cooking had her nose open. It smelled divine, and she was starting to feel a little hungry.

After she was done lathering and close to getting out, he came in the bathroom with the bottle and refilled her glass. The water had chilled, and she was ready to get out, but with the refill, she changed her mind and decided to stay in longer.

"What are you making, baby?"

"Pizza, with everything."

"Please tell me mine has extra, *extra* cheese."

"I do know how you like it, baby, so yours have plenty of cheese. I'm going to go down and finish up, and then I'll hurry back up here and take care of you." Kory was the sexiest man on the planet she thought. She'd never had a moment where she didn't want to devour him or not have him deep inside of her. He was sexy, smart, kind, and sweet, and she was the luckiest woman on the planet to have him.

"Oh, I'm done. I can get out now."

"Let me run down, take the pizzas out, and I'll be right back." He stood and left, and she went ahead and got out of the tub. Before she could dry and lotion her skin, her husband had returned. There were no words, just screams and moans as he pleasured her body to several orgasms. Afterward, they went down and enjoyed their pizza, salad, red wine, and then they hung out by the pool. Kory reminded her of all they had to be thankful for, and she agreed to stop obsessing over getting pregnant. They both agreed to stop the temperature taking, calendar watching, and pillows under the hips and get back to lovemaking, not baby making.

He was right. Only God could allow them to have a baby, so she had to move out of the way.

"That's good, Reesy. I always knew you could do great things, but you just wanted that fast life."

"I know, Amber, please don't remind me. I keep trying to leave my past in the past, but no matter what street I go down in this city, my past is in my face. Men I fucked and fucked over, women I spit on, cussed out, and stepped on. All the party people, still doing the same old shit, and if it weren't for my daddy, I'd leave this place. Get the hell out of L.A. Relocate, go someplace remote, quiet, maybe countryside, by a lake. Somewhere peaceful and serene and start over. You know, live a life like this," Tressa gestured to Amber's home and yard. "Like you with a husband a kid and a half," she said because Amber was already carrying baby number two.

"If you feel that way, Reesy, why don't you just tell your dad that you don't want to take over his company or even work there? Tell him how you truly feel. He'll understand, Reesy. Why won't you just be honest?"

"Two reasons," she said, and then paused before answering. She took a sip of her cool drink.

Amber eyed her like a mother would a child waiting for a lame explanation. "Those two reasons *are . . .?*" Amber inquired.

"I fought so hard and begged my father for an opportunity at his company for so many years, Amber, and now that I have it, I don't want to just walk away, and I don't want to leave it all to Tiffany. She's not my blood or my father's daughter from another mother, but he still thinks so highly of her, and I have to show him I'm just as smart and capable as she is. I can't abandon ship. I'm just as good as Tiffany."

Amber didn't speak, she just shook her head.

"What? Why are you shaking your head? What is that look for?" Tressa asked.

I'm Over It

Episode 16

Tressa

"Would you like anything else, Reesy?" Amber asked. They were out on Amber's poolside patio, enjoying the rays. Amber was clearing the table, and she asked before she headed back into the house.

"No, I'm good," she told Amber. She was so happy that she and her friend were close again. She didn't realize how awful she was before until she looked back on some of the conversations she and Amber had had in the past, when Amber tried to convince her to do the right thing, and that was mostly all the time they talked.

Amber returned with a pitcher of lemonade. She topped off both of their glasses, and then took a seat and put her feet up. "I'm so glad you came by today. I've been thinking about you a lot lately."

"Well, I had a day. I mean, I'm learning so much. I grew up in that studio and thought I knew everything about it, but turns out I didn't know a damn thing."

They both laughed. "Yes, hanging out there is an entirely different story than working there."

"Yes, it is, and I just want to make my parents proud, you know? I've messed up so much that I want my daddy to see that I am doing my best to be the best."

"Reesy, I thought you were over this competition and obsession to destroy Tiffany."

"I *am* over it, Amber. I don't want to rip her heart out of her chest with my bare hands anymore, and I don't even mind being partners with her. That is best for our business, because she *is* smart and more cut out for this than me. I know I'm going to need her to keep from losing everything that my father and Mike have built, but personally, I won't lie. I still harbor some ill feelings for some things, but trust me, I'm over it, Amber. I know I was on drugs and did a lot of evil shit, but she got Kory; she can't have my dad. That's what puts me on the defense. That's where I am sore, but I don't have it in for her anymore at all. She just can't have my daddy too."

"And she doesn't, Reesy. Langley is a supersmart man. After all, he is still giving you an opportunity to be a part of something we both know you don't deserve. Tiffany didn't move in on your father, Reesy. She just gave him all the things he wanted from you. You will always have your daddy, Reesy, so let the past truly be in the past and let it go."

"I'm over it, okay, and I promise you I'm not scheming, nor do I have any ill motives. I'm clean. I'm on the straight and narrow. I go to anger management, therapy, and even go to AA and talk to people who are where I've been. Tiffany and I are good. As long as we do well as business partners, I can stand her. Now, on the other hand, she does have an enemy out there. And she is close by."

"What do you mean?"

"There is this vindictive chick named Tracy Simms over at TiMax that just recently came on and said that Tiffany beat her outta a job over at KCLN. She still harbors ill feelings about it and is trying to come up with this plan to destroy Tiffany. It's comical to me."

"Did you tell Tiffany?"

"No, that's not my business."

"What? Tiffany is going to be part owner of your dad's company!"

"Yes, and this little nobody doesn't have a plan or any weight or clout. She is just a bitter-ass little idiot that needs to move on and get over it. She's pathetic. Juvenile, if I must say so myself."

"How do you know so much, Reesy?"

"Because she thinks I still have bad blood with Tiffany, and that I'm plotting on her too."

"And why would she think that?" Amber's eyebrow arched with curiosity.

"Because that is what I'm leading her to believe." Tressa gave a half grin.

"Why do such a thing if it isn't true?"

"So she'll trust me. She feels confident that we both have the exact same agenda. So if she comes to me with something life-threatening, of course, I'll alert Tiffany. Plus, I just like seeing her carry on. I have to contain my laughter most times. And, she *will* be one of the first ones to be cut from the team after Tiffany becomes her boss. TiMax is family, and as much as I hated Tiffany in the past, I'm over the past and moving forward with no animosity."

Amber looked at Tressa suspiciously. "For some reason, I'm having a hard time believing you, Reesy. After all, you really, really despised Tiffany once upon a time."

"Amber, relax. Trust, I honestly don't want any of that anymore. I just want to get my money, leave, and get on with the rest of what I have in this so-called life. I've done the most, Amber. I ruined everything for a lot of people, and everything I used to touch turned into shit. I'm serious when I say I want to get as far away as I can from here. I'm not the Queen of L.A. anymore. L.A. no longer loves me, and I don't love L.A." Her eyes watered because she spoke from the heart, but she didn't allow a tear to fall.

"You're serious, Tressa," Amber said looking deep into her eyes.

"Yes, more serious about it as I want to stay clean and sober. I keep myself busy at work and spend way more time than a woman my age should with my parents just to keep from falling off the wagon. Amber, it is so hard, and I feel if I just could . . . get away from here and find that small little place where no one has heard of me, I'll find a husband, have a couple of kids, and my dad will truly be proud of me for once in his life.

"You know I grew up thinking I was the queen of everything. My dad adored me and to make up for the thousands of hours he spent building TiMax, he just threw money at me. I have never shared this with a soul, Amber, not even my shrink. All the acting out and all the bad girl bullshit wasn't who I truly was. I was just craving the attention of my father. It was always late nights for him, Amber. Most times it would be days before I saw him.

"He'd be at work when my mom tucked me in at night and gone by the time I came down for breakfast. When I started to get into trouble was the only time my daddy showed up." Tressa let out a deep breath, and then a sigh. "I know it was stupid and a poor choice to make, but once I fell into bad-girl-bitch mode, it was like who I grew to become.

"Now, after I ruined everything and almost died, this is the one and only chance I have to be free. If I stick around here, I'm going to continue to crave the attention and the VIP treatment and the way bitches used to worship me. I need a new start, and my past is so close behind, I can't do it here," Tressa expressed. She then let the tears fall.

Amber reached over to comfort her. "I think you should be honest with your dad, Reesy. Your dad will understand."

"I can't, Amber. He's now sick and trying to make my momma happy and turn me into this suit that I never was. I am not cut out for this. I thought I was, but, Amber, I'm not. And then there is my mom. She cries every day in fear that my daddy is going to die. I can't tell him how I feel. I just can't right now."

"Listen, your dad *will* understand, I guarantee you," Amber encouraged.

"Maybe he will, but I won't do it. I want my daddy to die a proud man, so I have to forget myself and how I feel for once in my life and think of him like he has done for me time and time again. Once my daddy is resting in peace and I still want to fly the coop, I will. I know that Tiffany is more than qualified to run things without me. If I do have children, which I plan to, I'm sure my shares will be handed down to them, and I'm sure Tiffany will do the same for her offspring, but, for now, I'm all in."

"And you give me your word that you are not out to destroy Tiffany in any way. Not even a tiny bit. You are 100 percent sure that there are no ulterior motives behind that gorgeous face?"

"I promise you there are no motives. She has to run my dad's company because I'm not capable of doing it alone. In the meantime, I'll just keep a close watch on Tracy. I swear on everything that I'm over it."

"Good, now if you are still in the mood for shopping, let's go, because if my pregnant behind stays idle too long, I'll fall asleep." She stood, and so did Tressa.

"Well, come on. I'm not at my monthly spending limit, so let's go spend some money."

Dinner and Rewrites for Two

Episode 17

Tracy

She checked the time on her phone again and wondered what was keeping Colby. He was over fifteen minutes late, and she didn't want the food to dry out, trying to keep it hot for him. She didn't want to seem anxious or impatient, so she didn't call or text him. Then she heard her phone and rushed over to it. It was Mike again. She hit Ignore and sent a quick text to him.

Going over rewrites with Grant. What's up, baby?

A few moments later, she got:

Baby wants to play . . . I miss my mommy! How long will you be?

She replied, Not sure, baby. May not be able to play tonight. :-(

He replied, You said the same thing the last four nights, and baby is starting to grow angry. You don't want baby angry, do you? When baby's happy, everyone's happy.

She blew out a breath and knew he was right. Her job was still hanging in the balance. With only one show, that had still not aired yet, and with no new show ideas, she knew she didn't have a lot of leverage to play games. Especially not with the big boss, so she replied, Will rap it up soon, baby. Mommy's tits are full and ready for you to feast!

With that, Mike stopped texting. She looked at the meal she prepared for Colby and turned off the warmers. He wasn't coming, so what was the point? She didn't bother to text or call him, she just poured a glass of the chilled wine she had for them, and then waited ten more minutes before she texted Mike.

Is baby still hungry?

Yes, Mommy.

Give me an hour and I'll come feed u.

OK, Mommy.

She flopped down on the sofa and grabbed the remote and flipped through the stations, but nothing sparked her interest. She tossed it on the cushion beside her and let out a sigh. She was already showered, dressed to kill, and her makeup was flawless because, like Tiffany and most all of the staff at TiMax, they had a stylist and makeup artist who never minded making extra cash. She wanted to seduce Colby that night, so looking her best was a desideratum. Somehow, deep down, she knew that men like Colby, fine, arrogant, and cocky, would be a no-show. Having a little time to kill, she grabbed the remote again and cranked up the volume. One of her favorite shows, *Snapped,* was on, so she listened in. She sipped and by the time the show ended she had to rush over to Mike's, but she now had a plan to begin her operation to destroy Tiffany.

The show talked about a voice monitor that was planted, and the assailant had listened in on his victim's conversations, plans, and daily routine, giving him the leverage he needed to attack his victim at the right time. She knew Sundays was the slowest day, and she could get into Tiffany's office and plant a device. She had to find out something. That way, she could learn information that would help her in her plot to abolish her.

She wanted to run Tiffany out of town. She wanted to humiliate her so badly that Tiffany would want to live under a rock after she was done with her. To be so bitter over something like that from the past was crazy, and Tracy knew it, but for some reason, she couldn't let it go. For some reason, she wanted to knock Tiffany's ass to her lowest point, just the way Tiffany had knocked hers. "I have to show you, Tiffany, exactly what you did to me. You have to feel some of my pain. How did you swoop in and land my job, and then move so far up the ladder to where you are Mr. Green's next in line? You are an evil, selfish, thieving bitch, and you don't deserve any of it!" she griped.

"You will feel my pain. You will not ride off into the sunset while I have to suck old men's dicks and change nut-filled diapers just to get recognition. Oh yes, Tiffany Richardson, your ass is going to pay. You are going to feel me!" she declared.

She got up and went into her spare room where the walls were plastered with photos and articles of Tiffany. She had collected them over the years, and she obsessed over them even when she didn't want to. Her obsession was beyond her control, and there was no way for her to get over it unless she got even.

"You *will* pay, Tiffany. You *will* pay. This is far from over," she yelled at a wall decorated with captions of Tiffany. Breathing hard and heart thumping like a rapid erythematic beating drum in her chest, she began to slap herself. After a few stinging licks to her face, she punched her thighs. "Bitch, bitch, bitch, bitch, bitch, bitch!" she yelled repeatedly, over and over again until she was exhausted.

When reality set back in, she realized she bruised herself. She went to the bathroom mirror, and her cheeks looked as if she wore red blush from her self-inflicted slaps. "Get it together, Simms. You're not angry at yourself for being late, you are mad at Tiffany for taking your spot," she recited in the mirror. She snatched the cabinet open and grabbed her bottle of pills. She should have taken one before she slapped her own face and beat her own thighs, but she gave into the self-affliction instead of suppressing it with medicine.

Taking one without water, she put the lid down on the toilet and waited for the pill to relax her and the ability to contain her irrational thoughts of Tiffany and self-afflicting behavior. After almost ten minutes, she could feel the medicine doing its job. She was more tranquil now and felt like nothing mattered, not even Tiffany Richardson. She stood, turned on the water, and began to sing. She hummed the Jill Scott tune "Golden" as she combed her hair back into place and touched up her makeup, camouflaging the bruises from her slaps. She rubbed concealer on her thighs and sealed it with powder, hoping she wouldn't get makeup all over Mike's sheets because she didn't want him to question the marks she left on her skin from her punishing herself.

When she left the bathroom, she noticed the guest room door was still open. She hurried over to shut it. "Now who left this door open?" she questioned as if she was talking to someone else in her home. "We all know not to leave this door open," she said out loud as if she wasn't the only one that lived there. After shutting it, she went and trashed the meal she had prepared for Colby as she continued humming Jill Scott's tune.

After all of the pots and pans were empty, she loaded them in the dishwasher and poured in the dishwasher detergent. She made sure her kitchen was spotless before she headed for the door.

She drove to Mike's place as if nothing unusual transpired at her house. She smiled as she parked and decided to put Tiffany and her vendetta against her in the backseat. She got out and strutted to the front door and rang the bell. He let her in and welcomed her as always, and she let him do her body the way he did each time they were together, and she welcomed sleep when it was all over.

I'm in Control

Episode 18

Tressa

Tressa sat at her desk going over the numbers for the next season of *Boy Crazy*, and her eyes crossed. Over and over she coached herself saying, "You can do this, Tressa, you are a Green, and you're not just a lazy, spoiled brat, and you are no longer an addict." Hard work was something she had never done in her life, and it was still foreign to her. Getting up every morning and going to work still hadn't fully kicked in, and she thought of abandoning ship often, especially moments like this when everyone was gone for the day, and she was still at work trying to handle what was a simple task to the veterans that worked there.

Stressful moments made her want to snort a line or two, but she did her best to focus and fight off the urge. "You are strong, you are fearless, and L.A. doesn't control you, Tressa Isabella Green. Mind over matter, mind over desires, mind over feelings," she recited. Something she had learned in rehab. She learned that the mind was more powerful than emotions and feel-good fleshly pleasures. She was now in control, and she promised herself, her momma, and her father that she would stay clean. "One day at a time," she coached herself and got back to the graphs in front of her.

Since *Boy Crazy* had been one of TiMax's highest-ranking shows, she had to triple-check her work, because she didn't want to make any mistakes. She then knew why Tiffany was treated like royalty at TiMax, because everything about that hit show was brilliant. From the story line to the wardrobe, to the makeup, to the cast, there was not one negative thing to be said. The cast gave it their all, and then some, and the crew did not half step, so *Boy Crazy* would have a spot at TiMax for a very long time, and she was now a fan. She watched the show faithfully. Tressa smiled, and then said out loud, "How does she do it?" Her thoughts just jumped out of her mouth, and she didn't know she had a visitor standing in her office.

"How does who do what?" his voice jolted her out of her work zone.

She looked up, and her eyes landed on the last person she wanted to see standing in her doorway. The last person she needed to see, and she wondered what prompted him to show up at her office. A sudden wave of panic went through her body as if she had seen the devil. Why was he still there? His show was already done taping, so his visit was out of left field. She had ignored him, blocked him, and made sure she stayed as far away as possible from him, and somehow, he was standing in her office.

"Stephen, what, what?" she stuttered. "How did you get in here?" The sight of him not only surprised her, but it also made her extremely uncomfortable. She was strong, but what strong meant for her was staying away from her poisonous influences, and Stephen was just that, and in the worst way. Tressa had been on the straight and narrow, and Stephen was a friend that didn't take no for an answer, so she made it her daily job to stay clear and away from him.

"Nice to see you too, bitch," he said in his flamboyant, off-the-screen personality. He was a heart throb on television and played a straight, sexy role in his series, but not all of his fans knew he was really gay. There were rumors, suspicions, and even printed gossip about it, but nothing that was concrete, so his show did well.

He came in closer, uninvited, and Tressa thought she'd go into a full-panic frenzy. "So, missy, why have you deleted me from your Facebook, Twitter, Instagram, and Tumblr? Heck, even on Pinterest a bitch is not your friend. Why did you ditch me, Reesy? We were friends." He stood there with his body poised like a runway model, then crossed his arms over his chest and waited for an explanation.

Tressa took a breath and remembered what she learned in therapy about interacting with friends she has abused drugs and alcohol with in the past. "I didn't ditch you, Stephen. I decided to separate myself from the people who I indulged with. I am clean now, and no way could I have stayed this way if I continued to run with the same crowd and friends.

"As a recovering addict, you have to separate yourself, you know that. Nothing personal, but I had to let go of some of my old friends to begin my new journey. I'm clean, Stephen, and I want to stay that way." Her tone was even, direct, and stern. She meant it and hoped Stephen would not try to seduce her back into the life of addiction. It was always that "one line won't hurt you," she knew because she said that to Amber a billion times after she cleaned up.

"I'm no addict either, sister-girl, and I would have understood. Reesy, you are my girl. My ride-or-die bitch, so you know I would have never pressured you or forced you to indulge."

She knew that was bullshit, but she said, "I know, Stephen, but when you want to be free of that drug, or any drugs, for that matter, you can't be around it. You have to separate yourself completely to avoid temptation. Honestly, I could never blame you or anyone else for my habit, but for me . . . for me to remain clean, I can't be around it."

"So is that what rehab taught you?" he asked smartly and snickered. He went into his bag and pulled out a tiny zipped bag with coke in it. "I'm no expert on the matter, but you and I both know that you had it under control before the wedding bullshit with Kory and your trust issues with your dad. Look, Tressa, until Kory found that shit in your purse he didn't even know. You can snort responsibly," he suggested. He opened up the bag, licked his pinky, and dabbed a little on it. He licked his finger, sucking the contents clean, and Tressa's eyes were locked on him to keep from looking at the poison that she fought so hard to kick.

She knew what one hit would do, but she didn't want it. She liked her new life, her new clean life, so Stephen had to go. "Look, Stephen, a true friend wouldn't come up in here with drugs. A true friend would congratulate me, and lastly, a true friend wouldn't be mad because I turned my life around. Now, I am happy to see you, but if this is all that you came for, I'll ask you nicely to leave."

He grabbed his chest dramatically as if he was about to have a heart attack and took a seat in the chair on the opposite side of Tressa's desk. "Oh, since when does the Queen of L.A. ask nicely?" he retorted.

"Stephen, I'm no longer the Queen of L.A. I'm just trying to live a normal life, get along with my parents, and earn their respect. My daddy has put so much into helping me and giving me a job and my thousandth chance to do right by him and my mother. This was the hardest thing

I've ever done in my life, so again, be a friend and put that away. I don't need to see any type of drug or drink. We can catch up, hang out, or whatever you want, but I'm done with that shit, Stephen, and I mean it . . . seriously!"

"But we all miss you so much, Reesy. Look, you don't have to indulge, just hang."

With sincerity, she said, "No, Stephen, I can't. I don't want to hang or put myself in those circles anymore."

"Are you sure?"

"One hundred percent sure." Tressa was confident and so proud of herself. Stephen was very persuasive, beguiling, and slick, and could convince someone to sell their soul, so he had to go.

"Okay, then, bitch, I'll put it away. I come in peace. I just wanted to see your ass, that's all. I mean, security so tight around here now," he stood and pranced around her office.

"I know, Stephen. My father has taken extreme measures to make sure I stay clean."

"Well, he must not know me well." He went over to her side of the desk.

She stood, and they exchanged a hug. "I'm happy to see you, Stephen, and I want you to know I love you, but I had to kick the old out of my life to move forward with the new, and I had to separate myself from old habits in order to break them," she explained.

He moved back to the other side of her desk and took a seat. "I hear you, boo, and I'm not here to cause no trouble. I see that you are truly on the straight and narrow, and as your friend, I'll respect that, but if ever—" he tried to say.

"Never," she declared, cutting him off.

"Okay, bitch, damn! Can we still hit a club or two? I know you're a working girl now, but everybody needs a party. There are virgin cocktails, Ms. Thang."

"Rain check," she said with pleading eyes. She had work to do, and she wasn't strong enough to fight off evil devices alone. "I have a deadline, Stephen, and I'm still learning the ropes here. These figures alone got my eyes crossed. I have to focus on work. You understand, right? So can I please get a rain check?"

"Rain check, bitch, please! *Nobody* rain checks me. Today is Sunday, and you shouldn't be here in the first fucking place, and tomorrow is some type of bullshit-ass holiday, so come on, Reesy. Working on a Sunday is for no-ass-life idiots, and on top of all of that, you are the boss's daughter. Get in gear, bitch . . . I'm here to resurrect your status, boo. After all, you do know your ass is on the 'I'll be damned' list now?"

"I am? Are you serious?" She frowned.

"Yes, as serious as a fat kid with cookies in his pocket," he confirmed.

"Okay, bitch, one drink, and I have to get back to my office and get my work done. I can't be fooling with you, Stephen. If my dad knew . . ." she said. She stood and reached for her handbag.

"*That's* what I'm talking about. Reesy all up in da house," he cheered and danced to the beat of the rhythm in his head, and then started twerking.

"I don't know how these bitches don't know yo' ass is gay," she teased.

"It's image, baby. My people know how to do their jobs, and as long as those lonely, desperate, need-to-get-a-life bitches out there with their tubs of ice cream and bottles of wine are tuning into my show and buying up all my 'Must Be the Magic' series trinkets, a brother like me can have pussy when I'm in the mood for pussy and the dick, which I prefer, whenever I fucking want it," he gloated.

"You are still crazy as hell. Come on, and, Stephen, I can't stay out too late. I have work to do," she pouted.

"You'll be back before you know it," he said.

Tressa let Stephen lead the way. She had worked hard and did her best to stay clear of trouble, but like some things, not all things come to an end. She never made it back to work. She fell off the wagon, and she wondered whose bed she was in when she opened her eyes the next morning. She immediately began to panic. "Oh my God, my father is going to kill me," is what she said after she sat up and realized she had done the ultimate no-no. "Holy fuck!" she said and got up. Her head spun out of control as she tried to locate all of her personal items. "My purse, where the fuck is my purse?" she cried in a panic, scanning the room. She put on the items of hers that she could find, and she was completely dressed sans panties.

She looked down at the man that was sprawled across the bed and her eyes began to burn. She didn't know him, and she had no clue of what she had done with him. She spotted her shoes near the door and still wondered where her purse was. "Please, God, this cannot be happening, please, Jesus." She began to shake like a leaf. "I got to get out of here. I need to call for a car." She rushed over, grabbed her shoes, and when she opened the door, the place then became familiar to her. She was at Stephen's, and she wondered where that bastard was and why didn't he look out for her.

She made her way to the front of the house and was overjoyed to see her handbag hanging on the coatrack near the entry door. She hurried over to it, ignoring the banging in her head, and did a quick check inside to see if her items were still there. With a quick glance, her credit cards appeared to be all there, and her cash, gum, gloss, and other items were there. She went for her phone, and praised God, it was there. She quickly dialed for her car to come get her. She didn't look for Stephen. She just walked out of the front door and prayed her car would get there fast.

As soon as she got in, she cried because she could not remember a thing about the happenings the night before, and when it hit her, that that day was piss-testing day to get her next payment, she broke down in the worst way. She would go back to square one with her father, and she knew that her chance of being at TiMax was gone. Her dad would kick her out for good. Instead of going to the main house, she went to her condo, a place she hadn't been to in weeks because she needed time alone to figure out what was next. Leaving L.A. sounded better and better the closer she got to her home.

I Got You Now

Episode 19

Tracy

She planted a listening device in Tiffany's office. She didn't know what advantage that would give her, but she had grown desperate and had to try something—anything to sabotage Tiffany. She now knew her chances of completely destroying Tiffany were slim to none because she didn't have shit on her. Tiffany was squeaky clean, and everyone one adored her, but she didn't want to give up. She wanted to add some level of humiliation and shame to her life, so this was a happy start. As diabolical as she wanted to be, she wasn't, so she was tired of racking her brain for ideas. Now, maybe Tiffany would feed her something she thought as she crept back to her office after planting the small device under Tiffany's desk. She'd just listen in for a while and use whatever she could to gain power and control of the situation and do the ultimate . . . bring Tiffany down a few notches.

She grabbed her tablet, made sure she had the app downloaded properly, and hated she had no way of doing a sound check. She'd just have to wait until Monday when everyone was back at work. She left, and as she was leaving, she could have sworn she saw Tressa getting into Stephen's car, but she only caught a glimpse of the woman, so she wasn't too sure. It was a nice night, so she decided to walk to the parking lot instead of calling for a cart because she hadn't valet parked.

When she got to the lot, she ran into Colby, the last person she thought she'd see on a Sunday. "Perfect," she said when she realized it was him. She increased her pace so she could speak to him before he got into his SUV.

"Hey, there," she called out.

She caught the disappointed expression on Colby's face, but she didn't give a damn. She didn't give up so easily. When she wanted something or somebody, she went for it, so his partial frown wasn't a deterrent. She moved a little faster to close the distance.

"Hey, Tracy, what's going on? I didn't expect to see you here on a Sunday."

"I had a few unfinished businesses to take care of. Why are you here on a Sunday? We don't tape on Sundays."

"I was working with Bella. She needed me to go over some lines with her for tapings tomorrow, so I came through to help her out."

"Oh, so Bella the reason why you won't go out with me?" she asked inveigling. Colby was A-list, tall, fine and rich, and she wasn't going to give up so easily.

"No, Bella is not the reason, Tracy; you are the reason."

"What's wrong with me, Colby? I know you find me attractive." She was a gorgeous, five-seven, petite, yet curvy framed work of art. She could still go braless, and her curly tresses were always well groomed.

"You are attractive, Tracy, very," he said. She moved closer. "But you are full of drama."

"Drama! What?" she asked surprised as if she was clueless to his accusation. "How and why would you say that?"

"In the door, after you cast me for the lead, you pulled me to the side and went in aggressively about destroying Tiffany. You started bringing up my relationship with

Tiffany and how she dumped me and left me cold, trying to amp me up to join forces with you, and, that, my dear, was a total turnoff. When I met you, Tracy, our initial meeting, I won't lie, I was checking you. You are a gorgeous woman. During auditions and negotiations, I did consider asking you out, but as soon as I got this role, you like flipped the script and starting talking crazy and trying to recruit me to join forces with you. You are too old to be running around L.A. holding a grudge over something that happened years ago.

"Tiffany took your spot—big deal. This is a dog-eat-dog world, so get over it. So, no, Bella isn't the reason, Tracy. You turned me off, and I say this as a colleague who believes in this series. Let it go. Concentrate on this show and go on to do more great things. You are just as bright and talented as Tiffany, but the sad thing is, you don't know it. If you did, you'd ditch the drama." With that, Colby hit the button on his remote to unlock his doors. Tracy stood there stunned, unable to move or even speak.

"Good night, Tracy." He opened the driver's door, got in, and cranked his engine. Even after he pulled away, Tracy stood frozen in place.

"Did that bastard just call himself reading me?" she said before her legs moved. "Who in the fuck does he think he is?" she said as she sashayed to her vehicle. *"Get over it, get over it."* Why did he not get that Tiffany had knocked her ten steps back from her dream? Yes, she had a spot at TiMax, but she was nursing a grown-ass man to be there. "Wow, Colby, wow. Tiffany has your dumb ass under her magic spell too. She has all of y'all fooled like she is some kind of goddess, but I'm going to show her ass. She isn't as good as I am, and she is going to have to pay for what she did."

Tracy hurried to her car, got in, cranked it, and then hit the gas and sped out of the parking lot. The words of

Colby still stung her ears, and she no longer wanted his stupid ass. "You're just as dumb as Mr. Green and Kory, but I'll be the one on top—just watch. I'm going to make Mike give me just as much power as Mr. Green has given to his precious Tiffany. She may have put it on Langley, but I'm going to put it on Mike, and we will see who gets the last laugh!" Tracy declared.

She dialed Mike and smiled when he said he'd meet her at his playhouse. That night she planned to do Mike so well, he'd want to sign over his ownership of TiMax to her. She laughed out loud. "Oh yes, Mikey, baby, Mommy has something special for you tonight, baby. Let's play!"

I Couldn't Resist

Episode 20

Rose

It had been four days since Rose had seen Levi, and she was going insane. They both agreed that things were getting too heavy since they both said they'd just be "company" to each other, and that they should scale back. Levi had begun to spend more nights with her and fewer nights at the hospital. They'd stay up late talking, holding hands, and exchanging sweet kisses and caresses, but they refrained from sex.

"Look, Rose, I adore you, baby, but I need to put some space between us, baby."

Rose froze. That was the *last* thing she wanted to hear. "Why?" she asked sadly. She enjoyed every moment spent with him, and she hated when he had to go to work and leave her alone. The gallery was finished, and she had a few more days before the grand opening, and now with her new assistant trained and ready to work with or without her, her afternoons were filled with nothing to do.

"Baby, you know why. Every time I'm near you, I want to kiss you, touch you, and be close to you." He paused. "Rose, I wanna make love to you." He eyed her down. His dark brown pupils penetrated her, and she believed him to be genuine.

She was not surprised because she wanted what he wanted. She wanted to make love to him just as much. "And I, you, so I understand if you need to fall back."

"Baby, you know this is so hard for me. I'm just conflicted and want to do the right thing, Rose. You do understand, right, Rose? You know what I mean, baby, right?" he asked.

"I know, Levi, and it's so hard for me too. I mean, you are perfect. I love the way you look, the way you smell, the way you smile, the way you make me laugh. I love everything about you."

"And I, you. I have moments when I wish I never met you, and then I have moments where I want to give up hope, pull the plug, and move on. I just don't want to be an asshole about it. Like I wonder if I'm being selfish or if I'm not being patient enough. I'm so confused right now, baby. Can you understand that?" he asked. The look on his face was so serious, so intense, and Rose could feel his heart crying out to her.

That made her pull back from his embrace. "Yes, Levi, we definitely need some space. I don't want to weigh so heavy on your heart that you'd considered doing something because of me, and then resenting me later for it." The last thing she needed was for him to go and pull the plug on his vegetated wife because of her. She'd never be able to live with something like that. That would be too much for her.

"I could never resent you, Rose," he smiled, and then caressed her cheek.

"You say that now, baby, but if you make a decision based on us, and we don't work out, you will hate me, so we do need a serious break, baby. Just take some time and sort out what you truly want. Don't make any decisions based on me or how you think I'll feel, because I'll be all right. As long as you are happy, I'll be happy, babe." It wasn't easy, but she gave him a reassuring smile. Well, as best she could, considering the circumstances.

After a long pause, he agreed. "Okay, but I won't take long, Rose. If I return, that means we're going all the way." He locked his finger with hers. "I love you."

She blinked a few times and told him the truth. She wanted to lie and downplay her feelings, just to make sure he didn't do anything hesitantly for her, but she had to be true to herself and him. "I love you too, Levi, and if you don't return, I'll understand. I know you'd never do anything to hurt me."

He pulled her into his arms. "I know you will, sweetheart." He gave her a passionate kiss, squeezed her tightly in his arms, and then he was gone.

That was four days ago.

For Rose, it had been four long days of praying, begging God for strength to not call him, and praying for the best for Levi. To pray for him to choose her would have been selfish, so she just asked God for the best for them both.

Now Rose was sitting in her backyard, with a glass of red wine, watching the sunset. She wasn't heartbroken, but she was lonely as hell without him. She had gotten used to him being around. Now there was no him. She hadn't had love in a very long time, and meeting Levi was something that she least expected. She came out to L.A. to start over and launch her career, not thinking love would be on the menu. She wasn't the same old confident Rose she had once been.

After losing her gallery, damn near going bankrupt, she moved in with her sister and basically cut herself off from the world. She stopped going out, going on dates, and even attempting to fix herself up. She basically became her sister's live-in nanny and housekeeper because since her funds were nonexistent, she cooked, cleaned, picked up the kids, helped them with homework, and whatever else she could do to contribute to the house.

She got a little check from Amazon every now and then, because some of the pieces she had online for sale would sporadically sell, or she'd get a client out of the blue to call and request something unique. Tiffany would always send her a check here and there, even before she got the huge amount from Mr. Green, and finally, Rose found a job doing what she hated . . . taking pictures at the mall. Yes, she was a photographer, but she never wanted to be in the mall taking holiday photos.

It didn't pay much, but it was enough to give her sister something toward her living arrangement, but deep down, Rose was unhappy. Little by little, she gained more pounds, and after Tiffany's wedding, it was like the weight came on full force. Basically jobless, no place of her own, and the horrible incident with her sister thinking she was sleeping with her husband, she finally took Tiffany up on her offer to move out to L.A. To start over. Starting over was what she was confident she would do, but falling in love . . . She did not anticipate that at all.

She grabbed the remote and cranked up Anthony Hamilton's "Charlene," and then reclined on the chaise she was relaxing in. With her shades on, she closed her eyes and thought of him. The man she needed and wanted after such a short amount of time. There was just something about him that gave her chills. He was sexy, fit, and a bit mysterious. His deep-set eyes and devilish grin were sexy, and she wondered at times how someone so delicious found her attractive. She wasn't ugly, far from it, but she never expected someone so fit to even give her a second glance.

She sipped from her glass and put her drink down. Relaxing, she sang, "Come on home to me, Charlene."

"Baby," he said. She jumped. Her heart immediately raced as she sat up to find Levi standing over her.

"Levi, baby, you scared me to death. How did you get past the lock on the gate?"

"Your front door was unlocked, which is not smart," he admonished with a look. "I rang the bell, and since the music was so loud, I figured you would not hear it."

"You're right. I didn't, baby. Why are you here? Why aren't you at work? Where is your uniform?" she asked him back-to-back questions. Usually, he'd be protecting the citizens of L.A. at that hour, so she was shocked he was there.

"I'll be off for the next few days. We are going to lay Paris to rest on Friday," he said.

She blinked in confusion at first, but comprehension dawned quickly. "Awww, baby, come here," Rose said, and he joined her on the chaise. She held him in her arms tightly, and she wasn't surprised when he began to sob in her arms. "I'm so sorry, Levi. I know that was a difficult decision."

"I wanted her to wake up, I did, but I knew she'd never come back," he cried.

Her heart ached for him. "I know, baby, I know." She held him tightly and cried for him. She didn't know Paris, but she knew him, and what he told her in their numerous conversations about Paris, she was a great person and a wonderful wife. "Levi, if you need anything, anything at all, just let me know."

He moved out of her embrace. "I'm good for now." He wiped his eyes. "It's hard, but I know she died a long time ago. I just didn't want to not see her, you know, not be able to touch her or stroke her hair. She died months ago, but I was so selfish, I couldn't let her body go."

A tear fell to Rose's cheek. "I can only imagine, Levi. I've never been married, never lost a spouse or anyone remotely close. I've had boyfriends and dated, but I must admit, you are the first man I've ever loved."

He looked at her and caressed her face. "I love you too, Rose, and as much as I still love Paris, I decided yesterday

I wanted to move on with my life. I want something real, something tangible. I want to be touched, have someone to talk to, someone to laugh with, and someone to touch me back. All those things were gone when Paris got shot. Before I met you, Rose, I honestly thought I could settle with her just being here, but the more we spent time together, the physical exchange and the conversations until four in the morning and just when you wrapped your body around me when we slept . . .

"I fell in love with who you are, not your sex or what you have, but just to simply be with you feels right, and I know Paris knows that. I think she had a hand in me getting that call that night I met you, so when I signed the papers yesterday to lay her body to rest, I felt good. I felt relieved. I felt like a man making a responsible decision. I know she died awhile ago, Rose, but until I met you, I just settled with her lying there in that bed. No movement, no exchange, no conversation, and she couldn't touch me back." His head fell low.

He quickly lifted his head and looked into her eyes. Rose could tell he was looking for a sincere confirmation from her, but she said nothing. "I felt confident that I did the right thing."

"Are you sure?" she asked.

"Let me show you just how sure I am," he said going down on one knee. "I had my life planned out with Paris, and then life told me otherwise, and then I met you. I don't want to start over or meet anyone else. I want to build with you. Rosemary Lynette Jennings, will you marry me?"

Without hesitation the words "Yes yes yes!" escaped her mouth. The words sprang out of her mouth before he could remove the ring from the box. He kissed her and slid the ring on her finger. The diamond was small, but

Rose didn't care. She knew he wasn't a high roller, but he had a heart of gold.

"Thank you, baby, thank you."

"Oh my God, I can't wait to tell Tiffany," she beamed.

"Hold on, baby, hold on. I have to ask you a huge favor, and if the answer is no, I won't be mad at you," he said interrupting her celebration.

Oh Lord, Rose thought. *How he gon' propose, and then ask for a loan or something that may make me want to give the ring back?* "What is it, Levi?"

"I can't take you around my family and friends for a while. They all adored Paris, and if I show up with a new fiancée—" she stopped him.

"Enough said, Levi. I know what you're asking, and I believe it's for the best as well."

"Thanks for understanding, Rose. You know how family can be."

"Yes, I do," she said.

He sighed and dropped his head. "I can't stay long, baby. I have to go and be with my family. Can I come back tonight?"

"Yes, of course." She didn't want him to go, but she knew he had a lot to deal with.

"Thanks, baby. I'm so grateful to have met you."

"Me too, baby, now go and do what you have to do, and I'll wait up for you." The corner of her lips turned up slightly. She didn't want to seem too happy and come off insensitive, but she was excited that she was going to have a chance to be with someone. Someone she had fallen in love with. Someone she was extremely attracted to. Someone she hadn't "settled" for.

He kissed her. "Okay, I love you."

"I love you too."

He disappeared into the house, and a few short moments later, she got up to go and lock the door. Levi was right; it wasn't safe, no matter how great the neighborhood was. She locked the door, went for her phone, and called Tiffany to share the news.

I'm So Sorry

Episode 21

Tressa

That afternoon, Tressa sat out on her balcony looking out on the ocean. Her father and mother had called her ten-plus times, and she didn't answer. Her dad texted asking if she was okay, and she didn't answer that either. Her mind was blank. She couldn't gather one thought. All she knew is that she wanted to disappear. A tear fell, and then another, and then another, and the breeze chilled her face because she didn't wipe her tears away.

"I'm such a failure and an embarrassment. I just want this life to be over with God. I just want a new life, a new me, someone my father could be proud of. I can't see him like this. I'm a junkie, and it's impossible for me to stay clean."

After she gave the night before some thought, a few things came back to her, and she remembered telling herself *just one drink* and *just one line*. She actually believed that she would be able to have one hit of liquor and coke, but that wasn't the case. She fell right back into what she was accustomed to doing, the only thing she knew how to do best, and that was party, get wasted, and have a good time.

After she loosened up and let the pressure of her peers convince her how she was in control of the drugs and alcohol and not the other way around, she convinced herself that that bullshit was true and let her guard down. She tossed her suit jacket, undid a few buttons on her blouse, and let loose. She toasted, threw back shots, and inhaled a few lines. After that, she remembers kissing the stranger and letting him take her to one of Stephen's spare rooms. She hadn't had sex in over a year, so he didn't have to say much to get her out of her clothes. She shook her head when she thought about him penetrating her anally. She remembered the pain, the burn, but she was so high she took it.

Once the shock wore off, when she got home, the discomfort reminded her just how careless she had been.

"You are a stupid, spoiled, little rich bitch," the words seemed to be in Dolby surround sound in her ear as she thought about the words he said to her when he poked and pried her body from behind. Thinking hard, she remembered it was a nameless man that she had turned down several times before that was ugly as hell to her. He treated her that way and talked to her that way because he had finally caught her at her weakest moment, and she gave that bastard her body, she gathered, thinking about his cocky attitude when they went into that room.

Embarrassment, guilt, remorse, shame, and humiliation were the first words to overpower her emotions when she thought about what she had done. "You don't deserve another chance," she cried. She pulled her knees up against her chest, wrapped her arms around her legs, and sobbed so hard she thought she would hyperventilate.

She looked out at the water, and her eyes were so full of tears that she couldn't see it clearly. Her sobs grew louder, and then she heard her phone. It was her father again. "I'm sorry, Daddy. I'm so sorry, Daddy," she cried, looking at her phone, hoping it would stop ringing. "Please, Daddy, I've fucked up again, and I'm sorry. I can't face you and Mommy. I can't. I'm a failure. I'm a walking disaster," she yelled. "I'm a fuckup!" she continued. Two seconds later, her phone went off again and again. It was her father.

She reached for the phone, and her hand trembled uncontrollably. What would she say, what would she tell him? How could she tell him what she had done?

"I'm sorry," she whispered again. She got up and went inside, leaving her cell phone on the glass patio table. She shut the French doors and walked in a daze to her bedroom. She stood there and looked at herself in the mirror, and she didn't recognize who she was. She walked closer and touched it, but her reflection showed a pale-faced drug addict with no future, no hope, and no reason to live.

"Yes yes yes! Tressa Isabella Green, it's the right thing to do. They won't miss you. They will be relieved not to have to rescue you again. They will not have to be embarrassed anymore or ashamed. Yes, Tressa, it's time. It's the right thing to do." She swiped the tears from her cheeks and went into her walk-in closet. She looked at all the privileges she had her entire life. Her closet was the size of a small room, and she looked at the racks and racks of clothes, shelves and shelves of shoes, and the chest of drawers that lined the walls with drawers upon drawers of jewelry, things she may not have even worn in over five years, but expensive, designer-, and most custom-made.

Shelf upon shelf of hats and designer bags and other accessories—and that was the closet at her home, not nearly as massive as the one at her parents' place. "I don't deserve any of this. Daddy, you were right to give Tiffany my inheritance. I am a spoiled rich bitch, and I'm sorry for all the hell that you and Mommy have suffered because of me." She went over to a shoe box and pulled it down from the shelf. Then she opened it and sat on the floor. There it was, uncut and pure, and she knew it wasn't going to take much to be lethal.

She prepared it, fed it into the syringe, and then tied off her arm. She wanted to think twice about it, but she injected herself so fast to keep from changing her mind and released its contents into her vein. It burned like hell, but the heat of it was nothing compared to the sudden pounding of her heart. It thumped so hard against her chest, and her body started to jerk uncontrollably. She couldn't scream because within seconds, her throat filled with a thick saliva, and she felt herself choking.

What she imagined would be quick and painless . . . wasn't . . . far from it. Even though she was gone in less than five minutes, she felt every second of it. She couldn't control her jerking body or unclog her throat. She lay still for a while and just gurgled. The tears ran into her ears and hair as she lay there wishing the suffering would end. Her last thought before she took her last breath and her heart stopped was of her daddy. Her lips almost formed a smile, because Tressa finally felt free. She no longer had to impress, suppress, or strive for excellence. She had won the fight, and she thought she'd be free on the other side. As she inserted the needle into her arm, she prayed and hoped her parents understood, that she didn't want to cause them any more pain. She didn't want to suffer or cause them to suffer another moment.

Why Me?

Episode 22

Tiffany

Tiffany walked into the kitchen to retrieve her phone from the center island. She looked at the ID and wondered why Mr. Green was calling her. That Monday was a holiday, so she hoped he was well. He almost never interrupted her weekends and holidays, so she quickly answered. "Hello, Mr. Green, how are you?"

"Hello, Tiffany, I'm doing well, how about you?"

"I'm great. What's going on?"

"Nothing too much. I was calling to see if you have heard from or seen Isabella. Yesterday, my wife and I decided to take a little trip down the coast for a little getaway, and we were supposed to come back today, but since it's a holiday weekend, we've decided to stay longer, I've been trying to let Isabella know of our plans. The last time I spoke with her, she said she was working this weekend on a project you had given her."

"No, Mr. Green, Tressa and I hardly ever talk outside of work unless she has a work-related question, and I haven't spoken to her since I left TiMax on Friday."

"Well, normally, she'd go home, you know, to our estate, but my staff said she didn't come home last night. I've called her several times, and since the incident last year, we check in on her often, so it's not like her to not answer her phone. We now talk at least five times a day, and my wife and I have been calling and texting her all day."

"I don't know, Mr. Green. I have no idea. Have you spoken to Amber?"

"Yes, I tried her first, but she and her husband are in Vegas for a medical convention, and she hasn't talked to her either, and I don't want to be a worry wart, but I'm concerned about my baby. You know her past is not far behind us."

"I understand, Mr. Green, what do you need me to do? I mean, I don't even know where to begin to look for her," Tiffany said. Kory walked into the kitchen and gave her a questioning look, and she hunched her shoulders.

"Back in the day when Isa would party, she'd go to her condo on the beach. Can you start there for me? I mean, other than that, she'd be at the spa."

"Okay, but you know Tressa. She may not let me in," Tiffany said being honest. They had overcome, but Tiffany didn't know how welcoming Tressa would be.

"As long as she opens the door, let her know that her mother and I are worried sick, out of our minds. She may be trying to hide some new clothes or shoes because she may have gone over her monthly spending limit, I don't know, but I need you to get into her place to make sure, because I just have a funny feeling that something is wrong. We made a vow to each other to not go a day without speaking, and for her to not answer worries me. There is a gray potted plant that has a fake rock sitting on top of the soil. Under that rock is a key, so if she doesn't answer, please use that key and the gate code is 1172. The alarm system in her place is 4943.

"There have been times I've found her passed out after binges, and I need to make sure she's okay. I know we've had a good year, but my wife I have been watching her like a child since rehab, and last night was the first night we left her on her own since rehab. I was confident she'd be okay. She assured me she would, but I am on pins and needles."

"I understand, Mr. Green. Kory and I will head over now."

"Thank you, Tiffany. The only reason I'm calling you is because if there is an unsightly situation, I can trust you will keep our family business private and not rush off to the media or tabloids."

"Of course, Mr. Green. You can trust me. You know I'd never do that to you and your family. Kory and I will go and find her for you."

"Thank you, Tiffany, and please call me as soon as you locate her."

"I will, sir," she assured him and ended the call.

"What was that about?" Kory asked before she could put her phone back onto the island.

"Mr. Green and his wife are out of town, and they can't reach Tressa. He's concerned that maybe she had something to drink or used again, so he wants me to go over to her place."

"And you want me to go with you?"

"You are my husband. Of course, I do," she said and put her hands on her hips.

He walked over to her, pulled her close, and ran his hands down her back and cupped her bottom. She loved to be in Kory's arms, so she reached up and wrapped her arms around his neck.

"Baby, I mean . . . I know we are all trying to act as if the past is the past, but I'm not sure how cool Tressa truly is with us now. You say she acts the part at work, but this is Tressa we're talking about. No matter how much everyone thinks she's changed, I still have my reservations."

"Kory, get over yourself. Tressa didn't even want you back then," she laughed. "She was with you for her money, man," she continued to tease him.

"What?" his voiced raised. "She *wanted* me. I know that she did," he defended playfully.

"She didn't, and you are going with me, Mr. Banks."

He didn't argue. Tiffany threw on a sundress, some flip-flops, and they headed to Tressa's. Kory didn't need directions. He remembered where she lived because he'd gone there a few times when they were a couple. They parked, but Kory didn't move to get out of the car.

She looked at him with a side eye. "Let's go," she said.

"Nah, I'm going to stay in the car."

"Wrong answer, now come on, Kory!" Tiffany ordered. He undid his seat belt and got out. She followed him to Tressa's unit, and Tiffany knocked. A few moments later, after knocking like crazy, a neighbor opened their door.

"You might want to go inside if you can. She's in pretty bad shape this time," she said.

Kory and Tiffany looked at the elderly lady. "Bad shape? What do you mean?" Tiffany inquired.

"She got in this morning, and I could hear her crying out here while she tried to open the door. She was mumbling obscene words and talking as if she was scolding herself. About thirty minutes later, from my balcony, I heard her out on her balcony, sobbing. She was talking to herself, saying how she was evil, and her father would never forgive her again. The poor girl was saying so many bad things to herself and kept going on and on how sorry she was and saying. 'I'm sorry, Daddy, I'm sorry, Daddy,' and her phone kept ringing. Now I'm old, but I've heard her in some odd situations, but today was different. Never heard her cry so much or say 'I'm sorry' so many times.

"I knocked several times, but she never answered. She's not crying anymore, but I can hear her phone on the balcony. It's been ringing off the hook since this morning."

"Thank you, ma'am." Tiffany looked at Kory.

"You're welcome. I hope she's okay. I heard she got all cleaned up and got herself together. I liked seeing her smile and being nice, not how she used to be," the lady said, and then stepped back and disappeared into her condo. Tiffany went for the key that Mr. Green told her about. She opened the door, then she and Kory slowly walked in. "Tressa?" Tiffany called out, but only silence answered her. Kory went over to the French doors.

"There's her phone on the patio table," he said and opened the doors to get it.

"Tressa, it's me, Tiffany. Mr. Green wanted me to check on you." Tiffany spoke loudly so Tressa could hear her if she was in the other room. She eased closer to Tressa's bedroom. The door was wide open, but she didn't see Tressa.

"Maybe she left?" Kory said.

Tiffany turned back and examined the room. "Without her phone? And her purse is over there, so I doubt it." Tiffany turned back toward her room. "Tressa, it's me, Tiffany. Are you decent? I'm coming in," Tiffany yelled out as she entered the room. The bed was made, and her room was spotless. Tiffany went over to what she thought was the bathroom door and tapped. "Tressa, are you in here? Your parents are concerned," Tiffany yelled, but heard nothing. She opened the door, hoping Tressa wasn't in the tub sleeping. The bathroom too was spotless, but she saw a towel on the vanity. She touched it. It was still a little damp, so Tressa had been there.

She went to leave and saw the closet door was half-opened. Tiffany laughed. "Now, Tressa, if you are on this closet floor sleeping, I'm telling everybody at TiMax," she joked and opened the door. She saw Tressa's pedicured toes and feet. Apparently she was on the floor asleep on the other side of the dresser that sat in the center of her enormous closet. Tiffany laughed again, thinking Tressa was crazy to be on that floor sleeping and figured she may have had a few drinks. She proceeded to walk closer—and then let out a blood-curdling scream when she saw her.

Kory came running. Tiffany had fallen backward against the hanging clothes, and she luckily grabbed hold of some hanging items to keep from hitting the floor.

"What is it, baby, what's wrong?" Kory asked.

Tiffany started to shake and cry at the sight of Tressa's body. Kory looked confused, but he hurried over . . . and then he saw Tressa. There was blood oozing from her mouth and nose, and the barely dried foam around her mouth let him know that she had foamed at the mouth. "Baby, go dial 911," Kory yelled and went to try to aid Tressa. Her eyes were wide opened and when Kory checked, she had no pulse. Her body had already begun to feel cold. Kory knew she was gone. Tiffany slid down to the carpeted floor and sobbed. Kory closed Tressa's eyes and went to assist his wife.

He lifted her from the floor and helped her to the bed in Tressa's room. She cried so hard. He stayed close to her to comfort her while he called 911. He told the operator what happened, and he did his best to calm his wife down. "Shhh, baby, shhh. Calm down, baby, relax."

"Oh my God, Kory, why me? Why did I have to find her like that?"

"I'm sorry, honey, just relax. We have to call Langley."

"I can't, baby. I can't tell him this," Tiffany was hysterical.

"I know, baby. Come in the living room and I'll call him." He helped her to her feet, and Tiffany went out on the balcony instead. She sat shaking and could not believe what she just saw. That image of Tressa like that made her sob more and even harder.

She muffled her cries into her hands and heard Kory talking to Mr. Green. A couple moments later, the paramedics arrived and pronounced Tressa dead on site. Tiffany was horrified, and she cried all the way home. Kory agreed to allow some officers to come by their house for their statements, because Tiffany was too distraught to go to the station. After an hour retelling the events, the officers left, and Kory gave Tiffany two aspirins and stayed with her until she finally drifted off to sleep. Later, they headed over to Langley's house to be with him and his wife.

As Normal as Possible

Episode 23

Tiffany

It had been four weeks since Tressa's death and funeral, and the office was still in mourning. Tiffany had returned to work only a few days ago, because the image of finding Tressa's dead body took a heavy toll on her. She had a hard time sleeping at night, and she constantly had nightmares and frequent daydreams about it. Finally, she was starting to not see that image every fifteen minutes of her day, and it was slowly fading, so she was anxious and excited to return to work.

Mr. Green had been strong, but Tiffany had sat with him and Mrs. Green many evenings talking to them, holding their hands, and just being with them. Mr. Green still could not cope with the fact his one and only child was gone, and Mrs. Green barely talked, but she was there for them anyway, even if she just sat and held their hands.

Tiffany grieved for Tressa, herself, and for the Greens; she had to get back to work to get her mind back to normal. She walked into the building, and it seemed foreign to her, like she had been away much longer than four weeks. Her new assistant spoke softly that morning when Tiffany approached. "Good morning, Mrs. Banks, and welcome back. I have a ton of messages for you and whenever you are ready just buzz me so I can bring you up to speed on your shows and appointments. Your coproducers did well, and there were no mishaps or crisis while you were out, but we are all very happy to have you back."

"Thank you, Summer. I will only need a few minutes, and then I'll be ready."

"Yes, ma'am." She smiled brightly and gave Tiffany a slight nod. Tiffany went into her office and dropped her purse and briefcase in one of the vacant chairs in front of her desk. She and Tressa had some really bad blood once, but she missed her for some reason. She had secretly been so proud of her for her will to change, and she was looking forward to building a relationship and partnership with Tressa.

Working side by side had shown Tiffany that Tressa was no idiot; she was bright, talented, and a fast learner. She honestly saw the change in Tressa and had high hopes for her. Still baffled of what triggered the overdose, Tiffany decided to pack her stresses away and get back up to speed with work. She settled in, pulled her muffin from her bag, and sat at her desk. She powered on her computer, and then she shook. She swallowed hard and wondered why she had a huge lump in her throat. She tried to ignore the nauseated feeling that came on, but her jaws swelled, and her tongue told her to head to the bathroom before she blew chunks all over her desk.

She raced to her private bathroom, where she graced the toilet with last night's dinner. She stayed in place and waited until she felt it was safe enough to stand, and then she went to the sink. She turned on the water, rinsed her mouth, and looked in the mirror. She was a honey-toned woman, but it looked like her skin was three shades lighter.

"Come on, Tiff. It's okay. You can do this. It's a kick in the ass, but you can't get sick over it. The worst is behind you," she said and went down for another rinse. She dried her mouth and wet a towel and patted her head. "You are stronger than this," she encouraged herself, and slowly her color returned. She collected herself a few moments longer before she returned to her desk. She wondered why she got nauseated. She had had a lot of emotions, cries, and feelings since the discovery of Tressa's dead body, but never nauseated.

She grabbed her phone and went to her calendar. Going through this traumatic ordeal, she didn't think of her cycle, and it hit her that she hadn't had one for a while. After verifying her last one, she saw she was more than two weeks late. "Could it be?" she wondered. She counted, recounted, and two weeks was two weeks, and even though she had been under a lot of stress, she wanted to know if she and Kory had finally gotten pregnant.

She called Rose.

"Hello," Rose sang.

"Good morning, Ms. Rose. Why are you singing hellos?"

"Because my life is perfect. The grand opening was a huge success, sold over nineteen pieces, meaning your friend has a pretty positive balance in the bank, so I can start repaying you for everything, and last night, me and my fiancé finally consummated our relationship. Yes, I got the dick, and the dick was good," she said like a sports announcer announcing a field goal.

"Wow, well, I'm happy for you, Rose. I honestly didn't think Levi was truly the one, but, hey, I've been wrong before."

"Don't start that shit again, Tiff. You know he laid his wife to rest weeks ago and for us to finally make love is huge, you hear me? We just have to give it more time before we announce our engagement. We don't want his family to freak out. They may not take too kindly to him falling in love so soon, so just be happy for me. Levi is the kindest, most loving man I've ever been with in my life. Stop being so suspicious, Tiff, and be happy for me."

"Okay, okay, Rose, damn. I'll be happy for you two. From what I've seen, he is a good guy. Kory said he seems to be on the up and up, and Kory thinks he really loves you, so I'm not tripping. I'm happy for you."

Rose was quiet and blew out a breath.

"I'm so for real, Rose, I am, and I wish you two the best. But I called you because you have to do me a huge favor."

"First, thanks for your well wishes. Levi makes me happy, and once we are married like you and Kory, things will seem normal."

"I'm sure, Rose, but I need you."

"Anything, Tiff, what is it?"

"Don't get crazy, Rose."

"I won't, Tiff, what is it?"

"I'm late."

Rose squealed. "You are? How late?"

"A little over two weeks."

"What? Are you serious, Tiff? Did you take the test?"

"No, and that's why I'm calling. Can you leave the gallery and bring me a test?"

"Ummmm, yes! I'm on my way, girl. Oh my God, Tiff, what if you are?"

"I know, right? I'm like all over the place now, so please, Rose, get the test and hurry over here."

"I'm on it, darling. I'll be there soon."

"Okay, girl, thanks."

"Don't mention it." They hung up, and Tiffany called her assistant in to get caught up. When she got the message that Myah had been trying to get an appointment with her, she made sure that her assistant put Myah down for that afternoon. That would give her time to spend time with Rose and take the test. If it was positive, she and Rose could go out for an early lunch and celebrate, and if it was negative, she and Rose could still go out . . . so Rose could comfort her and dry her tears.

It seemed like hours, but forty-five minutes later, Rose was there. She brought three tests. Clearblue Easy, e.p.t., and First Response. Tiffany went into her bathroom, peed into a disposable cup, and dipped all three sticks into her urine. She and Rose made small talk and went back after four minutes to check the test—and they all read positive! Tiffany was pregnant. She and Rose jumped for joy. Tiffany wanted to be a mom so badly, and she was finally pregnant.

"Oh my Lord, Rose, can you believe?"

"No, and I'm *so* jealous," she teased.

"Don't be. Soon, you and Levi will be married, and you will be a mom too."

"Yes, ma'am. I'm so happy for you, Tiffany. How are you going to tell Kory?"

Tiffany paused. "Girl, I don't know. I want to do something crazy, out of the box, something that will wow him."

"Well, I'm no expert, but I saw this clip on Facebook where the man came home, and his wife told him to check the oven for dinner, and she had a bun in it."

"That's cute, but I want to blow Kory's mind. I want to top his surprises. Like when he was supposed to be on his honeymoon with Tressa, but instead, he proposed to me on the plane before the flight took off, so I need something clever."

"Okay, I see what you mean. Kory smokes cigars, right?"

Tiffany's smile got even brighter. "He does."

"So, get him two cigars, put them in a case, and put a blue strip on one and a pink strip on the other. Put a card or a note in the box that says . . . *It's a boy, or maybe it's a girl.*"

"That is a better idea. Let's head over to Jinx. It's not far from here. Oh my God, Rose, I am pregnant. Let's go and toast it up."

"Chile, please, I'll have champagne for you while you drink iced tea."

"Hey, I'm only a *little* pregnant, early pregnant, and trust if I didn't find out today, I would have inhaled a bottle of wine tonight after my day, so let me have my last toast, please, before this little one starts to develop organs and the important stuff."

"You are a true bad girl," Rose laughed. They headed out, but Tiffany assured Summer she'd be back for her meeting with Myah. They went to Jinx, a local pub, not far from the studio and Tiffany frowned when she spotted Tracy.

"What's wrong?" Rose asked. Tiffany figured she'd seen the expression on her face change.

"Tracy is what's wrong. I mean, seriously, it can't be a fucking coincidence that she and I keep running into each other. I'm not a scholar, but I *know* this is impossible."

"It could be your imagination, Tiff."

"It could be, but during my time off, I'd go by the office periodically and just say I'd mention to Summer that Kory and I were going to Melrose for dinner, and somehow, I'd run into her at dinner. I don't know, but it's like unreal."

"It's not that serious, honey. Now swallow the last of your last drink of this pregnancy so you can get to your meeting with Myah, and I can get back to my gallery. Josh is a great salesman, and he is hot, but nobody can sell my pieces as well as I can."

"Yes, you're right, and I'm not trying to block your hustle, but please go by the cigar shop for me and put my order in. I need to get back to TiMax."

"Girl, please. I owe you my life, so, of course."

Tiffany paused. She was tired of hearing those words, and she could already tell her hormones were in overdrive. "Cut!" she said with a stern voice.

Rose froze in motion. "Stop it, Rose, okay? Enough!" Tiffany said with sternness in her tone. "For the one-hundredth time, you don't owe me shit. You don't owe me a dime. The house is yours, the gallery is yours, the car is yours, and your profits from this day forward are yours. Mr. Green blessed me with over $40 million, Rose. More money than I could ever dream of in my lifetime. I still have a six-figure salary, and it is on the high end . . . so high, it's close to a seven-figure salary. My husband is a businessman, and he is soon to open his third location. Not only me, but our grandchildren will be okay, Rose; your children, my godchildren, will be okay. The minimansion Kory and I live in is paid in full, and we don't have a note on any of the four vehicles we own. My mother is now settled into a gated community with an on-call chef, housekeeper, and all she does is play bridge and calls a service when she needs groceries or the latest magazine or what have you.

"I came from nothing, Rose, nothing. You know it. You were there. When my brother was killed, there was no insurance. Thank God our church and community loved my mother so much that they raised the money to help bury my brother and give him a proper service. As soon as I got that money, the first check I wrote was to my momma's church. I say that to say this.

"We are blessed. Not me, but *we* are blessed, and I'd feed you, take care of you until there was nothing left if I had to, so stop it, Rose. You don't owe me a damn thing. We are sisters, and I'd give my last cent for you, so stop saying that shit. It pisses me off when you say that. We are even, so stop it," Tiffany cried. She was in tears by the time she was done. She loved Rose, and other than

Kory, Rose was the closest person to her in her life. Yes, she and Asia had a bond, but it was nothing close to hers and Rose's.

Rose stood and went over to Tiffany. "You are *definitely* pregnant. I've seen you cry, but never in a public place." She hugged her tightly.

"I know, and I'm now embarrassed."

"Don't be. I'm the one who should be embarrassed." She took a couple of steps back. "You have to understand that I never in a million years thought my best friend would be this successful and to become this popular and wealthy. You didn't have to do a damn thing for me, Tiff, but in my mind, I'm always thinking that I hope you know I'm not looking for any handouts and just because I'm your best friend doesn't mean I'm special. And I am truly and sincerely grateful for what you have done for me. I just don't want you to think I don't appreciate you or that I feel entitled."

"That's where you're wrong, Rose. Just because you are my best friend, the person I love as much as my husband, you are special. So please, Rose, just say 'thanks, Tiff.' Thank you is enough."

She hugged her friend again. "Thanks, Tiff. Thank you," she said, and the two ladies paid their tab and departed. Rose promised Tiffany she'd go by the cigar shop for her, and Tiffany made her way back to the office. She was just in time for her meeting with Myah, and Tiffany was excited.

Myah presented her first show idea to Tiffany, and Tiffany was amazed. "Myah, that is a great idea. I am overly impressed. I see you've paid attention."

"Yes, ma'am, I have, and Dee is like one of the coolest, most brilliant persons to work with."

Tiffany detected a glow in Myah when she spoke of Darryl, and that was weird. "Mee-Mee, you do know Darryl is gay, right?"

Myah hung her head low. "I know, but I admire him. He is so brilliant, Tiffany."

"Yes, he is Mee-Mee, and I know you are a single mom and long for a partner. We've talked about this before. Don't shoot for stars you can't catch is our motto, remember. We stay in our lane. Dee is a homosexual and as gorgeous, funny, stylish, and talented as he is, he will never be into you."

She sighed. "I know, but I've had a crush on him forever, and if he was straight, I'd surely make him mine."

Tiffany tilted her head. She could see Myah's heart, and Tiffany knew all too well how it felt to yearn for someone to love and be loved by. At that moment, she had a thought. "Myah, I'm not big on matchmaking, but Kory has an employee who divorced about eight or nine months ago, and he's dating. Now, he is fine, no kids, and I think you two may hit it off."

"I don't know, Tiff. He has no kids, and I have three. Not many men want a ready-made family."

"Well, between you and me, his wife left because of his inability to get her pregnant, and from what Kory tells me, he wants a family."

She frowned. "I don't know."

"One dinner. If you think he's lame, and you're not interested, no harm, right?"

Myah smiled. "Okay, that sounds like a plan," she agreed.

"Great, I'll call Kory and, by the way, Mee-Mee, I'm pregnant," Tiffany smiled.

Perfect Combinations

Episode 24

Kory

After marinating the meats he planned to put on the grill, he chopped veggies for the kabobs, and then made the potato salad. The baked beans were in the oven, and the corn on the cob was seasoned to go on the grill. His mom taught him and his brothers how to cook and always said they needed to know how to cook so when their wives give birth, or if she, unfortunately, gets ill, they can feed her and their children. That lesson had always stuck with him, but he hated cooking for guests.

Tiffany had declared that night to be "couple's night," so Rose and Levi, Asia and Edward, and Myah, newly matched up with Cameron—which Kory was completely against—were coming over. He told his wife when she asked that he wasn't into matchmaking, but after some persuading, he was on board, and to seal the night, his wife presented him with a gift, a gift that informed him that he was going to be a dad, so whatever she said from that moment on was golden.

His wife and he had finally conceived, and nothing could take away from the joy he felt for her and their happiness. He had high hopes for Cam and Myah and for Levi and Rose. Asia was already married and a new mother, so if the other couples tied the knot, it would be all good.

"So, Levi, how do you like being a cop?" Edward asked. All eyes landed on Levi. Edward was a banker, Kory a jeweler, and Cameron a jeweler as well, jobs totally different from law enforcement, and that's why he asked, Kory thought.

"Being a police officer is cool. I grew up in a rough area and after seeing so much crime and murder, I wanted to make a difference. I'm hoping to be a detective one day."

"And you will be, baby," Rose added and rubbed his arm. He smiled at her.

"Awww, y'all are so cute," Tiffany said.

"Baby, don't start the mushy stuff," Kory said, and everyone laughed.

"They are, and Cam and Mee-Mee, you guys look good together. We should do this once a week, turn it into a game/couple's night," Tiffany suggested.

"Once a week?" Asia frowned. "I can't leave China with a babysitter to hang out once a week. Maybe once a month."

"Well, we're game, right, baby?" Rose said.

"Sure, babe, this is cool, and if the food is going to be this good, I'll say yes," Levi replied before shoving a spoonful of baked beans into his mouth.

"I can host next week," Rose said.

"I can host the following week," Myah added. Cam smiled.

"Yes, that sounds like a good idea," Cameron said and looked at Myah. "I'd be happy to help you cook."

"You cook?" she asked.

"Yes, I cook," he answered.

"What else can you do?" Myah inquired.

"Hey, hey, hey . . . There *are* others at this table," Edward joked.

"Awww, Edward, baby, they are just getting to know each other. Remember when we met, it was like an instant connection," Asia said. "I wanted you the moment you said hello."

"Yes, it was an instant attraction, and I'll never regret meeting you, baby." Edward leaned in to kiss her.

"It was almost the same for us too," Rose added.

"Yes, I was feeling you from the moment we met," Levi agreed.

"Ummm, would anyone like more wine, another drink?" Kory interrupted.

"I would," Levi spoke first.

"I know why you're interrupting the *how we met* stories, Kory," Tiffany said.

Kory got up to refill glasses on the table. "What, baby? What are you talking about?" he said nervously.

"You know," she said.

"Hell, tell us," Asia encouraged.

"Well, first, I'll say to Cameron and Myah, I hope this will be a start of something great for you two."

Myah looked at Cameron. "I'm sure it will be. I mean, look at him; he's gorgeous," she joked, and they all laughed.

"So are you," Cameron added.

"Well, my husband knows it wasn't love at first sight for him. It was love at first sight for me, but not for him. When we met, we were still in high school."

"Oh my God, Tiffany was mad crazy in love with Kory. She talked about Kory from sunup to sundown," Rose spoke openly, and Tiffany shot her a look. "Well, you *did*," she giggled.

Tiffany sipped her iced tea. "I did, but *this* guy," she put her arm around Kory's shoulder once he sat back down, "this guy was too cool for me back then. He didn't confess his love until over fifteen years after we met."

"Damn, y'all known each other that long?" Cameron asked.

"Yes, but we hadn't stayed in touch the entire time, and when I ran into him, do y'all know he didn't even tell me he was engaged to Tressa Green?"

"Well, I was going to tell you at dinner, but Tressa, Lord rest her soul," Kory added, "was like, oh my God, *Boy Crazy* is like my favorite show, take me," he said doing a perfect impression of Tressa.

"Yes, and when I saw him standing there next to this bombshell, I almost passed out. My mouth went dry, my hands shook, and I was praying Rose would call at that moment, so I could get the hell outta there."

Everyone laughed.

"I'm serious. Imagine sitting across the table the entire evening with the love of your life and his beautiful, rich fiancée."

"Yes, Kory, you know you was wrong for that," Asia said and took a sip of her wine.

"Yes, Kory, you could have at least sent Tiffany a text," Myah said.

"Yeah, Kory," Rose chimed in.

"Hey, hey, hey, ladies don't gang up on me. In all truth, I had planned on telling Tiffany that night. I didn't want to just show up with Reesy, but she put me on the spot."

The men shook their heads. "Well, I'm glad that's not the story we have to share with our daughter," Edward said.

"Ha," Asia interrupted. "But we have to tell her that she was conceived before we exchanged vows, and she was born two nights after our damn wedding," she spat.

Everyone continued to laugh. "Well, Edward, my man, I got a better one for you. My wife was on life support when I met Rose, and meeting Rose helped me to make a hard decision."

The table stilled. No one said anything. It was an odd silence. "Hey, it's okay. It was hard letting her go, but it was for the best. I miss her. Rose lets me talk about her whenever I need to, and I'm glad Rose came along. If it hadn't been for her, I wouldn't have been able to move on with my life or let my brain-dead wife rest."

Rose grabbed his hand.

"I'm so sorry for your loss, Levi. I never had a chance to actually have a conversation with you, but I'm happy you came into my best friend's life too. You two met when you both needed each other the most."

"Yes, I'm sorry too. We've gotten to know each other a little better now, and I know that that was a hard decision," Kory added.

"It was, and I have my days, but Rose is my happy place." He smiled at her, and she pulled his hand to her face and kissed the back of it.

"Well, Myah, this has certainly been an evening. I don't know what stories we will someday tell our kids about the day we met, but so far, it's going to be a good one."

She returned a soft smirk and held up her wineglass. "I agree." He tapped his glass to hers, and Kory looked at a glowing Tiffany. She had that look of pride, and he knew she was glad she suggested that they introduce Cam and Mee-Mee to each other.

Kory put his arm around her shoulder and pulled her close. They all continued to exchange little personal stories, and Asia had everyone's sides hurting from laughing when she told them about her labor experience.

As the evening came to an end, Tiffany and Kory walked their guests out to their vehicles when they departed. The last couple to leave was Levi and Rose. Rose stuck around to help Tiffany clean up while the guys sat outside enjoying brandy and cigars.

No Weapons

Episode 25

Rose

"I can get that, Rose," Tiffany said.

"No, you can sit your pre
 gnant behind down on that stool and let me take care of this."

"Rose, I'm fine. I don't even feel pregnant."

"Well, you are," Rose said and began loading the dishwasher. Tiffany sat down.

"The doctor said everything looks good. I'm only seven weeks along, so I feel fine."

"And the vomiting?"

"Girl, it's horrible. It happens morning, noon, and night. That is the only sign that I have, other than my nipples being tender."

"Well, the sickness should pass by your second trimester."

"Yes, that's what my doctor told me, and how do you know?"

"My sister. Roslyn has four, remember."

"Speaking of Roslyn, have you two spoken?"

"No . . ." Rose sighed. "I've caller her, texted her. I've reached out to her countless times, but she won't talk to me."

"And James is still there?"

"Yep, as far as I know."

"So she can write you off, but stay with James? I've never understood that about women or men, for that matter. If she thought you two had something going on, how could she stay with him and be done with you?"

"Your guess is as good as mine. I can't let it get to me, though, Tiff. Levi said as long as I've done all I can do to reconcile with her, I should just let it go."

"Well, Levi is right. You know I didn't care for him at first, Rose, thought you too were moving too fast or thought he had a plan or some scheme to hurt you or get over on you, but he seems really nice and in love with you. You can't put a time stamp on love."

"That's the truth," Rose said and added detergent to the dishwasher. She got the surface spray from under the sink and wiped down the island and counters while she and Tiffany continued to chat. Once the kitchen was done, Rose poured her final glass of Pinot, and she and Tiffany moved in the family room off the kitchen and took a seat on the sofa and love seat.

The men entered. "Hey, babe," Levi said. "Are you ready to head out?"

"In a minute, after I finish this glass."

"Okay." He took a seat beside her, and Kory went over to join Tiffany on the other sofa.

"So, babe, Levi and I were talking about going to the gun range."

"Gun range?" she quizzed. "We don't even own a gun."

"Well, I will soon. Tomorrow, Levi is going with me so I can get a license and buy one."

Rose looked at Tiffany and hunched her shoulders. She already knew Tiffany was going to oppose that. Her brother was murdered due to gun violence.

"Kory, we live in one the safest neighborhoods in Cali. We do not need a gun."

"Tiffany, it doesn't matter where we live. There's nothing wrong with having a gun."

"A gun for what is my question?"

"Protection."

"From whom?"

"Tiffany, we are getting a gun, because I want one. End of discussion."

"Oh no, Mr. Banks, you don't give me *because I said so* on this matter," she said raising her voice.

"Baby, maybe we should go."

"No!" Tiffany snapped at Levi.

"Baby," Kory said.

"Don't *baby* me. You know how I feel about guns, and plus, we're having a baby now."

"Even more of a reason to get one. I want to protect my family."

Tiffany crossed her arms across her breasts. "We are *not* getting a gun."

"Baby, please finish your wine. We need to go," Levi suggested.

"No, stay, Mr. Levi. How did the conversation about guns come up anyway?"

"Guy talk and I'm sorry, Tiffany. I never suggested for Kory to get a gun. I just asked if he shoots, and that's it. I didn't mean to start no strife."

"No, Levi, it's not you, and I apologize for snapping at you. Kory knows how I feel about guns, and if he thinks he's going to have a gun in this house, he has another think coming." She stood over Kory and put her hands on her hips.

Rose polished off her wine and stood. "Yes, baby, let's go. This is a conversation that Tiff and Kory need to have alone."

Tiffany's head jerked in Rose's direction. "No, Rose, please don't go. I'm done with this stupid conversation." Tiffany flopped down on the sofa.

Levi and Rose looked at Kory.

"Please, guys, stay. Tiff and I will discuss this later."

"You'll be discussing this with yourself," Tiff returned.

"No, we are going to head home," Rose said. She went to the kitchen, washed her glass, and slid it into one of the wineglass slots mounted under Tiffany's cabinet. Then she returned to Levi's side. The room was quiet, and she could tell Levi was uncomfortable. "Come on, babe, are you ready?"

"Yes." He turned to Kory and Tiffany. "Thanks for having us, guys. Dinner was heavenly, and we really enjoyed ourselves, and we are looking forward to having you over next week," he spoke for him and Rose.

"Yes, Tiff, thanks."

She stood. "I'll walk y'all out."

Kory stood. "No, *we* will walk you guys out."

Tiffany shot him a look, and Rose hoped that Tiffany would give in. She never had a problem with guns and enjoyed going to the range with Levi. She now owned a gun, and she felt safer knowing she had it. Since Tiffany despised guns, Rose hadn't shared that information.

They got outside, and when she hugged Tiffany tight and long, she said softly into Tiffany's ear, "Don't be so hard on him. Kory is responsible, and he'd never do anything to put you and your child in danger."

"We're not—" Tiff tried to say.

"Tiffany, it's about *us,* not *I,* so *trust* him."

Tiffany frowned but nodded at Rose. "Let us know when you guys make it."

"I will." They got into Rose's BMW, and Levi pulled out of the Banks's circular drive.

"Baby, I'm so sorry," Levi said as soon as they got onto the main road.

"What for?"

"Causing problems with your friends."

"Baby, don't worry about that. I'm sure Kory will win her over."

"I hope so. I mean, if you never have to use your weapon, great, but it's better to have it and not need it, than to need it and not have it."

"I know, baby. It's just Tiffany's brother was killed when we were teens. He was shot nine times, and Tiffany has had this thing about guns ever since. Kory is smart, responsible, and he would never put his family in danger, so I know once he talks to Tiffany, she'll give in."

"Well, I didn't want to start any confusion."

"Babe, it's not your fault, so don't worry."

He smiled and reached for her hand. Rose felt a warm sensation all over her body. She was still processing the fact she had met someone so handsome and fit that was truly into her. She still couldn't believe her luck.

"You are incredibly beautiful, you know that?" he said, and then kissed the back of her hand.

"Really? You think so?"

"Yes, I think so."

"Why?" she asked. She shocked herself with that question. She wanted to know how someone as gorgeous as he was so into her.

"What do you mean why, sweetheart?"

"Exactly what I said . . . why? I weigh over 200 pounds, with rolls and dimples, and since I've been in L.A., I've seen some of the most gorgeous women on this planet . . . so why me? How can you choose me out of so many beautiful women?"

He chuckled.

"Levi, I'm serious."

"I know you are; that's why it's so hilarious."

"There is no humor in my question."

He stopped at a red light and looked over at her. "How often do you look in the mirror?"

"What?"

"How often do you look in the mirror?" he repeated, and then proceeded because the light turned green.

"A couple of times a day, why?"

"What do you see when you look in the mirror?"

"Levi, this line of questioning is confusing," she said with a scowl on her face. He wasn't making any sense to her.

"Rose, you are a highly intelligent woman. I doubt my line of questioning is confusing you. Now, I'll ask you again, but I will give you multiple choices. What do you see when you look in the mirror? Beauty, ugliness, pretty, or hideous?"

She was quiet at first. She didn't want to sound conceited, but she did see beauty.

"Answer my question, honey," he urged.

"Pretty." She didn't want to be vain about it.

"Pretty? Really? Why didn't you say *beauty?* You don't think of yourself as beautiful?"

"Look, Levi, I've had a few self-esteem issues in the past."

"I'm sure you may have, but *now,* how do you feel *now?* Be honest."

She hesitated again, but finally answered honestly. "Beautiful."

"So, if you can see beauty in yourself, why can't I?"

"Because guys like you never liked girls like me," she said sadly.

"Well, all guys are not the same, and people are attracted to different things, Rose. You are kind, gentle, smart, talented, creative, and what I see in you goes beyond your outer appearance. I love women, Rose, and I don't have a preference in size, skin tone, or figure. I am attracted to smart and talented women, and what kicked it up a notch for me is your work. You are passionate about something, and you followed your dreams. I was so proud of you on your opening night, and it gave me pleasure to watch you shine. If you lost weight tomorrow, you would still be Rose; if you gain weight, you will still be Rose. I'm too old and too much of a grown-ass man to get caught up on physical things.

"Looks, sizes, shapes, and all that jazz can change, but your heart is who you are."

Rose was speechless. "Wow, I've never had a man talk to me this way or to make me feel this way."

"Well, I'm not like all men, I'm just me. If you are insecure about the way you look, Rose, do something to make yourself more confident about yourself, but don't do anything based on how *I* feel, but do it because of *you*."

She smiled. "If I want to drop a few pounds, will you help me?"

"Of course."

"Well, I want to. I want to feel as confident about myself as I do about my art and my business."

"And you got my support 110 percent, and tomorrow, I think it's time to introduce you to my family."

"Are you sure? You don't think it's too soon?"

"I can't worry about that anymore, baby. Paris is gone, and I can't bring her back. I still love her in so many ways, and that may never change, but I am in love with you, Rose, and I want my family to get to know you too. I want my family to know how special you are to me."

He pulled into the driveway and hit the button to open the garage. He pulled in, and Rose sat with a wide grin on her face. Finally, things were working out, and she looked up and gave God a silent thank-you before she got out of the car.

What the Hell

Episode 26

Tiffany

Tiffany sat at the sixteen-foot oval table and waited for their meeting to start. She was so excited because she was going to share Myah's idea for her show. She knew it would be a hit, but the final yes would have to come from Mike. Since Tressa's death four months ago, Mr. Green had not returned to work, and no one, not even Mike, knew she'd be the one appointed to take Mr. Green's seat after all was said and done. She spent a lot of time with Mr. Green and a staff that he had put together to teach her what she needed to know to run the company as successfully as he and Mike had. All was a secret, and Tiffany couldn't wait until it was all a done deal.

Although Mike had told Mr. Green he was selling his shares of the business, no legal documents had been drawn up or signed yet, and the transaction hadn't occurred. It was more like a waiting game, and she and Mr. Green didn't push it because he knew that Tiffany wasn't ready to take over just yet. She still had more to learn. Although she was eager to make the announcement, she had to be patient, and she was as patient as she could be, and even more anxious to let Tracy's creepy ass go. She hadn't told anyone other than Rose and her husband, and she knew she could trust them not to share that information.

While she waited, she scribbled baby names on her pad. She and Kory had learned it was a girl, and they were at the name-choosing stage. Tiffany was now showing and finally able to wear the cute maternity ensembles she had purchased. Feeling confident and easy that morning, her mood shifted when Tracy walked in. She put on a fake smile and nodded as her annoying bitch ass took a seat directly across from Tiffany.

Great, Tiffany thought and sent up a silent prayer asking God to not let the meeting run too long. Tracy was going to be the first person she released when she took over, and she couldn't wait to give her, her walking papers. She had one show that was doing well, but her ideas were always corny; yet, for some reason, Mike would say they were great ideas. Two of those trite show ideas were scheduled to go into production soon, and if Tiffany had a say, she'd stop the madness before it got underway.

Tiffany went back to her baby-name list, but she could feel Tracy's eyes on her. They had this meeting every quarter, and every quarter was too often for Tiffany to be in the same room with Tracy, and she wished Mike would be considerate of others and show up on time for a change. Mr. Green would comment on his tardiness, but that never motivated Mike to get there by nine. It was always nine fifteen, and the last meeting he strolled in at nine thirty. Since Mr. Green wasn't there, they couldn't even start without him, just like that day, and Tiffany wanted to tell crazy-ass Tracy to stop gawking at her, but she kept her eyes glued to her pad and pen.

Finally, Mike walked in. "Good morning, ladies and gents, I'm sorry I'm late." Tiffany knew that shit was a lie, but she held a straight face. Mike put his briefcase on the table and opened it. "First, we are going to go over numbers and ratings as usual, and then after we talk about what we can do to improve, the floor will be opened for new ideas. Same routine, same format, so let's get started."

Tiffany did all she could to keep from yawning during that part of the meeting. She never had low ratings or rankings so she thought of baby names as Mike commented, admonished, and announced who'd be in their last season. Finally, after almost two hours of that, they were on new show ideas. There were slots for four new shows, and Tiffany was confident Myah's idea would be chosen.

"Ummm, I'd like to go first," Tracy said raising her pen in the air.

Tiffany almost laughed out loud, but she refrained and rolled her eyes instead. She didn't care if Tracy went before her because she knew Tracy's concept would not top Myah's. Tracy was nowhere near as creative as she thought she was, and Tiffany wondered why Mike showed so much interest in her whack ideas.

"Okay, Tracy, let's hear it," Mike said.

"Well, I want to do a show based on three single mothers that are struggling to raise their children alone. Urban community, middle class, though."

What the hell! was Tiffany's first thought, and then she thought her ears were playing tricks on her. Tiffany's eyes darted at the woman sitting on the opposite side of the table. That was Myah's concept. How in the fuck did she know Myah's concept? Myah told her that in confidence. The look on Tiffany's face was incredulous as she listened to Tracy continue with Myah's words—verbatim. Tiffany stood, and her mouth opened, and as soon as Tracy's evil ass paused, Tiffany interrupted. "I'm sorry, Mr. Harrington, but that is my junior producer's idea. We've been discussing this idea for months."

Tracy also stood to her feet and met Tiffany's gaze. "I beg your pardon," Tracy said with disgust. "I thought of this idea months ago, and I've shared this idea with Mike before."

Tiffany eyed the woman down. She knew that trick was as shrewd as she looked. "*Mike?* Oh, so we're on a first-name basis? I don't care what you discussed with Mike," Tiffany spat. "That idea is my junior associate's idea. We've been bouncing that idea around for weeks, months, even, and I don't know how you got wind of it, but to stand here in my face and suggest it as if it were yours is low, Tracy. You stole Myah's idea."

"Mr. Harrington," Tracy said turning to Mike, "maybe this pregnancy is affecting Mrs. Bank's mind or clouding her thought process, but you and I both know that this is not the first time we have discussed this idea, and for her to accuse me of stealing a show idea is contemptible."

"Tracy, if I wasn't pregnant I would jump across this table and—" Tiffany blared in rage.

"Ladies, ladies, ladies," Mike yelled over them. "Have a seat," he ordered, but they both remained standing. "If you ladies want to continue working at TiMax, you will sit! Now!" Mike yelled.

Tracy sat first, and after giving Tracy the nastiest look Tiffany had in her, she eased down into her chair. Mike began to talk, but his words fell on deaf ears. Tiffany's eyes were locked on the other woman, and all she wanted to do was whip her ass. To steal Myah's idea was low. There was nothing documented to prove that Myah came up with that concept months ago.

"Do you understand, Mrs. Banks?" Mike yelled, and Tiffany snapped back.

"I'm sorry, Mike, can you repeat what you just said." She hadn't heard him. Anger overshadowed her sense of hearing.

"I said that we will continue this in my office at a later time. I want to get to the bottom of this."

"No need, Mr. Harrington. She can have it. She needs something to resurrect her sorry-ass career," Tiffany spat.

"*Excuse* me!" Tracy said, shocked.

"You heard me. The numbers don't lie. Your current show is only holding strong because of Colby Grant. If it wasn't for Colby having a strong fan base and followers, that show, along with your hackneyed-ass new ideas would be off the network's roster. You are not cut out for this line of work. If you were, KCLN would have kept you." Tiffany knew that was a sore spot, but she meant to hit below the belt. She didn't care. Any cordialness she had for Tracy was gone, and Tiffany wished she wasn't carrying her first child because she'd put a Chicago South Side beat down on that bitch.

"Mr. Harrington," Tracy cried, looking for help.

"Mrs. Banks," Mike said.

"It's cool, Mr. Harrington, I'm done," Tiffany said and took a long drink of her bottled water. She wished she could go to her office and hit one of the bottles of booze. She only half-listened to the rest of the meeting, and as soon as she got back to her office Myah was at the door.

"So what did Mike think? Is my show on the roster?"

"Have a seat, Mee-Mee."

"Oh no, they hated it." Myah sat. "It's okay, I have other ideas, so next quarter we can submit another one. I'm patient. I'm learning so much."

Tiffany smiled, because if that had been the case, Myah was taking the news well, but she had to tell her the truth.

"Mee-Mee, that's not it," Tiffany said.

"Okay, then, what? You look defeated, boss."

"Myah, did you tell anyone—I mean *anyone*—about your idea? Anyone here? Cameron?"

"No, only you. Why? Talk to me, Tiffany, what's up?"

"In the meeting today, Tracy gave your concept as her show idea."

"What!" Myah's face resembled Tiffany's when Tracy started talking that morning.

"Yes. The exact same concept, and I have no idea how she knew what we spoke about, and Mike likes it, and since we never documented anything, I can't prove it was your idea and not hers."

"Tiffany, that is fucked up. This nontalented, corny-ass bitch steals my show idea, and there is *nothing* we can do?"

"I'm sorry, Myah, but no. We didn't record it in a file or log it, so it's our word against hers."

"That's some straight bullshit, Tiffany. I can beat her ass right about now."

"I know, but please don't. I think she and Mike might have a thing going. She called him Mike in the meeting and said they had *chatted* about that concept before."

"Well, you and I both know that Mike bangs anything in heels and a skirt."

"Yes, he is a player. How . . . I don't know because he is not a catch. Definitely not my type."

"Not mine either, but can you talk to Mr. Green, Tiffany?"

"I could, Myah, but we have no proof. Mr. Green is still grieving Tressa's death, and I don't want to go to him with this."

"I understand." Myah dropped her head.

"Myah, don't worry, sweetheart. You are going to shine here. I promise. This is just a small hurdle."

She stood. "I hope so." She headed toward the door. "If Tracy says a word to me . . . I mean, even if she says hello, I'm going to punch her in her throat."

"Just don't get locked up, Myah. You do have three kids."

She laughed. "Damn, I hate her ass."

"So do I," Tiffany said, and Myah made her exit. Tiffany took a few deep breaths and tried to calm down. She didn't need or want any stress during her pregnancy, and she couldn't wait until Mike was gone and she was appointed CEO so she could have Tracy's ass escorted off the premises. She knew the network had a contract with Tracy, but her awful show ideas would be the reason Tiffany needed to relieve her of her duties, and the more she thought about it, Tracy would be out the door before she could put Myah's idea into production.

Tiffany made a mental note to bring Mr. Green up to date on what happened that day, and she'd have to convince him that she felt capable of stepping up. She wanted Tracy gone so bad her entire body ached.

She grabbed her cell phone and dialed Kory.

"Hey, honey," Kory said when he answered.

"Hey, baby, do you have a minute?"

"Always for you, baby, what's up?"

"Tracy is what's up. She is a thorn, Kory," Tiffany whined.

"What happened now, Tiff?"

She filled him in on what had transpired that morning, and, as usual, Kory had soothing words to comfort his wife.

"So get through your day and I will take you somewhere special this evening for dinner."

"Someplace special, huh?"

"Yes, baby, anywhere you want to go."

"How about Angelini Osteria, on Beverly Boulevard? I may be working a little late, so we can meet maybe around eight."

"Sounds good, baby, just try to enjoy your day, okay? Remember, we vowed that we wouldn't let anyone or anybody stress us out during our pregnancy."

"I know, baby, but fortunately for you, *I'm* carrying her, and *you* don't work with pyscho-ass Tracy."

"I know, sweetheart, but focus on the future. You won't have to suffer her forever."

"True. I love you, Mr. Banks. I'll see you later."

"Love you too, Mrs. Banks."

They hung up, and Tiffany tried to get back to work. She hadn't spent much time in the studio lately because her focus was on learning how to run that company. She wanted to make sure she could not only maintain the stellar name that Langley and Mike built, but she was also going to bring a fresh, new, and edgier feel to the company. There were a lot of young, hungry, talented writers out there, and she planned to shake out the old heads that weren't producing hit shows and replacing them with newcomers who wanted to turn TiMax into the leading network for the most viewed and highest-rated shows.

It wasn't going to happen overnight, but since Mr. Green was happy with her vision, she was anxiously waiting for all transactions to be completed and Tracy, along with the barely-getting-by employees, will no longer be on TiMax's payroll.

Tiffany arrived at the restaurant a little after eight, and she was happy that Kory had already arrived. They were seated, and since it was a special night alone with her husband, she and Kory both agreed it was okay for her to enjoy a glass of red wine. That day had been stressful, so she needed something to help her unwind, and a small glass would be okay.

They ordered their appetizers, and they decided that work would not be a subject. They agreed to talk about the baby, names, and the new nursery. Tiffany had had a couple of designers to present ideas, so she and Kory were trying to narrow down the one they liked the most.

When wine and appetizers were on the table, they started with names. Tiffany took a sip—and her eyes widened when she saw her.

"What is it, baby? It's like you've seen a ghost."

"Unfucking believable, Kory. No way is that Tracy," Tiffany snarled. She could not believe her eyes.

Kory turned to look in the direction his wife was ogling. "In the red?" he asked.

"Yes, in the red. Out of *every* restaurant in L.A., she picks this one, Kory. Something is up. There is *no* way that I keep running into this woman. I mean, either she walks in within minutes after me, or I'll walk in to find her leaving. This is crazy, Kory."

He looked at Tiffany. "Baby, this *is* weird. Do you think she's following you?"

"I don't know, but I'm going to find out." Tiffany stood, but Kory stopped her.

"No, babe, sit," he said reaching out for her hand. He wouldn't let her pass.

"Kory, I need to confront her."

"No, you need to sit."

Tiffany put a hand on her swollen belly and eased back into her seat. "Why can't I go over there, Kory? This bitch is apparently stalking me."

"Tiffany, the best way to handle someone like her is to straight ignore her. If you go over and confront her, or make a scene, she is going to make you out to be the one who is crazy or paranoid. Stay away from that crazy-ass woman, Tiffany. You are pregnant. You go over and confront her, she gets out of pocket and goes off, and something happens to you or my kid, I'd snap her neck."

Tiffany laughed. "Okay, baby, I get it. I won't even look her way."

"Exactly," Kory said . . . and then that crazy bitch approached.

Tiffany's eyes almost jumped out of her head.

"Good evening, Tiffany, and you must be Kory." Tracy extended her hand. Kory didn't touch her. Tiffany knew he knew better. After a moment, Tracy drew back her hand.

"Tracy, you and I don't have shit to say to one another so why are you at our table?"

"Well, I wanted to say hello. I know we had a misunderstanding earlier—" Tracy attempted to say, but Tiffany cut her off.

"A *misunderstanding*, Tracy?" Tiffany gripped her dinner napkin and peered at Tracy. Through clenched teeth, she said. "Bitch, if you don't get your demented ass away from our table, you are going to need help getting up from the floor."

"Wow, I thought you had more class than that, Mrs. Banks. Aren't you pregnant? I swear hormones are crazy when you are with child."

Tiffany looked at Kory, tilted her head to the right, and he knew that look. His wife was about to flip that table over. "Tracy, it was nice to meet you, now can you please give us some privacy." Kory's tone was direct and firm.

The other woman backed down. "Sure, and it was a pleasure to meet you. See you at work tomorrow," she said to Tiffany with a smirk, and then walked away.

"Kory," Tiffany hissed.

"I know, I know, but calm down, baby. No stress, remember? You cannot let Tracy of all people get to you. She is a piece of work."

Their server approached for the dinner order, so he created a temporary distraction. Although Tiffany's appetite had escaped her, she ordered her favorite dish anyway. Once the server was gone with their menus, Tiffany kept her eyes glued on her husband and ignored the devil with the red dress on in the room. Tracy had sat at a table that made it easy to watch Tiffany, but Tiffany used her skills of temperance and enjoyed the rest of her evening with her husband as if Tracy Simms were no longer in the room.

It's Working

Episode 27

Tracy

Tracy headed toward Mike's with an enormous smile plastered on her face. She was finally getting what she wanted. It pleased her to know that her antics were starting to get to Tiffany, and she was working on Mike to get closer to the top. Mike was pretty much her key to being more successful, so she wanted him to give her more shows, more power, and more praises. Tressa's overdose could not have come at a better time. Rumor had it that Mr. Green may not ever return to work, and she has to be in Mike's good graces in order to move up the ladder for whatever position or station that put her over Tiffany.

She wanted Tiffany miserable, and she wanted her to become so irritated and uncomfortable at TiMax that she resigned. Tracy had listened in on several conversations where Tiffany had expressed her hatred for her, but she didn't give a damn, because she despised her ass just as much, and she wanted her gone.

After she had put on her best performance, she lay next to Mike in his bed and silently praised herself for a job well done. Before Mike could shut his eyes, she mentioned doing something else besides producing. Mike's reply was, "Something else like what?"

"I don't know, baby. Like more on the corporate side . . . maybe being the head of my department. I can tackle the job of ratings, rankings, and monitor the shows' progress and schedule. What you do, because I know you hate it. You barely walk in prepared. Most times, we can tell you've just taken a glimpse at the figures right before our meetings, and then you're never on time. You can just put me over our department, and that way, you can scratch the nightly series monitoring off your list."

"That's sounds good, Tracy, that would relieve me of that burden, but you know with a decision like that, I'd have to consult Langley, and there is the matter of seniority. If I suggest this, I'm sure Tiffany Banks would most likely be Langley's choice. She has the most hit shows and has been there the longest since a few veterans have moved on. Most likely, you wouldn't get the offer."

"What if Tiffany doesn't want it?" she said. She didn't want to be defeated. "Baby, Langley is not returning, and you can make an executive decision on how you want things to run. Langley doesn't have to even know until I'm already in it. I can give my shows to Tiffany and even Darryl, and you know everything they touch turns to platinum. It would be a win-win. Plus, I can let Tiffany's junior's assistant have the idea for *My Single Life* since they want to accuse me of stealing it, and we'll all be happy."

Mike was quiet at first, but then Tracy went there. "What's the purpose of being family if I have no privileges?"

"What are you talking about, Tracy?" he asked. She didn't understand why he was confused.

"I mean, I take care of you, Mikey, and as your mommy, that should entitle me to *something*. I don't want to start talking to the other moms about our relationship. Tiffany is expecting. I'm sure I can give her some parenting tips, though." His body shifted under hers.

"You and I both know that you don't need to discuss what goes on here. You gave me your word."

"I did, but I also assumed with my role you would make me privileged."

He let out a breath. "It does."

"Do you like what I do to you, Mikey?"

"You know I do."

"So me getting a new title overseeing my department can happen for me, right?"

"Tracy, I'll see what I can do, but I can't make any promises."

"Okay," she said, and then stood. She went over to her bag. "While I have your undivided attention, baby, can I show you something?"

"What do you want to show me, Tracy?" She could hear the impatience in his voice, but she didn't give a damn. Mike was a very wealthy man, and he wasn't paying her for her sexual favors, so she wanted what she wanted. She retrieved her tablet from her bag, then she got back in the bed, and he propped himself up an elbow.

"What are you showing, babe?"

"You'll see; it's a new show idea. You're going to love it." She pressed Play, and when Mike saw himself and her, in his playroom, his eyes bucked.

"Tracy, when did you record us?"

"The real question is when did I *start* recording us?"

Mike's dark complexion went pale, and Tracy knew he was terrified. "Okay, then, when?" he asked in a panic.

"Well, it was a couple of months ago when I got you that teddy bear. It is a nanny cam. I wanted to watch you while I was away and watching when I wasn't away is just an added bonus. Now, it did please me to know that you're saving this *special* thing for me only, so that is a plus, but there is nothing to think about, Mike. I know you can create any position you want, and I want Tiffany Banks to answer to *me,*" she thundered.

Tracy could tell Mike was nervous. She didn't know it would be that easy, but she knew he'd want to keep this part of his life a secret.

"Fine, Tracy, fine. I'll have your new contract drawn up by week's end."

"And my office?" she smirked. "I assume I'll be moving to a different floor."

"Of course, just promise me you will not let this footage go any further than this room. I don't want to embarrass my wife or my company. This stays between us, right? I mean, it's hard to find someone that is like me, Tracy, and the others, I paid for their silence, so if you want a higher position, it's yours."

"Thanks, baby," she leaned in and kissed him. "You're the best."

He gave her a half smile.

"I want to call a meeting to announce my promotion."

"Of course," Mike said. She caressed his face. She was overjoyed and proud that everything was working in her favor.

"Now come here, baby, and give Mommy's clit some attention," she purred. She knew the last thing Mike may have wanted to do was go down on her, but she insisted that he did. He wasn't the best-looking man, but his bedroom skills were off the charts, so she never had a problem with having sex with him. If she had to be honest, she had grown to like him. Hell, she suddenly felt like she could do anything. Make Mike leave his wife . . . become part owner of the company—hell, the sky was the limit, but for now, she'd enjoy the moment she was in. Now she was over Tiffany, and *she* called all the shots, and she couldn't wait to see the look on Tiffany's face.

This Is Where It Ends

Episode 28

Tiffany

The following week, when Tiffany walked off the elevator, she was bombarded with a lobby of producers, cast members, and her assistants. Everyone was talking about something, and Tiffany wondered what happened that day and so early. She hurried to her office and checked in with her assistant.

"Summer, what's going on? What's up with this morning's circus?"

"You haven't heard?"

"Heard what?"

Before she could answer, Darryl and Myah had made it over to Tiffany.

"Oh my word, turtle dove—Tracy! The shit is about to hit the fan," Daryl said, fanning himself.

"What's going on, guys? Someone just please tell me." Maybe there was a fight or a personal matter because Tiffany had just had brunch with Langley the day before and they were still on schedule, so it had to be some celeb, cast member drama, she thought. Boy, was she wrong.

"Well, your girl got a promotion," Myah spat.

"Who got what?"

"You heard me. Tracy is now the head of our department!" Myah barked.

"Says who and since when?"

"Since today. I don't know. But first thing this morning when I checked my e-mails, it said meeting this morning at nine sharp in screening room B to announce the new head of our division," Myah responded.

Tiffany laughed. "This has *got* to be a joke. I saw the alert, but I didn't open any e-mails this morning."

"No joke, honey bun," Darryl said and whipped out his phone. He went to his inbox and shared the message with Tiffany.

Her eyes scanned the e-mail, and all kinds of thoughts ran through her mind. She and Langley hadn't discussed that, and Mr. Green never mentioned speaking to Mike about it.

"Let's go," Tiffany ordered, and they all followed her to the screening room. *This is going to be good,* Tiffany thought to herself and couldn't wait to hear what Tracy had to say. They filed inside, and Tiffany, Darryl, and Myah took front-row seats. Losing patience, Tiffany's nerves were all over the place, but she tried to appear cool, calm, and collected. She should have gone straight to her office and called Langley, but she wanted to know what was going on first before she went to him.

After Tracy kept them waiting it seemed like forever, she finally graced the podium with her presence. She stood and waited for the banter to cease, and then she spoke. She cleared her throat, took a sip of water, and then adjusted the mic. All eyes were on her, and Tiffany wondered why Mike hadn't joined the meeting.

"Good morning, all. I hope everyone is well." She ran a palm over her lapel, and then continued. "I'm sure most of you got my e-mail this morning, so I'll get right to it. This company is one of the largest in the industry, and I am so happy to be a part of it. TiMax is known for . . ." she continued giving them all a history lesson on the network, something they already knew. Some sat patiently, but the sighs and breath releases had shown some of the staff's annoyance. Tiffany wanted her to get to the point.

"In conclusion, I am your new boss," she said with a smile bright enough to illuminate a deep hole in the ground. "From now on, producers and junior producers will report to me and consult me with any problems. I will be meeting with each one of you to have a one-on-one about your shows and to get you your new lineups. As for now, I don't have time to answer questions. I suggest you hold them and ask in our one-on-one."

"What the fuck just happened?" Dee asked. The room was no longer quiet.

Millions of questions were asked anyway, but Tracy said, "Thanks for your time; have a great day." She adjourned the meeting.

"I don't know, Dee, but I'm going to find out."

"I can't work under her, Tiffany. This is insane. Whose idea was this?" Myah objected.

"I don't know, guys, but I'm going to get to the bottom of this," Tiffany said. Dee and Myah stood and helped Tiffany's pregnant body from the low chair. They left the screening room, and Tiffany assured them she'd let them know when she had answers. She headed to Mike's office, but he was not in. She figured he wouldn't be. That bastard was the one who created that monster, and she knew Tracy must have been giving him sexual favors. To create a bogus position, give her a bogus title was the work of an idiot, and she knew Langley would pull the plug on that shit.

She hurried down to her office to let Summer know she was leaving. She had to get to Mr. Green. Talking to him on the phone would not suffice. She made a pit stop in her office to use the bathroom. The further along her pregnancy got, the more frequently she had to go.

When Tiffany was done, she walked out of the bathroom and dropped the paper towel she was drying her hands with. "Oh great," she said because the idea of bending was a task. Approaching six months, she felt like she was further along, and she looked as if she was too. She bent over, and before she could return to a full standing position, she saw a red light blinking under her desk. "What the . . .?" she said and moved closer to it. She didn't want to touch it, but she got up close to it. She instantly knew what it was.

She sat and didn't say a word. Then she reached for her phone and called Kory. She would give Ms. Tracy an earful that day.

"Hey, baby," Kory answered.

"Hey, baby, are you busy?"

"A little, what's up?"

"Okay, brace yourself for what went down this morning."

"Okay, talk to me."

"So I get in this morning, and there is an uproar in the lobby." She proceeded to tell him, play-by-play, making sure her tone was of one who was pissed. "Bottom line is, I'm done. This is where I go, because you know I can't work under that woman."

"Quit? What are you talking about, baby? You can't quit."

She knew Kory was in the dark, but she planned to call him right back when she got into the car to let him know the real deal.

"I can, and I will. I'm coming for some boxes, and I'm cleaning out my office today, so whatever you need to do to get out of there to help me, make it happen, Kory," she growled and ended the call. Kory tried calling her back a few times, but she purposely hit Ignore. Her desk phone rang. It was Summer. She hit the speaker. "Yes, Summer?"

"Mr. Banks is on the line."

"Tell him I'll call him back," Tiffany ordered. She wanted to roll on the floor laughing. That explained the show idea, the popping up wherever she'd be, and her face burned when she thought about the couple of times she and Kory made out in her office. Oh well, they *were* husband and wife. She stood and grabbed her things to head to Mr. Green's. She couldn't wait to inform him of this bullshit. She also planned to tell him about the recording device. After she was done, Tracy was sure to be back to being unemployed, and Tiffany didn't give a damn.

Surprise, Surprise

Episode 29

Rose

Rose hung up with Tiffany and went into her bathroom. She had avoided this, but it could wait no longer. She and Levi had been working out, and she didn't want to step on the scale, but she did. She looked down, and the numbers hadn't changed from the two weeks' prior number. She was just about ready to throw in the towel. She had been working out and giving it her all, but the pounds stuck to her body like white on rice. The first month, the pounds were falling off, and she had easily lost her first twenty-six pounds. The second month, it wasn't as many, but now she had lost forty-two pounds in total. She had gone down two sizes, and although a sixteen looked more attractive to her, she wanted to lose fifty more pounds, but the scale wasn't budging.

"What should I do?" she wondered. She called Levi, and he had said what he said to her over and over again, "Ditch the scale. The numbers don't mean anything. It's how you look and feel in your clothes."

"I hear you, baby, but I want to lose the pounds. Maybe I should see a doctor or a nutritionist."

"I guess, baby, but I have to go. I gotta fight crime."

"Okay, baby, I'll let you get back to it."

"Okay, I love you."

"I love you too. Are you coming home for your dinner break?"

"I'm not sure. I'll call you."

"Okay, baby, be safe."

She hung up, and then went for her tab. She googled a nutritionist in her area and after calling a couple of places, she made an appointment with the first person that could see her that day. She dressed, went by her gallery, ran a couple of errands, and then headed over to her appointment. She got there fifteen minutes early as the receptionist suggested and filled out the long medical history forms and consent forms. She waited, patiently scrolling Facebook on her phone until they called her. Then she gathered her handbag and the clipboard and went back.

The young lady was nice, and they exchanged small talk while she got her vitals and drew blood. The young lady then gave her a cup to take in the bathroom and give her a urine sample. Rose just wanted to know how to lose her stubborn pounds and wondered why they needed urine, but she went anyway.

Once she got into the doctor's office, she occupied her time reading the healthy eating and weight management posters. She checked her watch after ten minutes or so and wondered why they called you from one waiting room to make you wait in another room. After almost twenty whole minutes, the doctor finally walked in, and Rose was impressed that she apologized for the long wait.

"So, Rose, I see you've come in today to ask a few questions about weight management, right?"

"Yes, ma'am," she responded.

"Well, let's take a look at your vitals and results and I'll check a few things, and then we can discuss a plan for you and your body type."

"Sounds good."

"How long have you been working out, Rose?"

"A couple of months. At first, I was shedding pounds like melting butter, but now I'm not losing anything. I don't even have the same energy I started with, and now, I'm even a little sluggish."

"Okay," the doctor attentively listened as she did her exam. She listened to her heart, made her breathe in and out, and checked her glands and neck. After she looked down Rose's throat and checked her ears, she sat down and powered up her tab. "Well, you look good, although you are considerably overweight for your height; your blood pressure looks fine, and your heart rate is good. It looks like you're pregnant, so that could be the reason you're starting to feel sluggish and the pounds are not coming off."

"I'm *what?*"

The doctor looked at her. "You're pregnant," she repeated. The look on her face showed she assumed Rose knew that already.

"I'm pregnant? Are you sure?"

"You didn't know?"

"No, I didn't know . . . I mean, are you positive?"

"Well, that's the results from your urine test. When was your last period?"

"I haven't had a period in over a year. My periods have been irregular for as long as I can remember," Rose said. She could not believe her ears.

"Well, surprise, surprise. You are, in fact, pregnant."

Rose still couldn't believe what the doctor was saying. "This has to be a mistake. I mean, how, when . . . well, I know how, but . . ." Rose was baffled.

"Well, it may have happened after you dropped a few pounds. Sometimes weight can be a factor of infertility. You said you've lost over forty pounds, so with that, you were able to conceive. You should get with your OB/GYN to get more of your questions answered, Ms. Jennings. They can give you a more accurate timeline and start your prenatal care."

"Pregnant," Rose said again.

"Is this an unpleasant thing for you? Do you know who the father is?"

Appalled, Rose snapped. "Of course, I know who the father is. We're engaged."

"I didn't mean to offend; you'd be surprised nowadays, so please forgive me."

"It's okay, I'm just trying to take it all in, and I wonder how I'm going to tell him."

"Well, congratulations. We can still go over some healthy suggestions for you to maintain a balanced weight and good eating habits, but like I said, for your questions about your pregnancy, you'll have to get with your OB."

Rose nodded. She finished up her appointment with the nutritionist, and then called Tiffany. Before Tiffany could fill her in on what went on at Mr. Green's house, Rose said, "Before you say a word, I'm pregnant."

"What!" Tiffany screamed in the phone.

"Yes, are you home?"

"I am. I just walked in."

"I'm on my way."

Time for Change

Episode 30

Tiffany

Tiffany pulled up to Mr. Green's gate, where the guard greeted her with a bright smile, and then let her in. Once inside, one of the staff members told her where Mr. Green was. She showed herself to the outdoor patio, where Mr. Green sat with Mike Harrington. Surprised to see him there, Tiffany politely greeted them both.

"Have a seat, Tiffany," Mr. Green said. She sat, and one of Mr. Green's staff members came and filled her glass with lemonade. "Would you like anything else?" Mr. Green asked.

"No, sir, this will be fine," she said before taking a tiny sip.

"How are you feeling, Tiffany? How is the baby?" Mr. Green asked. Always before business, they exchanged personal banter.

"I'm doing fine, Mr. Green, considering the stress I'm starting to encounter at TiMax, and the baby is fine. My pregnancy is progressing well."

"And Kory?"

"He's well, Mr. Green. How are you and Mrs. Green?"

"Better. It gets a little better each day," he said softly. Mr. Green had had a few health issues, but that day, he looked good.

She grabbed his hand. "That's good to hear," she said giving him a warm smile.

"And you, Mr. Harrington?" Tiffany turned her attention to him. She never hated Mike and never thought anything ill about him, but that day, she wanted to slap his face.

"I'm doing well . . . considering."

"Well, let's get down to business," Mr. Green suggested.

"Yes, please," Tiffany said, eyeing Mike.

"So where do we begin?" Langley asked.

"Let's start with today's events, shall we? Mr. Green, did Mike tell you that he created a bogus title and promoted one of the absolutely worst, most inexperienced producers at the company?"

"Yes, Mike told me everything. Tracy has blackmailed my friend, and we are already working on that matter as we speak."

"So you were sleeping with her?" Tiffany scowled.

"Yes, I was, and I am ashamed of my behavior, and I am now ready to sell my shares, step down, and let the chips fall where they may. Tracy recorded us in some . . . let's just say highly personal acts, and I'd rather that information not be leaked. I'm taking some extremes measures as we speak to assure this doesn't get out. I have some pretty efficient people that will make sure Tracy doesn't become my worst nightmare."

"So instead of facing the music, you're going to cover it up?"

"What would you do, Mrs. Banks?" Mike countered.

Tiffany turned to Mr. Green. "So why am I here?"

"Listen, Tiffany, how Mike decides to handle himself has absolutely nothing to do with me or you. In over thirty years, I've never cheated on my wife, so morally, I can't stand the sight of him, but as my business partner, I have a responsibility to protect my company. I'm not happy with what Mike has done, but it's not my business. My only concern is TiMax. Mike will announce his resignation, and I will introduce you as our new CEO. I will also announce my retirement, and you will step into your role as the head of TiMax. You will have a top-notch staff to help you along the way, and until I'm resting in my grave, you know I'm a phone call away."

Tiffany looked from Langley to Mike and back to Langley. "So what if the Tracy situation doesn't go away?"

"Let me deal with Tracy," Mike interjected.

She looked at Langley. "Well, sir, I believe that I am ready, and I'm more than honored to fill your shoes. You and Mike did something truly great, and I will do my best to make sure TiMax continues to thrive and be as successful as it has been."

"Good," Langley smiled. "Now if there is nothing else, I'll be in touch, Tiffany. I want to chat with my old friend and partner for a bit."

"I understand." Tiffany stood. "Oh yeah, and by the way, your little side piece bugged my office. She thinks today is my last day."

"Let's keep it that way. She's at the spa getting a head to toe makeover on me, just so my guys can get what we need."

"Good luck with that, Mike," Tiffany snarled and rolled her eyes. She didn't have any respect for men who two-timed their wives.

Tiffany bent over and gave Langley a kiss on the forehead and gave his neck a tight squeeze. He was truly a father figure to her, and she knew she wasn't a replacement for Tressa, but she thanked God that she was able to be there for him and his wife. "Thank you, again, sir, and I'll talk to you soon." She left feeling good. She had no idea what Mike had gotten himself into, but that was of no concern of hers. She would go and clear her office and wait for the call from Mr. Green. She was going to enjoy those days off while Tracy floated around TiMax like a boss. The look on her face come announcement day would be priceless, and Tiffany couldn't wait.

Tiffany headed home and called her husband. She brought him up to speed on what occurred in the meeting with Langley and Mike, and then she reminded him that they had to go to TiMax and grab a few of her personal things from the office just to make it look real. They went over lines of what they would say as they gathered her things, and by the time Tiffany pulled into her drive she was laughing hysterically. She hung up with Kory, and as soon as she got off with him, Rose called. Tiffany answered. "Hello," she said. "I was just about to call you."

"Before you say a word. I'm pregnant."

"What!" Tiffany screamed in the phone.

"Yes, are you home?"

"I am, I just walked in."

"I'm on my way."

This Is the Life

Episode 31

Tracy

Tracy lay on the massage table and enjoyed the deep-tissue stimulation. She had her earbuds in her ears, and Joe was letting her know it must be magic and how she likes the way he gives her the magic, as he serenaded her with his smooth lyrics. Two highly skilled masters worked her over as they kneaded the back of her calves, thighs, buttocks, back, shoulders and arms. She had dozed off a couple of times, but she fought her eyelids to stay awake, because she wanted to experience every moment of her day, including her body treatments. Mike had set her up to have an all-day experience, and she figured making him hers was going to be her next task.

Taking him from his wife and becoming part owner of TiMax was just a couple of fucks away, and she was up to it. One of the masseuses tapped her and told her to turn over. She obliged and welcomed their hands as they made her front side feel as good as they had made her backside feel. The track changed to Jaheim's "Finding My Way Back," and she thought of her ex, Blair.

Blair was the love of her life, but when she let her position at KCLN slip through her fingers, he abandoned ship. He was the bridge to Bill Keiffer. He planned and schemed with her to get into the door, but she fucked it all up by being late. "Fucking Tiffany," she said aloud and caught herself. She hated her so much, and she had moments when she wanted to just choke the life from her body. She lost everything and all the work she invested with getting into KCLN with a show she knew could be number one, then Tiffany swooped in and took everything. Her body tensed. She knew she should not have been entertaining thoughts of Tiffany, especially now. Not in front of people, because she'd want to inflict pain on herself.

She'd beat her thighs, slap her own face, or run into a door or cabinet to discipline herself for losing something so important. Her life turned upside down in a blink of an eye, and Tiffany Richardson Banks was the only person that made her see red. She was the only person that she knew she could actually kill with her bare hands. "Harder," she instructed the professionals working out her kinks. The thought of Tiffany sent her into a space she hated to be, and until Tiffany was eliminated from the team and down to nothing like she had left her, Tracy would not be satisfied.

After her two-hour massage, she headed for a mud bath, and then after that came the beauty treatments. She showered and before she went to have her nails and toes done, she had her lunch; salad with a cocktail made her feel like a queen. After nails and toes, she was waxed, after waxing, she went for hair, and before hair, she had a snack and then makeup. She enjoyed a relaxing six hours of pampering, and when she dressed in the beautiful evening dress and sparkling shoes, she knew life with Mike would be a dream.

His car picked her up and took her to one of L.A.'s most exclusive restaurants. She and Mike had been out before, but that night, he was laying out the red carpet, and she had no complaints.

"Wow, Mike, this is beautiful. I mean, what will you tell people if they ask?"

"This is business, Ms. Simms. That is what we will say."

Her face beamed. "If that's what works, okay," she glowed. "Thank you so much for the spa treatments today. They really pampered me and treated me like a queen, and from my head to my toes, I feel like a million bucks."

Mike smiled. "Well, enjoy it, baby. Enjoy it while it lasts."

She frowned. "What does that mean?"

He cleared his throat. "Nothing, sweetheart. You look beautiful. When I look at you, I sometimes still can't believe my luck," he expressed.

She grinned. "Well, I'm glad you brought that up, Mike."

The server interrupted. They both put in their drink orders and appetizer selections, and then Tracy dove back in. "What I was saying, Mike, is . . ." she paused. "I've fallen for you. I know I wasn't supposed to, but I have, and I want you to leave your wife."

"Come again?"

She sat straight up in her chair and boldly repeated herself. "I'm in love with you, Mike, and I want you and me to be together. I want you to leave her and be with me."

Mike scratched his head and picked up his menu before replying. "Tracy, you know what it is. Now, I will wine you and dine you and fuck you appropriately, but leaving my wife is not a subject that you and I will have."

"Why not, Mike? Is it because you love your old-ass wife so much, or is it because my pussy isn't good enough to make me Mrs. Harrington?" Her voice rose, and the look on Mike's face was displeased.

"Lower your voice, Ms. Simms, and understand this. I fuck with you because you make my dick hard. I fuck with you because no other bitch has turned me on so much. I fuck with you because your pussy is good. And I am *not* leaving my wife. If what I give you isn't enough, get your conniving ass up and walk up out of here."

"You don't know who you are fucking with," Tracy calmed and brought her voice down. She gave him a cunning smile with her words.

He returned, "And you too, my dear, have no idea who *you* are fucking with. I can buy dozens of bitches like you with a finger snap. I met you. I was feeling you, and you turned me on. Now you think you can black-mail me and hold my balls in your little pocketbook. You are wrong, and you got me mixed up. Now what you are going to do is be good company, fuck me properly after dinner, and if you don't want to be on the do-not-hire list in the U.S., you will not threaten me again."

"You bastard," she spat.

"You dumb bitch," he returned.

"I can *bury* you. I *will* expose your dirty little secret."

"You try it. See, the difference between you and me is, I am a man with wealth, influence, power, and money, and if I wanted you to disappear, you'd be gone. That shit you pulled the other night was real cute, and I forgive you. Now, I got you where you wanted to be at the network so you can feed your little need to be in power, and you are still at the top of my fuck list, so look over your menu and figure out what you want to eat. This conversation is done," Mike spat.

Tracy almost fell out of her chair. She didn't fight or argue. She would have to show him better than she could tell him. She would simply go to the media and expose his ass, and then sue him. He wanted to play rough, then she would play rough. The recorded videos were her meal ticket. Oh, she'd play it cool and fuck him that night because his dick was damn good, but Mike aka Mikey had just checked the wrong bitch.

"The pasta looks yummy," she replied.

"I was thinking the same," he returned.

"Baby, let's not fight," she offered to break the hostile mood.

"Let's not."

"I'm looking forward to fucking you tonight."

"And I look forward to fucking you too."

She let out a breath and figured she'd handle Mike like she'd handle Tiffany and hold on to her footage a little while longer. It was some leverage, and she really didn't want to piss Mike off. But why had he been so cocky now? The other night, she had forced his tail between his legs. Whatever had gotten into him sent her into a brief panic, and she now had to reorganize her plans. She had to find a way to get back on top of the situation; and in the meantime, she had to chill.

Big News

Episode 32

Rose

It had been two days since Rose had learned she was pregnant and six hours since she was informed that she was approximately eight weeks along. She had a vaginal ultrasound, and still, even after seeing her little fetus on the screen, she could not believe she had gotten pregnant. She thought her chances would be never since she rarely had a period. If she got a period, she was amazed, because her body didn't act like a future mother. She never even thought much about being a mother. She was elated that Tiffany would be having a baby, but the thought of being a mother hardly ever crossed her mind.

She and Levi had never addressed that subject head-on, but he had mentioned he wanted to be a father one day. When he said those words, Rose smiled and didn't comment and didn't tell him that she may not ever be able to give him children. Now she was pacing the floor, waiting for him to come home so she could tell him the big news. They were pregnant. His family had welcomed her and made her feel like family, but they hadn't told them that they had plans to wed . . . and now a baby. Rose imagined that that wouldn't go over well.

She wanted a drink, a glass of Riesling or Pinot, but now that she was expecting, she refilled her glass of lemon water and waited for her lover to walk through the door. He spent at least six nights a week there with her, and they both agreed when his lease was up he'd move there.

She saw the headlights of his Mustang pull into the driveway. Her heart thumped against her chest, and her hands shook. "Ahhhh, I need a shot. I can't do this. I can't tell him. He is going to hit the roof. We're not married," she cried to herself, and then she heard his keys. She stood by the island in her tank and boy shorts. Her natural locks had a fresh shampoo and conditioning and the mango scent her stylist used on her hair was still loud and filled the air. She had a few squirts of her Very Sexy by Victoria's Secret, and she hoped he'd be happy and not walk out on her.

He entered. "Hey, gorgeous," he said.

"Hey, baby, how was work?"

"You don't want to know. I promise you these teens are getting worse and worse. I had to arrest a kid today that thought it was okay to beat up his grandmother—her own grandson. What would possess a person to do something so evil?"

"I don't know, babe," she answered and took his lunch bag. "Are you hungry? I made a pan of lasagna for you."

"Yes, baby, please." He leaned in and gave her a quick kiss. "You look so beautiful. You are glowing and your skin, baby . . . Did you go to the spa today?"

She laughed lightly. "No, I got my hair done, though, but that's about it."

"Well, you look so beautiful, baby. You are a sight for sore eyes. Baby, I promise you, if we ever have kids, I'm going to be a dad that is on it. I'm not going to let the streets raise my kid."

"Baby, our lives are not like some of the people you come across every day at work. The crime rate here is what . . . not even on the radar. Our children will have different opportunities than some of the kids you see on the streets at work."

"I know, Rosy. Meeting someone like you so classy, so put together, so educated . . . I never thought I'd have a key to a spot on this side of the fence. I'm grateful, and I'm not going to be doing this street work too much longer. Once I make detective, things will be different, baby, and I'll be able to do more around here. Once I get rid of my spot, every dime that goes there will go to you." His words were sincere, and Rose believed him.

"I know, Levi. I admire your drive. I respect what you do, and I will be honest, I want you to make detective, because every day when you are doing police work, I worry, and we need you, honey. We can't lose you."

He looked at her confused. "*We?* Baby, what do you mean we?" He put his holster on the island and sat.

She swallowed hard. "You remember the other day when you told me to stay off the scale?"

"Yes, I have told you pounds don't matter, baby."

"I know, Levi, but you know me. I overthink things, so I went to a nutritionist."

"Okay and . . .? What type of advice did they give you? I'm sure it was no different than what I've already been telling you."

"You are right, but she told me something that you had not."

"What? We've covered it all. Diet, exercise, and I showed you different techniques to target the areas you're not happy with."

"You did, baby, and everything you said was right."

"So what did I miss?"

"I'm pregnant."

He paused. He tilted his head to the right, and his brows furrowed. "What did you say?"

She swallowed hard and repeated herself. "I'm pregnant."

His eyes welled. He stood, paced the floor a few times, and Rose froze in place. He didn't say a word, and she had no idea what thoughts went through his mind.

"I'm sorry," she whispered.

He turned to her. "Sorry, baby?" he said and walked over to her. She trembled, and he embraced her and held on to her tightly. "That is like the best news I've ever heard a woman say to me, baby, I am . . . I can't believe it. You are having my child?"

She looked up at him and nodded her head. He wiped her tears. "Thank you, God. Thank you, Jesus," he said holding her face next to his. "Baby, I'm so happy."

"You are?"

"Yes, yes. You are beautiful, and I want to marry you now. Let's go to Vegas. Let's get married now."

"Right now, Levi? We can't. I want Tiffany there. I need my girl to be there."

"Call her," he said going for her phone. It was on the island. "Call her and Kory and tell them we need to go tonight."

"Levi, do you know what time it is?"

"I don't care, Rose. I want to marry you. I want to be with you, and if we have to do it tomorrow, that's fine too, but I want to marry you."

Rose dialed Tiffany. She was shocked she was wide awake. "Hey, girl. Did you tell Levi?"

"I did, and he wants to go to Vegas right now."

"What? Get the fuck out of here. Right now?"

"Yes, right now, but I want you to go."

She laughed out loud. "You want me to go to Vegas right now?"

"Yes. We can make it a one-day trip."

"Hold on," Tiffany said. "Kory," she heard Tiffany yell. A few moments later, Tiffany said, "Are you up for Vegas?"

"Why not?" Rose overheard him.

"We can pack a bag and be at your place in an hour," Tiffany confirmed.

Rose screamed. "This is crazy! Come on. We are going to Vegas!" Rose hung up. Levi went to shower, and they threw a bag together. Tiffany and Kory came shortly after, and they agreed to take the SUV. Tiffany sat in the back with Rose, and they laughed and talked the entire four-hour drive. They made it close to six in the morning and checked into the Bellagio Hotel. By five the next evening, Rose and Levi were married, and they hung out, gambled, and decided to leave the next day.

Rose was now a successful business owner, a wife, and an expectant mother. The only thing that weighed her down was that she and her sister still were not talking. After Levi had kissed her good-bye to head to work, she pulled out her phone. This was her last attempt to reconcile with Roslyn. She dialed her number and after the voice mail came on, she left her a message. "You know who this is. I didn't sleep with your husband; never did I ever even try to. I'm married now, and I'm having a baby, and I want us to fix this." She hung up. That was her last try. About twenty minutes later, she got a call.

It was from her sister Roslyn.

Under New Ownership

Episode 33

Tiffany

Tiffany squeezed Kory's hand tighter as she waited for someone to come for her. The press conference had begun over an hour ago, and Langley assured her after he and Mike spoke and answered all of the press and media's questions they would send for her to introduce her. The baby was doing flips, and Tiffany's stomach had a million butterflies fluttering about.

"Calm down, baby."

"I'm trying, Kory, but the baby is anxious; I'm anxious. I feel like I'm going to blow chunks."

"If you are, blow them now, Tiff. You have a big moment, and you don't want to blow chunks out there."

She squeezed his hand tighter. "I know, baby, I know. Why is this taking so long?"

"You know the press. They will ask the same damn question a dozen times, but reword it."

"True, by the way . . . off the subject, I hear Cameron and Myah are doing well."

"Yes, they are. You did well. I'm training him to manage the new location, and all he talks about constantly is Myah and her kids. He took her two boys to a game, and he is like already saying she's the one."

"Well, I hope it works out for them. I plan to promote Dee to be my right hand and give Myah that spot Tracy called herself getting. That way, Myah can produce and keep up with the series department. She already knows how to read the numbers and evaluate the ratings. Dee and I will continue to work with her on the producing side, but I know she will do great things."

"Wow, baby, listen to you. You are already delegating—and you haven't even been on the job a day yet."

"I've thought about a lot of fresh changes for a while, Kory. There were a lot of talented people that came before us, and those people are worn out and tired. I just want TiMax to flourish. Now the veterans will leave with a handsome package, but as I said, we need new age ideas. TiMax is going to be the number one network by the time I'm done."

"Do you, baby."

"You know I'm always doin' me."

"Tiffany," a voice interrupted. "They're ready for you."

She stood. "Baby, this is it."

"Go get'em, baby."

"I love you, Kory."

"I love you more."

Tiffany exited the room, and when she heard Mr. Green announce her name, she stepped out. Cameras were flashing, and Tiffany felt like royalty. Things happened so fast it was a blur. She answered all questions confidently and was happy when it came to an end.

She stood in what used to be Mr. Green's office, now her new office, with Mike and Langley.

"How do you feel, darling?" Langley asked.

"I feel good, sir. I'm ready to make you proud."

"You will do great, Tiffany, and I know you don't think too kindly of me, but you have my number as well. If you get stuck or need advice, don't hesitate," Mike offered.

"Thank you, Mr. Harrington. You are a brilliant man, and what you and Mr. Green did with this company is phenomenal, and for that, I have great respect for you."

"Thank you, Mrs. Banks. Now I must go. My wife and I have a plane to catch. We are leaving for Italy for a couple of months, so keep in touch," he said. Tiffany laughed on the inside. People with money could always make any obstacle "disappear."

"Safe travels, Mike," Mr. Green said, and they hugged tightly. "We did well, old man. Now it's time to sit back and watch the younger generation finish what we started."

Mike grinned. "Yes, indeed, and once Laura and I return, we will be by to visit with you and Estelle."

"Looking forward to it," Langley said. Mike made his exit, and Mr. Green turned to Tiffany. "This is only the beginning, kid. This moment right here is a moment I always dreamed of sharing with my Isabella," he sighed. His eyes watered.

"Mr. Green, I am so sorry."

"No no no, Tiff, no apologies. God is taking care of my angel now. I have to take it for what it is. Isa was my center, and no matter what, she was my baby. To tell you the truth, I'd rather her be resting there than to be here fighting drugs and alcohol and all of those demons she couldn't defeat."

"I know, Mr. Green. Tressa and I weren't close, nowhere near it, but I have my moments when I miss her too. After she had cleaned up and we worked together, I got to know a kind Tressa, a sweet person, and she was so smart. It only took once for me to tell her something and she'd remember. When I did have the pleasure of spending time with her, she left me with fond memories."

He wiped his face. "Yes, my Isabella had a side to her that not many people got to see or experience, and I miss her so much, and it still hurts so bad," he cried.

Tiffany rushed over and hugged him tightly. "I know, sir, and we all miss her." Tiffany gave Mr. Green all the time he needed. She sat with him and held his hand and listened to his stories about Tressa until he was ready to leave.

"You know you and Kory are welcome to come by the house at any time, and when this little girl makes an entrance, Estelle and I want to be there."

"Of course, Mr. Green."

"Call me Langley. I'm not your boss anymore, Tiff."

She smiled. "Well, you still own this company, so you are. I'm just the CEO, but I will call you whatever you like."

"Good. Now go and handle business with that Tracy person, and then get home and have a good time with your husband."

"Yes, sir," Tiffany said. They exchanged their last hug, and after Tiffany called in Dee and Mee-Mee to inform them of their new positions, she made her way to Tracy's office. She was surprised her name was still on the door, and even more surprised she was still there.

Tiffany walked in without knocking. This wasn't Tracy's house, and Tiffany didn't owe her an ounce of respect. "You're still here?" Tiffany said.

"I work here," Tracy snarled.

"Do you?" Tiffany held back her laughter. "Have you heard the news?"

"I have, and what does that mean to me?"

"That means you don't have a show, an office, a title, or a place at TiMax. Your badge has been deactivated since eleven a.m. The gates know that you are no longer on the list. Shall I continue?"

Tracy rolled her neck, and then looked up at Tiffany. Her eyes were filled with anger, and Tiffany, being six-plus months pregnant, should not have gone in there alone. Tiffany placed a hand on her belly, and then took a seat. She didn't want to entertain Tracy, but she was inclined to hear her parting words.

"Do you think this is over?" Tracy growled.

"Tracy, come on . . . What do you want? Sympathy? Forbearance? Tell me what are you talking about? This *is* over. You've only been here what . . . seven months and some change, and you are back where your sorry ass started from. I won't slander you. I won't prevent you from getting a job at another network, but TiMax is not a fit for evildoers like you. We are family here, Tracy, and we don't bug offices, prey on junior producers, or plot to destroy each other.

"You are a black woman with an attitude. You are holding a grudge over something that is so old, that has no bearing on your future. You have allowed that one moment when you think I took something from you dictate your actions, Tracy, and that's just crazy."

Tiffany eyed her and could see she was boiling, but she finished what she had to say. "I did not take your job, Tracy. I showed up, presented my ideas, and Todd liked them. When you showed up, it was up to you to defend your position, but you didn't, so I did nothing wrong. For months, I felt guilty; for months, I prayed for you, and now, here we are.

"You are blocking yourself, Tracy, not the other way around. Holding on to anger is destroying you." Tiffany stood. She was going to leave, but she wasn't hateful or evil like Tracy, and she made a decision. "I'm willing to let you stay on as a producer of *Grapevine*. It is a great show, some of your best work, and we can discuss new original ideas somewhere in the future. This is your last chance, Tracy; please don't make me regret it." Tiffany went to the door, but she heard a sound come out of Tracy's body that scared the shit out of her.

"Fuck you, Tiffany Richardson! Hell will freeze over twice before I work for you. I'm not a loser; *you* are, and I'm not done with you. You *will* see my face again!" she roared like a lion at Tiffany.

"Don't threaten me, Tracy. I'm not afraid of you. If you think you want to try me, you better be ready. I *am* a winner, and winners *always* win!" Tiffany spat before exiting. She took quick strides to distance herself from Tracy's office. She wasn't weak, but she was pregnant, and standing up to her was probably a horrible idea. She called security and told them to remove Tracy Simms from the building and to make sure she vacated the premises. She gave specific instructions that Tracy Simms was banned from their property and should not be allowed in the gate under any circumstances.

Then Tiffany called Kory and told him what happened after he left, and he insisted he'd come and pick her up. She didn't argue. She was happy to be home, safe and sound.

"Baby, about getting a gun . . ." she said as she pulled the covers back.

"Yes, what about it?"

"I changed my mind. I think we should," she said.

"Really?"

"Yes, really. I think I'd feel a lot safer with one."

"Okay, I'll call Levi tomorrow."

"Yes, baby, do that," she said and climbed into bed. Tiffany wasn't familiar with crazy, but the look on Tracy's face was like an evil, empty person, someone with nothing to lose. She didn't want to be afraid of her, but she always wanted to be cautious. She had a baby coming in less than three months, so she had to make sure she and her baby stayed safe.

You Will Pay

Episode 34

Tracy

Tracy sat at her desk and waited for security to open the door.

"Don't touch me," she said and stood. "I'm happy to leave, just don't put your hands on me," she repeated. They did not get aggressive. They allowed her to get her bag, purse, and two armed security guards escorted her to her car. She got in without force and handed over her badge and garage card.

"Ma'am, please make your exit now and do not return."

"Whatever, fat boy. If I was a real criminal, I'd run just to see if you can catch me," she said to the husky officer. If that was TiMax's finest, they needed to do some rehiring.

Tracy turned off the radio and headed home. She talked to herself the entire ride. "I'm going to get you—oh, I'm going to get you. Mike, you ugly grown-ass baby fucker, I'm going to get you and Tiffany. Your ass is going to suffer. I'm going to get you, bad baby, just watch. You two will be the last two people on this earth to fuck with me. You hear me?" she yelled. "You bitches have fucked with the wrong one," she spat, with spit flying from her lips. She stopped at a red light and slapped herself as hard as she could. *Whap, whap,* and another *whap* as she punished herself with two more slaps. "Fucking bitch-ass bitches, stupid fuck bitches, I am going to fuck you in the ass, Mike, fucking stupid bitch." She heard a horn. She looked up, and the light was green. She pulled off, but she was overwhelmed with emotions, and she couldn't control herself.

Whap, whap, whap, whap.

She continued to punish her face as she drove home. "You're a stupid bitch. A dumb bitch, a dumb bitch that changed a grown nigga's diaper," she ranted. *Whap.* "You stupid bitch, you dumb whore." She continued this behavior until she got home. Her face was numb and purple from the bruising, but that wasn't enough. She wanted to get her ammunition for the press. She opened her safe—and all of her files were gone. Video footage on her tablet of her and Mike's rendezvous gone. "Son of a bitch!" She quickly realized that her spa day was just a day for Mike to clean up his mess. Every tape and voice recording she had in her safe was gone. How they cracked the codes or got in was too much for her to figure out. All she knew at that moment was people with money had the power, and she had none. She had earned a few stacks from her time at TiMax, but with that, she'd only be able to be jobless for approximately six months; after that, she'd be penniless.

"You're so stupid, Tracy, a stupid dumb bitch," she admonished herself and went into her closet. She stood and looked at the straps she had hanging on the walls and grabbed the thinnest one. She stripped out of her clothes and sat on the ottoman in her room, and she gave her thighs fifty hard lashes. By the time she was done, she was sobbing uncontrollably and out of breath. She reached for the blanket that was nearby at the foot of her bed and eased back into the chair. Her thighs and face stung, but she knew she deserved that ass whipping for being such a failure.

She closed her eyes and prayed for sleep, but not before she prayed for revenge.

Baby Shower

Episode 35

Tiffany

Tiffany left the office humming a tune and smiling. Her baby shower was going down the next day, and she was superexcited. She was thirty-nine weeks and larger than life. Work was good, her marriage was perfect, and her best friends, Rose and Asia, were living in bliss. Rose was starting to show, and her gallery was not only doing well, it was doing so well Rose had to hire two new artists because now that she was pregnant, she couldn't keep up with the demand. One of her new employees was a painter, and the other was a sculptor. He specialized in wood, but either way, they turned over profit, so life was great.

Levi had quit the force and was now working as a jeweler at one of Kory's stores because Rose could not stand the fact that she could lose her husband in the line of duty, and they were having a child. Although Levi wanted to be a detective, with his first child on the way, he agreed with Rose. Kory assured him that he'd manage his fourth location within a year when he opened it, but for now, Levi dedicated himself to learning what he needed to know to be able to run his own store.

"Baby, please bring in the bags from the back of my car," Rose told Levi.

"Rosy, I know, baby. Please let a brother get a sip of water first," he said.

Rose went over to kiss him. "I'm sorry, baby, and if I wasn't carrying your big-headed kid, I'd go myself," she jabbed.

"Oh, Lord, am I going to have to hear this until delivery?"

Rose rubbed her stomach. "Yes, sir, now go get the bags," she ordered.

Tiffany laughed. "Rose, leave that man alone. He is sweating from doing everything you've ordered him to do."

"So? And I have a waddle in my walk now because of this baby. I am close to six months, Tiff, and look at me. I know it's a boy, but is this Baby Huey? I'm huge."

Tiffany laughed. "Rose, you are talking to a pregnant person that cannot see her feet. I have to rely on Kory and a mirror to see how my cankles look in shoes, so stop. This is the beauty of motherhood."

"Oh, really?" Asia interrupted. "Mi so glad, I didn't blow up like you two."

"Get yo' skinny ass outta here, Asia. Nobody asked you," Rose snapped.

Tiffany laughed out loud. "Well, I will be glad when this little girl makes her appearance. I am so tired of being pregnant."

"Me too," Rose said.

"Girl, please, you still have almost four months to go."

"Hell, I'm still tired."

"Baby, where do you want this?" Levi interrupted.

"Over by the gift table." She poured the salsa into the bowl. "Tiffany, I don't know why you came early. You were supposed to get here when all was done."

"Well, Kory said he had to pick up the baby's gift and wanted to surprise me, so I'm here. I can always go outside and chill by the pool."

"Yes, go," Asia instructed. "Let me and Rose finish up here."

"Yes, go outside."

Tiffany left the kitchen and went outside. She relaxed on a chaise and thought about wine. "Lord, when this is over, I am going to drink a gallon of wine. With a straw," she laughed out loud. She began to let her mind wander back when she lived there and how she'd sit out by her pool and think of show ideas and chat with Dee or Mee-Mee on the phone. She thought of the times it would be snowing at home, and she'd tease Rose about being out by the pool.

Those were fond memories, and she cherished them. She loved her home at one time, but now she had grown to love the home she and Kory shared. Her old home was for entertaining, and she wondered if Rose thought about expanding the backyard to lay sod and adding a security fence around the pool. She was having a baby, and the guest room in that two-bedroom home would transform into a nursery.

She smiled until she drifted off to sleep. She dreamt of her baby and Rose's and Asia's baby playing together. Her dream was so vivid and colorful, and their kids were happy. Then her dream shifted and she saw Tressa. Tressa was as beautiful as the day they met, and she stretched out her arms. "Tressa," she called out in her dream. "What are you doing here? Why did you leave Mr. Green?"

Tressa laughed. "I didn't leave my father. I just wanted peace, and there was no peace there."

"Wait, Tressa, I don't understand, why are you here?"

"Call me, Isabella. My daddy loved Isabella, so call me Isabella."

"Okay, Isabella, why did you leave us?"

"I left for me," she said, and Tiffany jumped. She woke up out of her sleep, and her heart was racing. She was breathing fast, and she was frightened by her dream. She sat up straight and reached for her bottle of water that was on the little table and drank it all. A few moments later, Asia called for her.

"Huh, what?"

"Come on inside. Everything is ready for you and your guests are starting to arrive," she said.

Tiffany took a few moments to get herself together, then she stood. Her stomach was large and low, and she had to go to the bathroom bad. She went inside, went to the bathroom, and then went to enjoy her baby shower. She wondered what was keeping Kory, so she texted him. He didn't reply, but a few minutes later, he walked in. It was a coed shower, so they did things that both men and women could enjoy, and after she had opened all of her gifts, Kory gave her his. It was three charm bracelets; one for him, one for her, and one for the baby, and on all three charms, it had a mommy, daddy, and Kourtney charm. They had agreed to name her Kourtney a couple of weeks ago, and Tiffany was happy with her gifts.

She and Kory headed home and settled into bed. At four a.m., Tiffany was jolted out of her sleep with pain. She lay back down, but ten minutes later, there it was again. "All right, now, little one, relax . . . I didn't eat that much salsa," she said rubbing her belly.

She nestled back next to Kory, and ten minutes or so later, another pain. "Kory, baby, wake up," she shook him.

"What, baby, what is it?"

"I think I'm in labor."

"Why? What's wrong?"

"I've had the same pain to hit me ten minutes apart, Kory, and it is not gas," she stressed. She went to the hospital one night because gas had hit her so bad she thought it was labor, but after a Sprite and a few windbreakers, she was better.

"Okay, baby, but we should—"

"Awe, awe, awweee," she panted. "If you are going to suggest waiting, wrong answer, Kory."

He got up and threw on some clothes. He helped her into a summer dress and flip-flops. By the time they made it, her contractions were five minutes apart. The nurse checked her, and she was at five centimeters dilated, so they paged her doctor. By eight twenty-five a.m., Tiffany and Kory were parents.

Tiffany called Rose and Asia, and then she called Mr. Green. She could not wait for Langley and Estelle to arrive to introduce them to their daughter. Rose and Asia vacated the room when the Greens made it, and Tiffany handed her to Langley.

"Kory and I would like you to meet Ms. Kourtney Isabella Banks." Estelle gently rubbed her head, and Mr. Green teared up.

"Tiffany, I know you are not my daughter, but can you let her call me Pop-Pop?"

Tiffany smiled brightly. "Yes, indeed."

Kory kissed the side of her head, and she allowed Mr. and Mrs. Green time to bond with little Isabella. She wasn't a replacement, but she would make sure her little Isabella was a part of their lives.

"She is going to be spoiled beyond belief," Langley said as he handed her back to Tiffany.

"*No muy mal estado, aunque,*" Estelle said in Spanish. Tiffany and Kory both looked at Mr. Green.

"She said, not too spoiled, though." They all laughed.

Two days later, Tiffany and the baby were home. Everything was perfect, and Tiffany couldn't have asked for more.

It's My Time to Shine

Episode 36

Tracy

Tracy sat in her car watching the Banks's home like a hawk. She had camped outside their home for the past two months, and she had their routine and schedule down. Now that Tiffany had had the little bastard child, she would be home, and it was finally time for Tracy to make her move. She'd wait until Kory leaves for his morning run. She planned to get in and get out as quickly as possible. She didn't want to wait until Kory left for work, because that wasn't consistent since he'd come and go at different times, but he always did his morning run at the exact same time.

As soon as she saw Kory leave the house she got out. He'd leave from the front door every single time, and she never once saw him lock the door. She crept up to the house and hoped no nosy neighbors saw her. She didn't know if Tiffany would be sleeping or up or what, but she knew she'd be off her game. She had had a baby four days ago, so she knew she probably wouldn't put up much of a fight.

Heart racing, palms sweating, hands trembling, Tracy approached the front door. She turned the knob, and the door opened. She didn't open it wide because she tried to be as quiet as possible. She pushed the door shut and looked at her watch. She only had twenty-five more minutes to go in and take care of Tiffany, and then get out of Dodge. She should have hurried to the second floor, but she paused and looked around Tiffany's beautifully decorated home.

It looked as if it belonged in a magazine, but she didn't have time to admire the décor or design. She crept up the stairs trying to be as quiet as she could, but the step before the last one made a sudden noise. Tracy froze.

"Baby, are you back?" Tiffany called out.

Tracy said nothing.

"Baby, can you please get a bottle for Isa," Tiffany said.

Tracy was glad she spoke, so she wouldn't have to guess what room she was in. She inched her way to the room where she heard the sound come from. Then she boldly walked in.

"I'm not your baby."

Tiffany gasped. "Tracy, what are you doing in my house? Why are you here?"

Tracy looked at her in her huge Cal king-sized bed. Her bedroom was just as spectacular as the rooms she saw on the first floor.

"It's my time, bitch, and it's time for you to pay up for everything you've done to me." Tracy pulled out a gun.

"Please, Tracy, I just had a baby. Please put that gun away. If you want a job, I'll give you a job. Money, I have plenty, just please put that gun away."

"Don't! You sorry piece of shit. How dare you say please or beg me for anything! You think you're better than me!"

"No no no," Tiffany whispered and shook her head. She held her baby tightly in her arms, and Tracy was ready to do what she came to do.

"Put the baby down, Tiffany."

"Tracy, please don't do this. I'm a mother. My daughter needs me. Don't do this. We can work this out."

"Shut the fuck up!" Tracy yelled. She was at the end of the road, and the only thing that would give her satisfaction is putting a bullet in Tiffany's head. "Put the baby down now!" she demanded again, and Tiffany laid her infant close to her, near her thigh.

"You can do whatever you want to me, Tracy, but please, I'm begging, don't hurt my baby, don't hurt Isabella, please," Tiffany begged.

"Fuck you and your baby!" Tracy said and squeezed the trigger—but she didn't squeeze it before Kory got one off. His bullet caught her in the head, and her bullet caught Tiffany in the right shoulder.

Tracy went down, and Tiffany wailed in pain.

Through tear-filled eyes, Tiffany watched Kory as he stood in the doorway with his gun still drawn and aimed at Tracy's body on the carpet, and Tiffany assumed she didn't make any more moves after he put his gun down. Kory went to her body first, knelt down, and made sure Tracy was incapacitated, and then he rushed over to Tiffany. She shook uncontrollably. Blood was everywhere, even on their newborn. Kory called 911, and then he picked up the baby.

"Is Isabella okay, Kory, is our baby okay?" Tiffany moaned. Kory quickly examined her to make sure she wasn't hurt. The only blood on her was Tiffany's blood. Isabella cried loudly from all of the excitement, Tiffany figured, but she wanted to make absolutely sure she wasn't hurt. He held Tiffany close, even though she had a bullet in her arm.

"I'll never let either of you go, baby," he cried holding them tightly. Tiffany was sobbing and shaking so bad that Kory said. "Baby, you're going to go into shock. You have to calm down," but that didn't make her shaking subside.

"Tiffany, baby, you *have* to calm down. Breathe, baby, breathe. Isabella is okay, baby, and we need you to breathe, honey," he instructed.

Tiffany looked up at him and nodded her head, but still shook uncontrollably. "How did you know?" she cried to Kory. "How did you know she was up here?"

"I left from here so fast this morning that I forgot my headphones. When I came back into the house to look around for them, I heard everything on the baby monitor. Luckily, we keep one of the guns locked away downstairs, because I would have been defenseless otherwise. The gun over there in the nightstand would have been too far for you to reach."

"I didn't hear her come in, Kory. Even if I would have, I would have thought it was you. Thank God you came back when you did. She came into my house to kill me, Kory. She wanted to kill me," Tiffany cried.

"I know, baby, and it's my fault. I never lock the door in the mornings. I didn't know that nut was lurking around," he said, and then held her tightly until they heard the police and paramedics. He moved away and went to the top of the stairs. "We're up here," he yelled, and within seconds, the paramedics and the police were in the master bedroom. They stabilized Tiffany to get her to the hospital. Although Kory wanted to ride along with Tiffany, he had to stay and answers questions and assure they removed Tracy's body from his home.

He sent Tiffany and the baby to the hospital and dealt with the police. Finally, they removed Tracy's body from the bedroom. Blood was everywhere. Kory called Rose to let her know what happened. He called Langley after he got to the hospital, and Mr. Green ordered him to stay with Tiffany like a concerned father. No way would Kory leave his wife's side, but he assured Mr. Green that he would.

Later, Rose, Asia, Mr. and Mrs. Green, Myah, and whoever could fit in her hospital room were there to see her. The staff warned her about all the people and noise, but Mr. Green ordered that she be put in a private room, and no one bothered her again about the noise and the many visitors. By the time Tiffany was released to go home, Kory had suggested that they get a hotel for a few days until their room was cleaned and all the traces of the tragic day were no longer visible. When they got home, their room looked as if nothing ever happened.

Thanks to Mr. Green, her house felt safe again because he had cameras installed, their circular driveway that was once open to enter from the street had a huge gate that required a code to enter. Their home was now fenced in, front and back, and although Tiffany thought it was a bit much since Tracy was dead and no longer a threat, she was grateful and felt like she and her family would be safe. Mr. Green made sure Tiffany had everything she needed and promised her as long as he lived he'd take care of her like a father.

Three weeks later, Tiffany returned to work and took things day by day. She learned to appreciate all she

had and the people she loved, and she promised herself
that she'd live life to the fullest and let the past be what
it was . . . the past. Asia and Edward conceived again.
Rose and Levi had a healthy baby boy, and Myah and
Cameron got engaged. As for Dee, let's just say he is *too*
fly and to *all about himself* to fall in love!

The End